Be Mine

Copyright

Second Edition, February 2023

Paperback ISBN: 978-1-961966-28-4

Published by: Carxander Publishing
Minnesota

Opening Quote

Yes, you want her. Look at her, you know you do. It's possible she wants you, too. There's one way to ask her. It don't take a word. Not a single word. Go on and kiss the girl.

Kiss The Girl by Khail West

Chapter One

✗ Breetana ✗

I stare at the woman in front of me in complete amazement. How in the hell can a grown woman throw a tantrum in the middle of a fucking place of business? At Shaw Incorporated, an elite financial investment company, no less. How? But here we are. No shame. No filter. Just a grown ass woman throwing a tantrum.

"You don't have any idea who I am! I'll have your job by the end of the day!" the random girl yells at me.

I glare, finally reaching my breaking point. Honestly. This has been going on for five minutes. Maybe not the full out tantrum. But she stepped off the elevator five minutes ago. I cross my arms over my chest. "With all due respect, none of which you deserve, that isn't happening. Now get out."

She screams and stomps her foot. Actually screams and stomps her foot. I would laugh if I wasn't so fucking shocked it happened in the first place. In. The. Middle. Of. An. Office. Building. Unbelievable.

"I'm Chase's fucking girlfriend, you stupid fucking bitch!" She continues to rant and rave and push past me to get to my boss's office.

I'm forced to physically stop her, which is not easy. I'm like five feet one. She has to be five feet nine inches, and she's wearing heels. I catch movement at the edge of my peripheral.

Chase Shaw.

He's just come around the corner and is slowly backing away. I glare at him.

Coward.

"If you make me call security up here, I'm gonna be so pissed off," I growl.

This chick has the balls to glare. "You wouldn't dare."

I laugh and shove her back just enough to get her off me. "Oh, I assure you. I will. I don't want to. But I absolutely will. So. Here's what's going to happen. You *are* going to leave like the grown ass adult you are. You *are* going to forget about Chase Shaw because you don't, and never will mean a damn thing to him. And you are *never* going to show up at this office again. You want to confront him? Do it somewhere that is *not* a place of business. Get out. This is your last warning."

"You're such a bitch. It's fucking unbelievable how you're even still employed here."

"I'm sure it has everything to do with my looks. Can't be because I'm good at my job," I say as sarcastically as possible. "Now leave." I cross my arms over my chest and face her down again in a show of power I have never in my life exuded.

"You'll regret this."

"I regret a lot of things. Throwing you and all of Chase's conquests out is typically the highlight of my day." I give her a humored smirk as I look her up and down like she's the ugliest thing I've ever seen in my life and means nothing to me.

She screams again and stomps to the elevator. I breathe a sigh of relief when the doors close. I lied to her. I *hate* having to deal with Chase's conquests, but not because of how they act. It's because I'm so incredibly jealous of them. Makes me feel so stupid.

Chase slinks out of his hiding place with a huge grin on his face. I'm fighting tears of hurt like I usually do after dealing with one of his stupid girls. There have been so, so many over the last three years I've been working here. It never gets easier to deal with them.

"That was fucking brilliant!" he laughs.

"You... you absolutely do not pay me enough to deal with your conquests." I blink a few times because I don't want him to see me cry as I go back to my desk, which is positioned strategically in front of the doors to his office. I glare at him as I sit down. Hiding behind anger is the only way I can deal with him right now without bursting into tears.

"Oh, come on now. How many have you actually had to deal with?" Chase asks casually. He has no idea what he does to me. No idea how I feel, and how hard it is.

"More than you know. I just never tell you."

"Because you're so good at your job. I don't know what I'd do without you."

"You'd fall apart. And have pissed off women interrupting your meetings."

He leans on the ledge in front of my desk and continues to smile at me with his trademark smug, cocky grin as he laughs. I would never tell him, but I love his laugh. I love the way he fills out his perfectly tailored, thousand-dollar suit. I love that he's so muscular, and that he towers over me. I love his piercing, deep, ocean blue eyes. I even love his stupid, cocky grin.

"You're probably right."

"Seriously." I shake my head and choke back a sniffle. "I can't do this anymore. I swear to God, I deal with one of your conquests every single week." I look down quickly so he doesn't see the hurt flash across my eyes. It's getting harder and harder to hide my feelings for him every day. Harder and harder to see all of these other women in his life. I blink a few times again to make the tears go away.

"Jealous?" he asks cockily.

Yes… but I won't tell him that. I can't. He's the only man who has been in my life over the past eleven years who has the power to tear me apart. I don't even know when it happened. I have to be strong.

"It's just… it's not in my job description to deal with them. One of these days, you're going to sleep with some crazy ass psychopath, and I'm going to be the one dealing with the consequences of your actions." I take a deep breath before continuing. I hate what I'm about to do, but I've been thinking about it for so long. I love my job more than anything, but Chase is too much for me. He breaks me more and more every single day. He doesn't even know it. "I love my job, but I have to resign. I can't deal with them anymore. It takes away from what you actually pay me for. I can't do my job if I'm dealing with them. I'm hoping you'll still give me a good reference."

He shakes his head and looks me dead in the eyes. "I'm not accepting your resignation."

"What? You can't -"

"I'm not letting you resign. I'll pay you more."

I swallow and look up at him. "That isn't the point, Mr. Shaw."

"Chase. We've discussed this. You've seen my house. You've saved me from many awkward morning after situations. To you, I'm Chase."

I point at him. "That. That right there. That's the point. I've saved you from many awkward morning after situations. What Executive Assistant does that?"

"A good one." He shrugs like he's shrugging it all off. He looks around the office and glances at the clock on my desk. "Come to my office. We'll talk."

I vigorously shake my head. I know if I go in there, I'll give in and stay. I can't do that. "It's Friday night."

"I know. I know. The one night I'm not allowed to keep you because of girl's night. You'll make it in time, even if I have to drive you there myself."

I glare at him. Using my girl's night as an excuse failed epically when it usually doesn't. It was my last and only resort. So, I stand and follow him to his office. I love the way he walks and hate myself for it. He waits for me to walk in ahead of him and closes the door behind us.

"So, what's it gonna take, Breetana? What's it going to take to make you stay?"

You. Not sleeping with all of Chicago's female population and paying attention to the woman in front of you. Ugh. Such a stupid thought. I'm not even his type. Yeah. He has one. Tall. Model thin. Makeup galore. Heels and designer clothes.

I sigh and turn, surprised that he's directly behind me. His scent is intoxicating and, for a moment, I nearly forget my name. I take a step back, more for my own sake than anything else. I need to think. And I can't do that when his ridiculously expensive cologne that makes him smell like Heaven is assaulting my senses.

“I've made my decision, Chase. I've been battling myself on this for months. It's hard for me to deal with all of this.”

“Why? You never seemed to have an issue over the past three years. Why now?” He takes a step towards me.

I take another one back. “I've just finally hit my breaking point. That's all.”

“I don't think so.”

I keep stepping back as he comes closer to me. “I don't have to justify myself to you. I don't even need to give you a reason.”

“You're right. You don't.” He's nearly touching me with his body. My ass hits his desk, and I gasp. “But I think after three years you owe me something.”

“Chase,” I breathe.

“Something, Bree,” he whispers.

I close my eyes. If only I could tell him. If only I could tell him how jealous I actually am. How hurt I am when I come face to face with a woman he slept with the night before.

I feel his thigh against my leg. I swallow hard and open my eyes, trying to be brave. “I can't tell you. I can't. It's unprofessional. I just... I have to resign, Chase.” I put a hand on his chest and try to push him back, but he grabs my wrist and turns it so he's holding my hand. “Chase.”

“You're the best Executive Assistant I've ever had. I'm not letting you go. So, tell me your demands.”

I can't help but notice he doesn't let go of my hand. How his thumb is rubbing soft circles against it. I suck in a breath. “An extra weeks vacation this year,” I blurt out. I knew his power over me would make me relent.

“You already get three weeks a year,” he says, narrowing his eyes.

“My sister is having a baby. Her fiancé left her, and our parents are dead. She's the only family I have left. I need to go home to help her when she has the baby. The extra week would help me ensure she's set up before I leave again.”

“Where's home?”

“Silver Bay.” I can tell he has no idea where Silver Bay is when he looks at me, confused. “It's a small town in Minnesota. An hour or so away from Duluth. Silver Bay's population is like five hundred people. Everyone knows each other," I say it with a little more vengeance and disdain than I intend.

"So you want to be away for a month... in some small-town place in Minnesota," he says incredulously.

"No. I don't want to. But my sister is going to need me." I take a silent breath as he takes a step back and walks towards the couch he has in his office. "If that isn't going to work for you, I'm sorry, but she's everything to me."

"I get it, Breetana. I just don't know how I'm going to manage without you for an entire month. I can barely get through a week without you." He turns back towards me, and I sigh. It takes all my resolve, but I begin walking towards the door in his office, wiping a tear as I go.

"I'll have my resignation for you Monday morning." I attempt a smile but fail as more tears burn my eyes. Chase grabs my hand and pulls me towards him. I slam into his rock-solid chest and gasp for the second time in like three minutes. "Ow. Ouch."

"Seven days a week in the gym," he says with arrogant pride as he holds me close to him. I love the way he feels. His arms around me are like nothing else. I fight to keep breathing. And to keep my resolve. "What else do you want?"

Oh, God. You. You, Chase. For three years. Just you.

I take a deep breath and put my hands on his chest, trying to push away.

He holds me tighter. "What else, Breetana?"

"Chase. Please. Don't. Don't do this."

"You have me begging you to stay. You could ask for anything, and I'd give it to you, Breetana. As long as you don't walk."

I steel myself and take a breath. If this is the only way he'll let me go, then he asked for it. "Fine. I want an extra week of vacation. I want a raise. Because if I have to deal with people like her and fight back my own jealousy, I should get something in return. And I want you to -" I cut myself off and put both hands over my mouth. My eyes go wide.

Oh God. I admitted it. I admitted jealousy. I've never been able to keep things from him. He's always been able to get me to talk no matter how hard I try to keep to myself. I don't talk to anyone. Well. Hardly anyone. I look up at him, and he's grinning from ear to ear. I shake my head.

"Jealousy?"

"No. I didn't mean -" I shake my head again like I'm warding off the words that just spilled from my mouth. He sits and pulls me into his lap. His blue eyes sparkle mischievously. "Chase. Please. I... I didn't mean -"

"You did. And you want to know a secret?" He has one arm securely around my lower back, his hand resting on my hip. His other is very slowly running up my thigh as his eyes rake hungrily over me. I can only nod. "I've known. For a very long time."

My heart skips a beat. My breath hitches. He leaves a trail of goosebumps and fire as he makes his way lightly up my thigh. "It's so unprofessional and unethical," I whisper.

His eyes stop on my lips for a moment before continuing to my eyes. His hand has stopped on the upper part of my leg. Under my skirt. His thumb is resting against my panties. I'm instantly wet for him. How the fuck did I let this happen?

He gives my leg a squeeze. I'm hypersensitive to where his thumb is. Every part of me is screaming for him to touch me, but my mind is telling me to run. I can't move. My mouth has gone dry, and I'm afraid to breathe.

"And my hand under your skirt isn't unprofessional?" he chuckles.

"Chase…" It's part whisper, part plea, and I have no idea how the words even come out at all. I close my eyes and lick my very dry lips.

"Yeah?" he whispers back. He runs the back of his hand along the outside of my panties. I can't hold back. I kiss him, and it's all it takes. The kiss becomes feverish in seconds. Our tongues twine with one another. It's all I've ever wanted. *He* is all I've ever wanted.

He pulls at my panties, moving them aside and running a finger from my clit to my center. I moan into his mouth as I grip his shoulders. Every part of me is tingling and throbbing for him. I couldn't pull away from him if I tried. My body wouldn't let me. I need him. I need to feel him. It's been so long since I've been touched like this, but I've never wanted anyone else to.

Just him.

He slowly pushes a long finger inside me, and my eyes fly open. He feels so much better than I've ever dreamed, and I've dreamt of him like this a lot. I let my legs fall open wider, really having no control, as he gives me long, deep strokes. He twists slightly, and my head falls back.

"Mmm…, Chase… oh…" I close my eyes again as he licks my neck, then kisses it as he gives me a second finger. "Oh! Fuck… yes…"

I grind my hips against his fingers as his lips meet mine. He twists them inside me again, and I tighten around him. His magical fingers are doing more for me right now than mine or any of my toys ever have.

He quickens his pace as he presses his thumb against my clit and starts rubbing. He expertly gives me just enough pressure as he continues his masterful strokes and kisses me long and hard. The pressure builds inside me until I can't take any more. My tongue tangles with his as I grip his shirt. My pussy starts pulsing around his fingers as my legs shake, and I come harder than I ever have.

I quietly whimper into his kiss as he slows his thrusts and rides me through the best orgasm I've ever had. "Mmm… Oh, Chase…"

"That was fucking sexy," he whispers as he nuzzles my neck. He slowly pulls his fingers out of me and grips my hip. He quickly shifts me so I'm straddling him. He slides his hand up my body and runs it across my tits as he reaches down with his other hand and starts unbuckling his belt.

My reverie is immediately broken, and I shake my head. It doesn't work.

The belt.

Flashbacks start, and I can't fight them back no matter how hard I try.

No, no. Not this. Not now. Please not now.

I suck in a breath and try to keep my attention focused on Chase. I beg myself to not allow the break about to happen. It only helps me enough to keep myself in the present day instead of letting the flashbacks overtake me. The break I didn't want slams over me like a tidal wave.

"Chase. I... I'm sorry. I can't." I can't look at him. I thought after so many years after what happened to me in Minnesota, I'd be okay, but I'm not. I blink several times and take a few deep breaths as he watches the sudden change in my behavior.

"Breetana? What happened? Are you okay?"

I look up at him long enough to see the concern in his eyes, so I look down once more. I've wanted him for so long. But I haven't had sex in years. And only a few times before that. All but one of those times was against my will. I don't even know if at the time that it was consensual counts as sex. I barely remember it. I was just as traumatized afterwards as… every other time it was forced on me.

But that's not even everything. Not nearly.

Chase reaches up to wipe away a stray tear. I hate myself for showing weakness in front of him.

"I… oh God. You're going to think of me so differently," I whisper.

"I sincerely doubt that."

I take a deep breath, still refusing to look at him. "The short version is when I was a Freshman in college, I got drunk at a party. When I woke up, I was laying in a bed with no clothes on. It was... I mean, flashes came back to me. It… we were drunk. I was young. Stupid. I got hurt." I look down, ashamed at my lapse in judgment but more ashamed that if I tell him everything, he'll throw me out. I left out so much.

My uncle.

The hospital.

The bullying.

"Why would I think of you differently?"

"I…" I can't tell him. I can't tell him everything. He'll hate me. He'll think I'm a slut like everyone else.

"I know there's more to it than that, Breetana."

"Damn you and your CEO senses." I try to smile, but can't. Instead, I take a deep breath. "I don't want to talk about it right now. Please don't make me. It's... not everything but the rest is embarrassing, traumatizing, and completely my fault for letting it happen."

"Bree. I won't make you talk about it, but whatever happened to you... I know it had to have been something that hurt you deeply. I doubt it's your fault. You know you can trust me."

I don't know why he's being so sweet, or how we even ended up like this. With me in his lap. With him holding my hand. I don't even know when he took my hand.

I'm not his type. His type is tall, gorgeous models. I'm not anything like that. I'm really short. I have hips. I have an ass. It's not huge, but it's there. Models don't have asses. They also don't have boobs. I'm a D cup. Sometimes a double D, depending on the bra. How can he possibly be attracted to someone like me? Is he even attracted to me at all? He can't be. I'm just another conquest.

"It's hard to talk about, Chase. I'm so sorry."

"I've known you a long time. I know you're hiding something. But I won't push it." He narrows his eyes in a challenge. "Right now."

I know he won't let this go, but I'm grateful that he is right now. "Thank you."

He smiles and reaches up to touch my cheek, tucking a finger underneath my chin and forcing me to look at him. He kisses me again, and I can't help but melt into him.

He drops his hand to my neck and runs it slowly down my shoulder and arm until he reaches my ribs. He trails it across my back and pulls me closer as he deepens the kiss, slipping his tongue inside my mouth.

I shift slightly and reach up to run my fingers through his hair. It's impossible to resist him, no matter the thoughts about myself running through my head. And I do want to be like this with him. It's like a war is raging, though. Part of me is screaming to get out of here. That not only won't this ever work, but that I don't deserve for it to. That Chase is a player. That Monday, it will all be awkward. I'll be just another girl.

The other part, though, she's begging for him not to stop. Screaming how much she wants him.

He slides his hand to my hip before gliding it to my ass. He gives it a light squeeze. "Is this okay?" he asks against my lips.

I nod and moan softly as he starts rubbing his hand up and down my bottom. "Yes."

He gives me his cocky grin, and I smile. He catches my lips with his again, and our tongues begin their dance once more. I'm so lost in him. Even if it doesn't last, the fact that he can make me feel like this, wanted, for just a little while is enough.

He runs his hand down my leg and under my skirt when he comes back up. He starts rubbing my bottom again over my silk panties. "What about this?"

"Yes." I want him so much. He makes it hard to think.

"Good. You're beautiful. Do you know that?" He catches his thumb on my panties and slips his hand underneath them so it's firmly on my ass. He kisses along my jaw to my neck. I kiss his head. I love his hair. It's unkempt and a mess, but it's perfect on him.

"How did I go from resigning from my job to sitting on my boss's lap?" I ask, whispering.

"If you've wanted this as much as I have, it's not hard to figure out."

We spend more time kissing, his hand resting comfortably on my ass. Finally, Chase pulls away, smiling at me. He gives me another sweet kiss on the lips before gently moving me off his lap and standing. He reaches a hand out to me and pulls me up to him.

"I hate to let you go, but I promised you wouldn't be late to girl's night. So. You've negotiated an extra week's vacation. A raise. And whatever you want, including sex when you're ready and whenever you want with your boss. That's what will get you to stay?"

I swallow with a blush. It's a start. But there's only one thing I want. "Um…" I pause.

After several moments, Chase groans. "Breetana. You're fucking killing me, sweetheart."

I look up at him and try to be brave. "I think I've made it clear how I feel about you, and how upset dealing with your conquests makes me because of those feelings. I wanted to resign because I can't handle that anymore. It hurts too much. I can't handle the other women. I just want it to be… us."

He purses his lips. "I don't do exclusivity. I never have."

My heart shatters in my chest. I knew those words would fall from his lips. I know I'm not the kind of woman who would ever be able to knock Chase Shaw off his feet. I force myself to stand my ground, though I'm not sure how I'm still standing at all. I allowed myself a brief moment to believe maybe I could be the girl who changes him, but that thought is stupid and never ends well for anyone.

I nod. I refuse to cry, even though it's all I want to do. "Then I walk, Chase. Because I can't handle the thought of you with anyone else. You wanted honesty. You wanted to know what it would take. That's what it'll take. Thinking of other women touching you makes me crazy. I know I'm allowing jealousy to get in the way of my job, but I'm being truthful. It hurts seeing that when I know, and now you know, how I feel. I can't do this to myself anymore."

I can't believe how bold I am being right now. I never am. I usually just ignore my wants and needs. I put everyone else ahead of myself. I don't open up to anyone. Only my sister and best friend. And Chase, but only when he makes me. Yet, I just put myself on the line and told him how I feel.

"Breetana." He rubs his forehead. Like it's physically painful for him to think of himself with me.

The tears I'm fighting sting my eyes once more. "Sorry, Chase. I'm not like you." I can't look at him, or my resolve will weaken. "I can't do what you do. After my past, I can't just have sex and have it mean nothing. It's not me. It will never be me. I can't just walk away knowing that tomorrow night, or later tonight, you'll forget about me and be with someone else. That? Doing what we just did? Having you be like that with me? Being patient and understanding? That meant something to me. It meant everything to me."

I can't tell him everything now. I probably would have if he'd asked me to. Maybe not tonight, but I would have. I opened up a little, though, and it wasn't enough. It's never enough. *I'm* never enough. I push away from him, hard, and begin to walk out of his office, but he grabs me around the waist and pulls me to him, my back against his chest.

"You know it's not like that. I'm not going to forget about you or find another woman tonight. What happened? What are you so afraid of, sweetheart? Just talk to me. Tell me, so I can understand."

"Chase. I just can't. I'm not like the people you date and sleep with. I need more than that. I can't be a once and done thing. I was so stupid to allow myself to fall for you in the first place. I know what you're like. I should've known I wouldn't have a chance. I've never been good enough. I never will be. My uncle was right about me. I really am nothing more than a whore. A slut for letting what just happened between us happen at all."

I start to cry, unable to stop the wave anymore, and quickly release myself from his grip so I can run from the office before he sees how weak I am. How ridiculous I am for crying over him. For something we never even had. I run to my desk to grab my purse, then nearly sprint to the elevator. I keep pressing the close button after I step inside as Chase runs out of his office, seemingly past the shock he probably felt at me running from him. It's probably a first.

"What the fuck? Breetana! I never said that. Any of it! I'm not upset! Wait a second!" He reaches the elevator just as the doors close, but he's too late to stop them. I scream inadvertently when I hear his hands slam against the doors. I breathe a sigh of relief, but I'm so confused. I swear I saw guilt and pain cross his features as soon as he saw I was crying.

It couldn't have been. Chase Shaw doesn't care enough about me. No one does. How could I be so stupid? It's like college all over again. I thought I had found someone to accept me for me, but I was wrong. So wrong. I paid the consequences, just like I had paid them when I fought off my uncle.

I wipe vigorously at my tears as I near the bottom floor. I don't want anyone to see me like this. Security is the only people here at this time of night, but I'm not taking chances. If they question what's wrong, I'll break into a million pieces.

I get off the elevator at the bottom floor and shoot the security guard a smile. Reese Bryant. Thank God. He's nice to look at and really sweet. Also my best friend and one of the few people I can't hide my emotions from.

"Hey, gorgeous. Off to girl's night?" he asks, giving me a brilliant smile.

"Actually, no." I feel my eyes start watering and Reese is immediately around the desk and at my side.

"Hey, what happened?"

I shake my head as I take a deep breath and choke down the sob threatening to escape. "Can you come over tonight?"

Reese looks at me before he nods and glances at the clock. "We'll take my car." He hands me his keys. "Go wait for me. I'll be out as soon as my relief gets here. Won't be long."

I nod as I rush to the car and let myself in. I lock the doors and cry uncontrollably.

I need to forget Chase Shaw exists.

I have to forget everything that happened to me. Forget the reason I ran from Minnesota.

I need to push everything away like I've always done.

If I don't, it'll shatter me this time.

Chapter Two

⚔ Chase ⚔

I'm completely taken aback. I've seen women cry. Hell, I've been the cause of many of their tears. I never cared.

But Breetana.

Seeing her cry is like a sucker punch to my chest. I stop fucking breathing and feel like the biggest asshole in the universe. I just almost fucked her. In my office. She confided in me. I'm pretty sure she told me one of her deepest and darkest secrets. She confessed her fucking feelings. Bared it all.

And I fucked up like I usually do.

"Fuck! Fuck! Fuck!" It's a good thing there's no one else on the top floor. It's just my office, my conference room, my gym, a sitting area for when my clients are waiting for me, a private bathroom for Breetana, and her desk. If anyone else saw me right now pounding my fists against the wall as I swear, my suave image would be tanked. "What the fuck is wrong with me?"

I storm into my office and slam the door behind me. I have an hour of work left to do, but I can't do it. The thought of sitting behind my desk infuriates me. Especially when I start thinking of Breetana and what she'll be doing tonight to forget about everything that happened between us.

I want her.

I have for a long time, but I settled for intense flirting because I didn't want to push boundaries. I have a rule. No interoffice dating. I put that rule in place for myself. I had made that mistake before. When I first started the company, I had a fling with a woman in my accounting department. When I broke it off, she started spreading rumors about herself, and told everyone she heard from someone else that I had been talking about her and spreading the rumors.

Thank God I had a good management team. Her manager came to me with concerns. We talked it out and fired her. Her performance also sucked, and she had a huge attitude problem. She tried suing for wrongful termination. I settled out of court to make it go away and slapped her with a permanent gag order. The day after she signed and accepted, I wrote the policy and implemented it.

Everything was fine until Breetana walked into my conference room for her interview. She answered every question with enthusiasm and honesty. She blew the interview out of the water.

She's smart. She doesn't put up with my bullshit. She's never been afraid to stand up to me. But she's also incredibly guarded, and she's never once opened up to me about anything important. I'm good at getting some things out of her, but never anything *truly* important.

Until tonight.

The only reason I know about her girl's night is because I once needed her help preparing for a Monday meeting. She didn't tell me no, but I could read her disappointment. I knew she was upset with me, and I pushed her until she finally told me why. It's the only way I get anything out of her.

She told me it's the only time she gets to spend with her friends the entire week, but that her job is important to her, and she'd do whatever it takes to be successful at it. She didn't ask, but I vowed never to keep her from her night out again.

It's unlike me. I don't do that for anyone. If there's work to be done, people stick around until it's fucking done. I didn't get where I am by allowing people to skip out on deadlines. Now, I have her schedule meetings only in the afternoon Mondays, so she doesn't need to stay late to help me prepare for them.

"Fuck!" I plop down on my couch where I just had Breetana in my lap and take out my phone. I contemplate calling her, but I call my best friend instead. I need him to talk me down.

"Hey, bro! What's up?"

"I fucked up, man. I fucked up bad," I breathe into the phone as I collapse against the back of the couch.

"Uh oh. What happened?"

"Remember that chick from last week?"

"The blonde?"

"Yeah. Well, she showed up today at my office spouting off some bullshit about her being my girlfriend. Breetana, the fucking saint she is, kicked her out."

"Like usual. She's gotten pretty good at it, too. What's the problem?"

"She was jealous." I shake my head as I growl the words out.

"Oh… dude. That's, uh... I guess that's good for you, right? You haven't been able to stop thinking about her since you hired her."

"That's not the problem. The problem is she was so jealous and fed up with my bullshit that she told me she was resigning. I almost stopped breathing. Right there. So, I pulled her into my office so we could talk." I pause as I try to steady my suddenly racing heart. I fail with spectacular ferocity.

"And?"

"Fuck." I'm so pissed off at myself I can barely speak. "I told her to tell me what she wanted. She told me she wanted an extra week off this year to go home to be with her pregnant sister. And she wanted a raise if she was going to have to tamp down her jealousy over my conquests."

"She... actually said she was jealous? That doesn't seem like her at all."

I shake my head as I glare at the window overlooking Chicago's skyline. "It's not. She went red with embarrassment as soon as the words left her mouth. It was sexy as hell." I smile a little at the thought of how cute she looked, then snap out of it and glare back out the window. "Next thing I know, I have her in my lap with my hand on her pussy."

"Fuck. Seriously? Come on, Chase."

"I don't need you to beat me up about it. I feel guilty enough," I growl. I steel myself again. Telling him about my sexual relations isn't something new. We both talk freely about it. It's telling him what happened after that I'm having an issue with. He's going to be just as pissed at what I did as I am. "I fingered her. There was a lot of kissing. After she came, I flipped her around intending to continue, but she stopped me. I'm not used to being stopped, but she did it. I was a little taken aback, but it's the fucking reason that floored the fuck out of me."

Taylor sighs. "What was the reason?"

"Something that happened in college. She wouldn't give me all the details, but she thinks it's her fault. And something happened with her uncle. I don't think she knows I picked up on that, but I think he's got her convinced that she isn't worth anything, and that she's a whore. But that's not even the worst part, Taylor."

"There's more?" He sounds exasperated. I can't blame him.

I start rubbing the bridge of my nose. "After it was all said and done, I repeated her demands. An extra week. A raise. Sex with me when she's ready and whenever she wants. She tells me that she also wants me with no other woman."

"So? She's the woman of your dreams. You've told me every time you pick a woman up that if you could just have her, you'd give it all up cold."

I close my eyes and sigh. "I told her I don't do exclusivity."

Taylor is silent. I can almost see him staring at the phone in his hand incredulously. Finally, I hear him let out a long breath. "Fucking Christ, Chase. Have you lost your mind?"

"She walked out. Well. Ran. I was shocked for a couple seconds and couldn't move. When I finally did, I couldn't get to the elevator fast enough to stop her. But I did see she was crying. I don't think I've ever seen that level of hurt in anyone's eyes before."

"Can you blame her? Really?"

I don't say anything. Instead, I stand and head straight for the whiskey I keep in my desk. I don't bother with a glass. I drink it straight from the bottle as I curse myself for fucking up the one thing I've always wanted. A real relationship with the woman of my damn dreams.

I hear Taylor slam something down, and I jump a little. "Fix this. That's my advice. Fix it before you lose her for good."

"Pretty sure that ship has sailed and sunk." I take another drink. The liquid burns on its way down, and I relish in it.

"Fix it, Chase." Taylor doesn't give me a chance to respond. He hangs up, and I take another long drink.

Probably not the best thing to do in my state of mind, but I decide to head to the club she always goes to on girl's night. I made it my business to find out just in case she needed something, but I never told her that.

All I know right now is Taylor's right. I have to fix this. I can't let her resign. I really would fall apart without her. I refuse to lose her. I'll do whatever it takes.

XXX

I walk into LYTE and head straight for the bar. I can get a good look at the dance floor as well as the booths and tables where people are sitting. The bartender gives me my usual beer without my asking. I don't come here when I know Breetana is here with her friends, but I do come here a lot. I take a long drink as I scan the club. There's a sea of people, but I'd be able to spot Breetana anywhere.

The problem is I don't see her. I grab another beer and walk through the club keeping my eyes peeled for her. Her shiny blond hair. Her sexy as hell curves. She's nowhere to be found.

The club is filled with girls dressed in slutty clothing holding fruity drinks with whipped cream. There are men in business attire hitting on all the young girls. There's sexy, very dirty dancing. A couple people look like they might be fucking on the dance floor.

I finish off my beer and go back to scanning the crowd. Breetana isn't here. I've come to that conclusion already. I don't know whether to be thankful she doesn't have guys pawing at her, or if I'm pissed off even more that I can't fix this unimaginable fuck up I've managed to put myself in.

I also realize with a sickening punch to my chest that I'm the guy in the business attire. I'm the guy who walks into these clubs with Taylor and picks up random, sexy girls. I'm the one usually making out on the dance floor. I'm no stranger to finding a dark corner in the back and having my way with my fling of the night. I'm thirty-four years old, and I act like a fucking teenager.

All I've wanted for three years is Breetana. I just let her walk out of my life like an idiot. It's time for me to grow the fuck up.

XXX

(Two Days Later)

Chase: We need to talk, Bree. Just… call me, okay?

It's the fifth text I've sent today. I've tried calling her, but she's ignoring them. I gave her Saturday to relax. I needed it, too. I spent the entire day going over every little detail of all of Friday. Everything from when I walked in and saw her sitting behind her desk to when she ran out of my office, and I saw her cry.

She's so beautiful in the morning. She's beautiful all the time, but mostly when she's concentrating hard and doesn't think anyone notices her. I don't think she ate lunch Friday. No. She didn't. I know she didn't eat. I need to make sure she starts doing that. If I can get her to stay.

Fuck. I have to get her to stay.

Chase: Please give me a chance to talk about this, Bree.

I drop my phone on my table and head to my bar. I don't usually drink much, but this weekend, I don't think I've quit. I can't stop thinking of Breetana walking away from me.

The pain in my chest when I saw her crying.

I'm losing it. I'm losing it completely at the thought of losing her.

This is such a new thing for me. I'm so good at shutting off any of my feelings. I don't mind being considered cold and aloof. I thrive on it. But I *hate* that *she* thinks of me that way. I hate that she sees me as everyone else does. As Chicago's playboy. I hate that I acted the way I did with her. That I shoved her away because she made me feel something and it scared me.

I sit down with yet one more bottle and glance down at my phone.

Nothing.

"Fuck." I take a long drink of my beer.

I lost her. I absolutely lost her. I took advantage of her for years. I made her open up to me, and then I pushed her away. I don't blame her for hating me. I probably made her feel like I just wanted to add her to a long list of girls I fucked. Chase Fucking Shaw adds another notch to his belt.

Fuck. I'm so fucked up. She was right to run. She's better off nowhere near me.

I lean my head back as the edges of my vision start to blur. It's been a long time since I've gotten blackout drunk. I down the rest of my beer and make my way to my bedroom. I bounce off a couple walls and fall up the stairs. By the time I get to the top, my house feels like it's flipped upside down. I close my eyes a second before opening them again and starting for my bedroom once more.

When I finally reach it, I strip off all my clothes and fall into the bed facedown. I don't bother with covers. I can't fucking feel a damn thing right now anyway.

Except the pain and emptiness left from Breetana leaving. No amount of alcohol will ever take that way.

But fuck if I won't try.

Chapter Three

⚔ Breetana ⚔

(The Next Morning)

I spent most of Sunday typing out my resignation, throwing it away, restarting it, throwing it away again, and doing it all over. Chase was relentless in trying to get a hold of me, but I couldn't talk to him. I knew he would somehow talk me into staying, and I can't. Especially after the sweetness and tenderness he showed, then the words he said after. It hurt to know I had opened up to him, even a small amount, and he closed off from me. I told him something I had only told my sister and best friend.

I feel the tears sting my eyes again. I've been crying since I woke up yesterday morning. I didn't watch movies with Reese. I cried into his shoulder the entire day and all of the night before. I told him everything I had refused to talk about with anyone. I just wanted to forget.

Reese listened. He tried to talk me out of resigning, and tried even harder to get me to talk to Chase, but I couldn't. Can't. I hadn't told Chase everything that happened to me in Minnesota, even though Reese wanted me to, but what's the point? He'd never settle for me. Never commit. He said it.

I sigh and look at my clock. Eleven in the morning. Chase still hasn't shown up to work. He hasn't responded to my phone calls. He had one meeting this morning. It was the first one in nearly two years I had scheduled on a Monday morning, but it was only because of how important it was. I made sure he knew. I even put a reminder in his phone just to make sure he didn't forget. I had gotten here early to drop my resignation on his desk, making sure he wouldn't be here when I did it.

When he didn't show by eight for his nine o' clock meeting, I started calling him. When he still wasn't here when his meeting showed up, I had already resigned myself to having to cover for him.

So, I did. I took the meeting myself. I got his client to re-sign with us. Then I texted him again and called. He still hasn't responded. I growl low under my breath as I start calling to cancel his afternoon obligations. By noon, I still haven't heard from him and decide that I need to check on him. Why? I don't know. Maybe it's the good Executive Assistant in me or something.

I gather my stuff, and a half hour later, I'm standing in front of his ridiculously large mansion on the outskirts of the city. I never understood why people need homes this large. And then I met Chase Shaw, and everything made sense. It's all about ego.

I let myself in with the key he gave me and enter his security code. I've dropped off his dry cleaning many times. I've had to pick up files for him and drop other things off over the years. I've never seen any staff here, but I know he has a housekeeper.

Which is why I am so surprised when I walk in and see beer bottles all over the table in his living room and takeout containers littering his dining room table.

I sigh and call his housekeeper.

"Good afternoon, Ms. Carter. How may I help you?" the housekeeper asks when she answers. I've had to call her often enough that my number is saved in her phone now.

"Hey, Mary. Mr. Shaw had a rough weekend."

"Oh, yes. He called me and told me not to bother him today. He said he wasn't feeling well."

Like hell. He's fucking hungover. He'll call her but not answer for me. Fuck him. Instead, I say, "I'm overruling him, Mary. Please get here when you can."

"Yes, ma'am. I can be there in a couple hours. I'm just finishing another job."

"No problem. Thank you, Mary. Have a nice day." I hang up and start walking up the stairs to his bedroom. He *is* going to pay for this.

I walk into his room, not bothering to knock, and stop breathing at the sight. He's sprawled on top of his blanket on his stomach… completely naked. I get dizzy and nearly fall over before I regain my composure and take a few deep breaths.

It isn't fair.

At all.

I worked myself up into such anger, and then I walk into this. He's gorgeous, and he knows it. I hate that I'm staring. I *hate* that my chest is tight. I *hate* what he does to me. I *hate* that I fell for him. I *hate* all of it.

I shake my head, force myself to look away, and then walk to his windows. I smile to myself a little vindictively as I throw open the shades, letting light flood his dark room.

Chase buries his head in his pillows. "Please. For the love of fucking Christ," he whimpers.

"You missed an important meeting." I turn to him, forcing myself not to focus on his very naked and well-muscled body.

"I don't fucking care, Breetana. Go away," he hisses.

I laugh sinisterly as I let the anger take over. "Torturing you after all you've done to me is so much more fun."

"Stop it, Breetana. You wouldn't even answer your fucking phone so I could explain." He sounds pissed off.

I glare. "Is that why you refused to answer mine today?" I fold my arms over my chest.

"Go away, Breetana. Close the fucking shades."

"Get up."

"No."

"You're acting like a two-year-old, and you smell like a brewery. Get up and take a shower."

He mumbles obscenities that I can't totally understand into his pillow as I turn and head to his bathroom to turn on his shower. After checking the temp to make sure it's hot, but not too hot, though I don't know why I care, I walk back out to his room.

He hasn't moved.

"Chase, I'm not kidding. Get the fuck up right now." I fight the urge to slap his incredibly toned ass.

He growls. "Breetana. Go away unless you want to end up underneath me in this bed."

My heart skips a beat at the image, but I force myself to focus on how upset with him I am. "Tempting offer, but you smell awful. I won't be someone else's conquest. *Ever.* Go take a shower."

I leave the room taking a deep breath. I hate seeing him like that. Despite everything, I hate seeing him hungover like that, and in so much pain. I know his head has to be hurting. It took all of my willpower not to crawl into bed with him and rub his head until his headache went away while he was nestled on my chest.

Damn him for making me feel like this. I should hate him. Something must be seriously wrong with me. I must be more fucked up than I thought.

I walk into his kitchen and sigh. I can't let him suffer so I start looking for ingredients for my miracle hangover cure. I created it in college for my roommates. I didn't drink much after my freshman year, but they did.

I find coffee and start brewing it. I can't find chocolate. He must not be a sweets type of person. I dig in my purse for the few pieces of chocolate candy I always keep in there and throw them in a blender. I then cut up a ghost pepper from his fridge and toss it into the blender with the chili powder I found in a cabinet. When the coffee is done, I pour it into the blender with everything else and blend it together. When it's done, I pour it into a glass and wait for him.

After what seems like hours, but is only maybe twenty minutes, Chase enters the kitchen looking sick and exhausted. He's wearing sweatpants and a hoodie. I raise an eyebrow. I've never seen him so incredibly dressed down.

He glares at me. "Why the fuck haven't you left yet?"

"Because unlike *you*, I actually have a heart. Though I have no idea why I'm crazy enough to waste it on you."

I hand him the glass, and it's his turn to raise an eyebrow. "What is that?"

"Something to help with your hangover. I promise you won't die. It'll work. Drink."

"It looks like poison." He eyes it suspiciously and wrinkles his nose.

"It doesn't taste good, and it's spicy as hell. But it will work. Just trust me."

He sniffs it and makes a face before he shakes his head and downs it. He gags when he's done, and I take a small pleasure in watching him suffer. "No way that's going to work. Fucking gross. That's the worst thing I've ever tasted."

"Really? The worst?" I shoot him a glare, and he smirks at me. I shake my head, take the glass, rinse it and the blender out, and put them in the dishwasher. I turn back to him and smile as he stares at me, confused.

"What the fuck?"

"You're welcome."

"How did you do that? What's in there?"

"Coffee, chocolate, chili powder, and a ghost pepper." I take a deep breath and start to leave. "I canceled and rescheduled the rest of today's meetings. I said you were sick. Mary will be here in a little while to clean up. I'll see you tomorrow."

Chase grabs my arm. "Bree. Please. We need to talk."

"I've never let anyone call me Bree. Only you. That's another thing that hurts. I let you in, Chase. At least a little. I could've let you in all the way because I trusted you. I don't do that. I have one real friend and my sister. That's it." I don't look at him. I don't move. I don't try to remove his hand. I just stand there looking at the floor.

"I know I fucked up. I know I hurt you. Just give me a chance to make it right." He gently and tentatively touches my cheek. "Just give me a chance to show you I can do better. Be better."

"Chase. I... I'm sorry. I can't."

He steps closer to me, his body nearly touching mine. He gently touches my chin and lifts my face so that my eyes meet his. "You're not the one who needs to be sorry. I am."

"I shouldn't have expected you to give up your lifestyle for me."

"Don't you see? Bree, I've never wanted to. Until you. It scares the hell out of me."

It takes me a long time, but I finally allow myself to reach up with a shaky hand. I touch his hand that's on my cheek and lean into his touch.

It's happening. I'm relenting. I've prided myself since I left Minnesota on how strong I've become. Not a pushover. Tough.

Chase is the only person who I can't seem to do that with.

"Breetana. Please. Don't resign. I know you love your job. I'll give you your extra week. I'll pay you more. I'll give you whatever you want. I'll treat you better. I won't take advantage of you anymore. Don't resign from a job you love because I'm an asshole."

"That sounds nice, but you know that's not the full reason I want to resign. I can't stand seeing -"

"No more women."

I stare at him completely startled. "W-what?"

"No more women. Just you."

"Chase... I... I don't -"

He cuts off my stammering with a sweet and incredibly tender kiss. His arms slip around my waist, and my body molds itself to his. I wrap my arms around his neck, and he lifts me off the ground.

After a few moments of bliss, he pulls away. "I'm breaking company policy for you. Company policy that I created."

I nod. "I know. I'm sorry." I blush.

"How do I get you to stop apologizing? It's my company. I can change the policy."

It's hard to hide my excitement at finally getting what I've wanted for so long.

Him.

I smile.

He smiles back at me as I stare in his eyes. "What?" he asks.

"I don't know what to think right now. I'm scared that this is all a dream. I thought Friday night was all a dream that turned into a nightmare. Yet, I have nervous butterflies at the thought of you actually wanting to be with someone like me."

"Someone like you?" He puts me back on the ground, and then grips my thighs just below my bottom. He lifts me so easily. I wrap my legs around his waist, and he turns from the kitchen towards the stairs and starts walking up them. "What do you mean someone like you?"

"Not a gorgeous supermodel with long legs, and no ass or boobs. Someone who hates makeup just as much as heels. Someone who prefers jeans to a skirt any day of the week. Someone who prefers to stay home, watch a movie, and have something homemade for dinner instead of going out to some fancy restaurant."

Chase grins before he kisses me. "You can't possibly be any more perfect. You're fucking gorgeous. You don't need makeup. I like that you don't wear heels. I love how I tower over you. Makes me feel tough. Like I can protect you from anything." He kicks his bedroom door closed and walks me to the bed as he kisses me. When he gets there, he drops me in it and climbs in after me. He pulls me close to him. "Stay with me. We can watch a movie, and I can make you dinner."

"You cook?" I smile and kiss his chin. He's running his hand across my hip, my ass, up my back, and then back down.

He grins cockily. "I'm really good with my hands."

"I am in no way surprised and can't wait to find out." I wink at him, and he laughs before leaning down to kiss my neck. I've never felt this way about anyone.

"Say the word, and I'll happily give you a demonstration. And thank you, by the way."

"For what?"

"Saving me from the worst hangover of my life."

"That's what Executive Assistants are for."

I feel him smile into my neck as he kisses it again. "Are you going to stay?"

I sigh and close my eyes. "I don't need a raise," I whisper. "I just want the week extra."

"And me?" he asks a little reluctantly. "I can't tell you how much I want to hear you say you want me."

"And you," I say softly. He exhales in relief, and I turn to kiss his shoulder.

"You're really giving me a chance? Us?"

"Yes."

"Fuck, Bree," he whispers. "Thank you. You won't regret it."

I hug him as tightly as I can, and suddenly feel him start to unzip my dress. "Chase…, what are you doing?"

Flashbacks.

Not again. I swallow hard and force my mind to focus on Chase. Just Chase. He won't hurt me. He's not like them.

"You're sexy as fuck in this dress, but I bet you look better out of it. I promise I won't touch you unless you want me to, but I really want to see you. I've imagined you naked and in countless different positions in my office. Let me at least see if my fantasies live up to the real thing."

I close my eyes and take a deep breath as I sit up slightly to slip my arms out of the dress. He's not them. This is Chase.

He takes off his hoodie and grabs my hand. He puts it against his hard length and rubs it over himself. I stare at him, eyes wide. My hand shakes, but he keeps it steady. The last time I had my hand like this against a man's hard length, I was crying and trying to pull away. Chase isn't forcing me. I know I can pull away. I just don't want to. He makes me feel okay. Like I'm safe. And I really do want him. I want all of him.

"Wow," I whisper as I let him rub my hand against his hard, large cock.

"That's what you do to me. Every fucking time I see you."

I kiss him softly, then sit up on my knees next to him so I can remove the dress. I sit next to him in nothing but navy blue panties and a matching bra. He licks his lips and smiles as his eyes roam over me.

"Beautiful. I want to know what size bra you are because your tits are as perfect as you are, but I don't want to scare you away again." He pulls me back down next to him and wraps his arms around me.

I take a breath. "I'm a D. Double depending where I buy the bra. Which is never going to be from Victoria's Secret. They say double D, but they lie."

He laughs, and I smile. I really love his laugh. He runs his hand over my hip and my stomach until he is just underneath my bra line.

"Will you let me touch you? Over your bra? I won't take it off unless you want me to."

I bite my lip, forcing myself to stay in the moment. "Okay." The fact that he keeps asking me if things are okay makes me feel so loved. Special. So much more in control of this situation over the others.

Comfortable.

He doesn't take his eyes off my breasts as he slowly runs his hand over one of them. He squeezes gently and rubs his thumb in small circles over my nipple. I close my eyes as it immediately hardens for him. He slides his hand across my chest to my other breast and does the same thing while he kisses my lips, my jaw, and then my neck. He continues to my collar bone and kisses the mounds of each breast before stopping and looking up at me.

"Can I keep going? Over your bra?"

I nod and run my fingers through his hair as he pushes me a little ways on to my back, but not all the way. He kisses over my bra to my nipple. I can feel his tongue lick it through the thin material, and I let out a soft sigh. He kisses his way to the other one and lavishes it just the same.

"Chase…"

"I love when you say my name." He gently bites my nipple before kissing it. His hand slides down my stomach, coming to a rest just above my panty line. "I don't want to stop, but I don't want to push you either. I know I've touched you before, but you ran right after. I'll never do something you don't want me to. I'll stop whenever you say."

Tears sting my eyes at the thoughtfulness. The sweetness. I still can't tell him. Not now. I don't want to lose him. Not after the possibility of having him after so long. "I'm so sorry I'm like this," I say quietly.

"I'll wait for you, Bree. Eventually, I want to know what happened to you to make you so afraid. Your breath is quickening, and I know it's not because of where my hand is. You're scared, baby. I hate that you're afraid of me."

He's right. I love the way he makes me feel, but I'm fighting back tears and panic. I know he isn't going to hurt me, but I'm terrified. Flashbacks threaten to overtake me, and I feel myself begin to shake. Chase moves his hand to my lower back and pulls me close to him as he lies down. I bury my head in his firm chest as his hand comes to rest on my butt. He kisses my forehead.

"It's not you I'm afraid of," I whisper after several minutes.

"Tell me what happened, Bree," he whispers back.

I shake my head. "I can't. Not right now. I don't want you to hate me."

"Breetana. I don't know what happened to make you so afraid, but whatever it was, I can damn well guarantee that it wasn't your fault. I will never hate you. For anything. Ever."

"I'm a mess, Chase. I thought I was over everything and moved on. It's been so long, but everything just randomly floods back. I'm just... I... I don't know what to say. I just don't." I bite my lip. I know he'll hate me.

"Sweetheart, listen to me. You said your uncle told you that you're a whore, and you accused yourself of leading me on and said that he is right. None of that is true. You aren't a whore or a slut. I don't know why he called you that or how you could ever believe it. You're the most beautiful woman I've ever seen. You're sweet. You're fucking perfect, Breetana. I would never think of you like that. Ever."

I stare at him a moment as I try to gather my thoughts. Finally, I speak. "I just don't understand you. How can you go from a cocky playboy who has slept with all of Chicago's female population, and then suddenly be so sweet? And genuinely attracted to someone who is totally opposite of everyone you've ever dated?"

"I haven't slept with all of them. Maybe ninety percent," he says teasingly. I swat his chest. He laughs and catches my hand, turning it so he can kiss my palm. "I don't want anyone else, and that scares the fuck out of me, Bree. I mean that."

"I'm sorry," I say quietly.

"But I am absolutely willing to face that fear," he continues as if I said nothing. "Maybe one day soon, you'll trust me enough to tell me what happened, but until then, I'll take this as slowly as you need me to. I'm going to prove to you I'm worthy of the second chance you gave me. I'll break down those walls you've put up piece by piece until you understand that I'm not going anywhere. That this is just as new for me as it is for you, and that I'm working on my fears just like you are." Chase holds me close to him for a long while, and eventually, I start to believe that maybe he won't go anywhere, but I'm scared.

I feel Chase take a deep breath before he kisses me softly on the lips before he gets out of the bed. He puts his hoodie back on and grabs a t-shirt from his dresser.

He hands it to me. "How about that movie?"

I smile and take the t-shirt. Chase sits next to me and kisses my neck just where it meets my shoulder, and I sigh. "That may be my new favorite place for you to kiss me."

"Then, I'll make sure I do it all the time." He kisses the other side of my neck in the same place and reaches around to the band of my bra. "Can I unhook this? I won't take it off. Just unhook it so you can change into my t-shirt and be comfortable when we watch that movie."

"You're so sweet, Chase. It's so unlike you. You're usually so cocky and self-assured and flirty. Sometimes, even more so with me than anyone else."

"It's a carefully constructed persona."

"Why? Why not be the genuine man all the time that you are with me sometimes?"

He looks in my eyes and smiles as he leans forward to kiss me. "Because when you're worth as much money as I am, people want things from you. I'm less approachable if people think I'm a dick."

"How do you know I don't just want something from you?"

"Because you, baby, have never asked me for anything. You've always been honest with me. You aren't afraid to stand up to me or call me out on all of my bullshit. Most people just give in and do what I want. No questions asked. But not you. It's one of the things I find insanely attractive about you."

I smile and lean forward, meeting his lips. "You can take it off. If you want to." I glance down at my bra and give him a soft smile.

He looks at me longingly before he takes a deep breath. "I probably shouldn't. I'll unhook it, but if I take it off, I'll want to touch them." He unhooks it and lets me go, being the gentleman I'm falling even more in love with. He leans forward to kiss my forehead before he gets up.

He starts walking to his bedroom door to give me privacy, but I decide to be a little playful. I take off my bra and throw it at him. He catches it and looks at me. I smile as I sit there on his bed, completely topless. He growls before jumping on his bed, climbing on top of me, and pinning me to the mattress with his body. His entire body is hard as granite, but I'm more interested in his cock against my thigh.

Chase makes me feel pretty. Wanted. Two things I've never felt. He makes me feel safe. He helps keep the flashbacks at bay, even when they sneak up on me. I just need to focus on him, and how he makes me feel.

"You're playing a very dangerous game."

"Maybe I just really want you to touch me without the bra on."

"And if I do that, I may not be able to stop." He presses his hips closer to mine, his impressive cock growing harder by the second. "Do you feel that?"

I look up at him through hooded eyelids. "Yes."

"That's how I was earlier when you woke me up. I was instantly hard for you. I had to fucking get myself off in the shower just so I could put these sweats on." He sets feelings off in me that I never feel around anyone but him. A tightness in my stomach and chest. That tingle between my thighs that I've only felt when my own hand is between them.

"Chase…"

He kisses me and then gets off of me, obviously adjusting himself so I can see his reaction to me. "I know you're not ready for all of me. Please get that t-shirt on, Bree. You're killing me."

I put the t-shirt on, biting my lip with a soft smile, and he pulls me up. He takes my hand and leads me down to the den. There's a TV screen that takes up nearly the entire wall.

"My God," I whisper breathlessly.

"Eighty inches. This is my favorite room. I don't let anyone in here." I look around as he grabs two drinks out of the mini refrigerator. He hands me one. I'm in awe.

"You... remembered I like Strawberry Banana Naked Juice?"

"It may not seem like it, but I remember everything you've said to me. And I pay attention. You always have one for your breakfast because you can't eat early in the morning. And you have one in the afternoon to up your energy after I've run you ragged, and you've skipped lunch. Which you *are* stopping, by the way. I don't care if I have to order lunch for you myself. You need to eat."

"I can't get over how sweet you are."

"Not many people see this side of me."

"Your secret is safe."

He laughs and walks to the couch. I follow and start to sit down next to him, but he grabs my hips and pulls me into his lap. "Right here. This is where you belong."

"In your lap?"

"Damn right."

We settled in to watch a movie. When it's time for dinner, I sit with him in the kitchen while he cooks the most delicious steak I've ever eaten. We talk and laugh. Hours later, I yawn and decide it's time to leave, but I don't get a chance to tell him.

"Stay with me," he pleads again.

“I already said I wasn't resigning,” I say, confused and sleepily. I yawn again.

He chuckles. He runs his fingers through my hair, and I lean my head on his shoulder. “I meant stay here. With me. Tonight.”

“I have no clothes for tomorrow for work, Chase.”

“So? Drive home in the morning. I'll meet you at the office. But stay. With me.”

I'm tired. I don’t want to drive, and the thought of sleeping in his arms is too good to pass up. “Only if I get to sleep with you, and you keep your arms wrapped around me the whole night.”

“Done.” He lifts me up and kisses me.

I'm asleep before we even get up the stairs.

Chapter Four

✗ Chase ✗

Breetana's hair smells like coconut. I get a hint of coconut on her skin, but I can't place what else. Vanilla maybe? It's so unique to her, and I can't get enough. I hold her tightly to my chest, her back to me, as I breathe her in. I make a mental note to buy and keep whatever shampoo and body wash she uses.

"Chase?" she murmurs sleepily.

"Yeah?" I ask with my face buried in her hair.

"This is definitely my new favorite way to sleep."

I chuckle as I kiss the place on her neck that she told me she loves when I kiss and smile at her content sigh. "This is my new favorite way to wake up. You. In my arms."

"Mine, too."

I keep her securely cuddled into me for a few more minutes before I sigh and force myself to release her. "I don't want to, but I guess I should probably let you get home, so you can get ready for work." I get out of bed, and she looks at me shyly as she stays curled under my blanket. I smile "What are you thinking, baby?"

“Well, I was thinking that maybe if we do this again, I could leave something here I could change into.” She pulls the blanket up further to cover how her face is turning a furious shade of red, and I can't help but smile at her. Her shyness is so sexy.

“Bring an overnight bag next time. What kind of body wash and shampoo do you use? I'll buy it for you and keep it here so you don't need to worry about bringing it.”

“I can bring it. Really. It's not a problem.”

I smile at her and walk to my bed. I climb on top of her and pull the covers down so I can see her face. I kiss her. “I'm buying it. End of story. Write it down before you leave.”

“Very well, Mr. Shaw.”

I groan and kiss her neck. “You're going to kill me.” I force myself off of her. “We're both going to be late for work if I stay in that bed any longer.” I grab her bra off the armchair I threw it on last night and take it with me to the bathroom, smirking the entire way.

“Chase! What are you doing? I need that! Do you know how hard it is to drive without a bra when you’re my size?”

“I'd give just about anything to be that seatbelt. But this stays here. You aren't getting it back unless you play a game with me later and earn it.” I don't look back as I close the door to the bathroom.

A second later I hear her laugh. I smile to myself as I put her bra on the vanity and start my water. I have a full day of meetings I’m not looking forward to. Hopefully, Breetana will be up for playing a very sexy game with me to get me through my day.

XXX

I step off the elevator and see my nine o’clock meeting, Anthony Calaway, waiting for me in my sitting area. Breetana is tucked in a corner talking quietly on her cell phone. She looks crestfallen. Like she’s about to cry and is barely holding it together. I immediately head towards her, but Calaway steps into my path. I nearly growl but take his outstretched hand instead.

“Mr. Shaw. I'm happy you were able to squeeze me in.”

"Of course, Mr. Calaway. Why don't you head to the conference room around the corner? There should be coffee and pastries."

As soon as he releases my hand, I step around him and head straight for Breetana. I take her hand and lead her to my office. As soon as I close the door, I take her in my arms, and she nearly collapses against me. I hold her close while she continues her conversation.

"Kiki. I know, sweetie. I'll take care of it. I'm so sorry." I can only hear one part of the conversation, but I'm pretty sure the person she's talking to is crying. "Sweetie. I'll fly out there and bring you here. It'll be okay." She sniffles. I raise an eyebrow and look down at her. She looks up at me and bites her lip as she frowns. She buries her head in my chest and takes a deep breath before continuing. "Kiki. We'll figure it out. I'm so sorry. As soon as I have my ticket, I'll call you." She pauses as she listens and tears immediately spring to her eyes. She bites her lip again. "Don't worry about me. It'll be okay. I promise. I'll be okay. I'll book it right now." She says her goodbye, and then screams in frustration as she throws her phone across the room. It lands on my couch.

I don't let her go. "Woah. Hey, baby. What happened?"

"Why can't they leave her alone? She's done nothing!"

"Who? Talk to me. Who was that?" I try to stay calm, but her sudden freak out has my heart rate spiking

"Why do they have to fuck with her, of all people? She doesn't deserve this!"

"Honey, I have no idea what's going on. What happened?" She pulls away from me and storms behind my desk. She folds her arms across her chest as she stares out the floor to ceiling window at the Chicago skyline. I follow and slip my arms around her waist, pulling her tightly to my chest. "Please tell me what happened. I hate seeing you upset. Let me help."

She lets out the breath she's holding, and my heart breaks when I see the tears falling from her eyes. "Remember my sister?"

"Pregnant. Yes. Fiancé left her."

"He's very influential in Silver Bay. Even surrounding areas. After he left her, he started saying that she cheated. He wasn't sure the baby was his. They've been together since high school. She was so in love with him. He cheated. She caught him. Now, three months later, he's destroyed her reputation. Her business. People call her a slut. She's been propositioned by people who have known her most of her life. She can't even go to the grocery store without being sneered at and harrassed."

"I'm sorry, baby," I whisper in her ear.

"She lost her business. She had to close it. No one came in. Not a single person. In three months. She went through her savings. She tried to get a loan and can't because he's so influential. Bankers won't even hear her out. And now she's losing her house. She has to be out by Sunday, Chase. They foreclosed on her."

"Shit. How are they doing that so fast? Why didn't you tell me? I can help. I can buy the deed to her house and buy out her business, so she can reopen."

"I didn't know about it. She didn't tell me it was this bad. She can't reopen even if you did buy her out. No one comes in. She has no customers anymore. He's ruined her. She has nothing. Someone threw something through one of her windows today, Chase. She left her house. She was so scared. Drove to Duluth, but she has no money to pay for a hotel." Breetana breaks down in tears. I kiss the side of her head. "She's in her car in Canal Park!" she sobs.

"Put her up in a hotel. Use my credit card."

She takes a few deep breaths to steady herself, and I have to give her credit for being so strong. She shakes her head as she wipes her eyes. "That's not necessary. I can put her up. But I have to go, Chase. She's eight months pregnant. She needs me."

"Use my credit card," I command. "As for you leaving to get her, I'll take care of it. I'll have my plane ready for take-off tonight. We'll fly out there together, rent an SUV to drive back in, and I'll get movers for your sister's stuff."

"We? Chase, you have a follow-up with Blake Stanton on Thursday."

I shrug. "Reschedule it. Reschedule everything after today. After my dinner meeting, we'll take off. You'll have to pack a bag for me when you drop my dry-cleaning and suits off."

"Chase…"

"I'm not leaving you to do this alone, Breetana. I saw how you reacted to the very thought of going back there. Whatever happened to you has something to do with there, and I won't let you deal with it on your own." I kiss the back of her head. She turns in my arms and wraps her arms around my waist. I bend to kiss her and let my hands slip to her perfect, full ass. I give her a gentle squeeze before pulling away. "Take your time to calm down and know that if you ever need privacy, you can come in here. Anytime." I give her a quick kiss, and then head to my first of many meetings.

When I get to the conference room, my team has already gathered. As they lead the meeting, I text my pilot. In twenty minutes, I have a flight plan, and a car reserved. I chip in when I need to during the meeting and text Breetana.

Chase: Do you want the flight plan? I'll email it.

I don't wait for an answer. I just do it.

Chase: Forget it. I emailed it to you. Reserve a suite for us, and one for your sister, as well. Think checkout Sunday works?

Breetana: That works. I'm worried about having enough time to get her set up here, though.

Chase: We'll take the week off and get her set up. I'll find her an apartment. I haven't taken time off in a long time.

Breetana: In ever.

She's right. I've never taken time off.

Chase: No reason to before. Now I have you.

Breetana: Chase… you're so sweet.

Chase: Only for you.

The rest of my morning goes slowly. I order lunch for Breetana and I to eat in my office. We both have been busy and need the break. Bonus is that I really, really love being with her.

I expect my afternoon to be just as tedious as I settle back into the conference room. I smile as I take out my phone. Time for the game to begin. If she's willing to entertain me. Hopefully, it will help get her mind off the shitstorm about to happen as soon as we leave tonight to get her sister.

Chase: I know you're getting ready to leave, but go into my office, strip down to your bra and panties, sit on my desk, take a pic, and send it to me. Play my game, and I'll give you your bra from this morning back…

Breetana: Chase! Are you joking?

Chase: Please, Bree? I'm dying here. I'm so bored. I need something to get me through.

It takes her a few minutes to respond, and I pray it's because she's doing what I ask.

Finally, my phone vibrates in my hand, and I look down. Sure as shit, she did it. My cock immediately springs to life, and I have to fight a groan. I adjust myself and angle my own camera at my hard-on to discreetly snap a pic.

I send it.

After ending the meeting and waiting for my next one, Breetana responds.

Breetana: That for me?

Chase: God yes. We may have to take advantage of the bedroom on my plane.

Breetana: You have a bedroom on your plane?

Chase: Damn right. And I really want to see you naked in that bed.

Breetana: Oh yeah? And what would you do to me?

Here we go. This is what I wanted.

Chase: First I'd lick you from your hot and wet pussy all the way up to that sexy thing they call a clit. Then, I'd make you suck on my middle finger, making it all wet.

I answer a few questions in the meeting and wait for Breetana to answer.

Breetana: Mmm. Yummy. And then what?

Chase: And then I'd put that finger into that hot and wet little pussy and move it deeply inside you while I sucked on your clit. And when you start bucking against me and begging for more, I'd give you a second finger. I'd finger fuck you and lick and suck your clit until you shatter and scream my name.

Breetana: Holy God. Chase. I'm so wet right now.

I choke back another moan.

Chase: Oh yeah? Touch yourself, and tell me how wet your panties are.

Breetana: I'm at the tailor's, but how about on your way to dinner, you call me? I think I can do something about that hard-on you have there.

Chase: Fuck, baby. Are you talking phone sex?

Breetana: If you're really, really good.

Chase: If it means hearing you touch yourself, I'll be a fucking saint.

Breetana: I should be at your house by then. On your bed…

I clear my throat and force my attention to the meeting to compose myself. She gives as good as she gets. I couldn't be more fucking delighted.

Chase: The other day, you wanted to run from me. Last night, you nearly cried when I touched you. Now, you're okay with sexting and phone sex? Not that I'm complaining…

Breetana: I just... I guess I'm starting to feel like maybe you won't hurt me. Especially after today. You're just so willing to drop everything to help my sister. Even though some of the meetings you're rescheduling are so important. I'm not used to it. But maybe it's kind of fast for this.

Chase: I won't hurt you. You're different then everyone I've been with. You always have been. It's why it scares me so much. I actually want to spend time with you. I'm not used to missing anyone like I do you when you aren't near me. As for helping your sister, you're important to me, Bree. If I can help you or someone important to you, I'm going to.

Breetana: That.

Chase: What's that mean?

Breetana: Proof that underneath your cocky, asshole exterior, you are incredibly sweet.

I smile down at my phone.

Chase: I don't care about a lot, Bree. I have a few friends, my mom, my company, and you. What I do care about, I'm viciously protective of, baby.

The rest of my day goes just as slowly as the first half of it. I truly hate meetings. I've always been hands on with my company. I like sitting down with people and convincing them to trust me with their investments. But sitting in meetings explaining to my clients what I'm doing and why I'm doing a good job for them bores the ever-living hell out of me. It's why I hired staff.

Sometimes, my VIP clients expect VIP treatment, though. Which means they want me in these stupid meetings.

When it finally ends, I make my way down to my waiting limo. I don't know how sitting in a conference room exhausts me so much, but I yawn as I settle in for the drive. I push the button to make the partition between me and the driver go up. I hate when they make small talk. I'm about to spend three hours of my life talking to someone. Don't have any desire to make small talk with someone I don't even know.

I take out my phone and call Breetana. I just need to hear her voice.

"Hey. How did the meetings go?"

I smile and yawn again. "How do I end up feeling more tired sitting around than I do after a two-hour workout?"

"Two hours? Holy shit."

"Sometimes I need to de-stress. The gym is my out."

"You sound so tired, baby."

"I am. Just wanted to hear your voice."

"Should I not tell you that I just got to your house and am laying on your bed?"

I groan. My cock immediately springs to attention as I smile. "By all means. Tell me everything. What are you wearing?"

"You saw me today. You know I was wearing a red satin button down with a white skirt."

"Was? Don't think I missed that."

She laughs, and I smile wider, loving that she laughed because of me. "You don't miss anything, do you?"

"Not often." I reach down to adjust myself.

"I'm lying on your bed wearing nothing."

I drop my phone. "Holy fuck." I pick up my phone, and she's laughing. I inhale sharply. "Nothing? Please send me a picture. I'm begging you."

"Okay. Hang on," she says shyly, and fuck if I'm not rock hard. Adjusting myself isn't going to work. I quickly unbuckle my pants and release myself just as her picture comes through.

"Fuck me, Breetana."

She giggles as I stare at the pic. She's leaning against *my* headboard on *my* bed completely naked. I start stroking myself. "I don't look too awkward, do I? This is all new for me."

"No. God no, baby. You're beautiful. So beautiful that I'm stroking myself right now."

"Oh… um… should I… touch myself?"

"You are adorably shy. Run your hand down your body. Think of me. What do you want me to do to you?" I ask huskily, my voice dropping low.

"I'm touching my chest."

I chuckle. "Rub your nipples. Squeeze them between your fingers."

She gasps and moans, and I squeeze myself a little tighter while I continue stroking. "Chase…" It's a whisper, and I close my eyes. "I'm running my hand down my stomach and touching between my legs."

"Yeah? How does it feel?" I breathe into the phone. I twist my wrist as I stroke.

"So, so good." Her soft breathing and sighs make me harder, and I quicken my pace.

"I don't think I've ever been so hard."

"Are you still touching yourself?"

"Yes. I'm so close for you, baby."

"Me, too. Mmm…"

"Put the phone down by your hand, Bree. I want to hear how wet you are." I need to hear how wet she is. She does what I ask. I can still hear her breathing and moaning while the sound of her wetness joins in. It's like a symphony just for me. "Bree. Good Christ. You're so fucking wet."

"Oh! Ah… Chase. I'm gonna... Oh…"

I listen to her breathing and moans until my own release is on top of me. I lean forward and grab some cocktail napkins from the mini bar. "Come for me, Breetana. Are you coming?"

"Right now… Oh, Chase!"

My name on her lips is all I need. My release spills out of me into the napkins I grabbed. "Ah... Fuck, Bree." I stroke myself through, finishing in the napkins and cleaning up as she comes down from her orgasm. "You have no idea how much I want to be the one who does that to you. I'm fucking jealous of your fingers, beautiful."

"You'd be really jealous of my vibrator."

The easy way she says it, like getting herself off with a vibrator is the most natural fucking thing in the world, floors me. I damn near choke. "What?"

She laughs. Hard. I pack myself away and buckle my pants. "I might not be that experienced, but you don't think I've never touched myself before, do you?"

"Jesus Christ. You're gonna be the death of me, gorgeous."

"Have a good dinner."

"Order something. Or make something. You need to eat. I hate when you skip meals. I see how exhausted you get."

"Yes, Mr. Shaw."

"Breetana…," I moan.

She laughs. I smile and lean my head against the back of the seat. "Hurry home, okay?"

"Not going home. I'll order you a car. Meet me at the airport. The driver will take you straight to my plane. I'll hurry the dinner along. And for the record, I hate fucking dinner meetings."

"I know, babe. But Preston is an important account."

I sigh and rub my temple. Of course she has to be right. "Make sure you pack casual clothes for me. No suits. I'm sick of them."

"Okay. I'll take care of it."

I say goodbye and hang up as the driver pulls in front of the restaurant. I can't stop thinking about her saying to hurry home. Like it was just as much hers as mine. I love it, but I have no idea why. I've never wanted to share my home with anyone. I hadn't taken any girls home, ever. I always took them to a hotel. A penthouse suite because I have pride, but never to my home. I've never allowed anyone into my den like I had her. Only Taylor and my mother.

Wanting to wake up next to her every day, to share dinner with her every night, it has never been something I wanted with anyone. I haven't been able to get her out of my head since I first saw her, but now? Ever since I kissed her in my office, I can't imagine life without her. I don't even want to, and it scares the ever-living fuck out of me.

Wanting her scares me.

Needing her scares me.

Missing her scares me.

Her not being in my life, though… That scares me the most.

I take a deep, steadying breath as I walk into the restaurant. What in the hell has she done to me?

Chapter Five

⚔ Breetana ⚔

I find myself yawning as I step out of the black SUV Chase rented for me. The day has been so incredibly long and trying. Kiki called me several times bawling her eyes out, and it tore me apart more every time. I feel so bad for her. I hate that I'm here, and she's sitting in a hotel in Duluth dealing with this on her own.

I also feel so guilty for everything that happened with Chase. Here I am, having the time of my life with such an incredible and intensely attractive man while my sister is alone. It's a young relationship, but it's perfect already. My sister, though, is hurting. I'm heartbroken.

"Ms. Carter?" a deep male voice says. I smile softly at him. "Hi. I'm Mr. Shaw's pilot. I'll be flying you to Duluth tonight."

"Oh. Um. Thank you." I shake his extended hand and smile tiredly. He smiles warmly in return as he lets go of my hand. He's tall and kind of young. He looks like he may have flown for the Air Force or something. He stands straight and proud like someone in the military.

"I'm going to finish our pre-flight checklist while we wait for Mr. Shaw. The staff will take care of your luggage for you."

"Perfect. Thank you."

He leads me to the plane, which is gorgeous, and helps me climb the stairs while the flight's staff efficiently take care of the luggage. Incredibly efficient. Just like everyone who works for Chase.

As soon as I step aboard, I'm in shock. The plane is just as gorgeous inside as it is out. It's sleek and elaborate, but so is Chase in every way. I can't help but smile as I slowly walk around.

Just then, a guy pops out of the plane's bathroom, and I jump as I let out a squeak. "Oh!"

He's not quite as tall as Chase but his presence is just as dominating. So is the gun on his hip. His smile, however, is easy going and warm. He extends a hand. "Hey. Didn't mean to scare you. I'm Taylor. You must be Breetana?"

"Yeah. Um…" I glance around before taking his hand to shake. He has a strong grip, but he's still gentle.

"I'm a friend of Chase's. More like family. He asked me to come along. I hope that's okay with you."

"I... I mean, of course. He just… he didn't say anything, that's all." I can't hide the disappointment I feel. I had actually psyched myself up to take things a bit further with Chase, even though it might seem fast, but I don't know how that will happen now with someone else traveling with us. I sigh.

Taylor gives an easy laugh. "Hey, don't worry. It won't be a long flight, but there's privacy in the bedroom in the back of the plane. I won't hear a thing!" He laughs again as he sits down. My cheeks immediately turn fifty shades of red before I have a chance to turn and hide it. "Chase will be a bit. He just left the restaurant. Come sit. Keep me company. Tell me about yourself and how you got my dick of a brother to fall for you."

"Holy fuck, Taylor," I breathe. "You're incredibly perceptive and don't mince words at all, huh?"

"Nope. Not in my nature. Come sit."

I have to laugh as I sit in a seat across from him. "You first. I'm at a disadvantage. What do you do? How long have you known Chase?"

"Since we were kids, actually. We grew up together. Right next to each other."

"Oh. What was that like?"

"We were middle class. Went to a public school. By the time we hit high school, we both were pretty big ladies' men. Neither of us wanted to be tied down. By the time we got to college, our reputation preceded us. We spent a lot of time partying. And a lot of time in clubs. We enjoyed Chicago's nightlife."

"And you still enjoy Chicago's nightlife."

"Not nearly as much as before. We try to go out twice a week. But with our jobs, sometimes it doesn't work out."

"What do you do? For work?"

"I'm a Lieutenant. With Chicago P.D. I work mostly in gangs and organized crime." His chest puffs up with pride. I can tell he's definitely proud of what he does. "Your turn. I'm dying to know. What about you makes Chase forget there's other women in the world?" He leans back in his seat and crosses his arms over his chest as he levels me with an intense stare.

I smile softly and look down at my hands. "I honestly don't know. I've liked him for a long time. As a boss, he can be a lot to handle. And I hate both his reputation and all of the women that show up trying to get his attention after their time together ends. To me, directly, he's always been so nice, even though he tends to hide behind that persona he's built. It's different when we're alone. After I first started working for him, my car broke down. I'm from a really small town. I can manage buses, but Silver Bay and Duluth don't have trains or anything like Chicago has."

"It can be overwhelming."

"Yeah. Anyway, I called and told him what happened, and that I was trying to figure out the transit system and would be late. I was actually crying because I was so nervous he was going to fire me. I'd seen him in meetings, and even with some other staff members. He's very no nonsense. He doesn't like excuses. But instead, he told me not to worry about it. That he'd send a car for me, and we'd figure it out."

Taylor smiles. "That doesn't sound like him at all. His last assistant was fired for something similar. She was late getting back from lunch because her boyfriend's car broke down. He fired her on the spot."

"I know. That's why I was so surprised. When I got to work, he had me meet him in his office. I figured he wanted to fire me face to face. But instead, he hugged me. Asked if I was okay and if there was anything he could do to help. I jokingly told him to get me a car that didn't have two hundred thousand miles on it, and one that didn't have a chance of blowing up at any time. He knew I was joking. We laughed about it. The next morning, though, Chase was outside my apartment building waiting for me."

"Uh oh."

"Yes. That's what I thought. He was standing next to a sleek, black Camaro with a giant bow on top. I wasn't sure what to think."

"I remember him telling me about that, actually. It was a while later, but I knew right then he had a thing for you. Chase has never cared about anyone. A few of us, I guess. But really. Other than me, his mom, and maybe one or two other people? He really doesn't give a shit about anyone."

"I know. And he's done things like that ever since. When I'm not feeling well, he senses it. He's made me go home a few times to rest and sent a delivery service with chicken soup for me. None of his other staff calls him Chase."

"Yeah. He prefers Mr. Shaw. Makes him feel like there's a barrier up there."

"He insists on me calling him Chase."

"The other day. He called and said you wanted to resign. Why?"

"You really are a cop, aren't you?" I smile.

He chuckles. "Sorry. Really. I'm pretty protective of Chase. He can handle himself. I know. But he's worth a lot of money. People know that, and you know as well as I do that, if given the chance, they'll take advantage of him. I don't want that. Chase is as much family to me as I am him. We've been through Hell together. Honestly, he's part of the only family I have. Him and his mom and one other person."

"Aww. I really love that. And I understand. I do." I pause and sigh, leaning back in my seat. "Over the past three years that I've been working with Chase, I've just... I've fallen for him. More and more every day. And not because of the money or anything. It's because of how he is with me. Even when others are around. He's guarded, but never like he is with others. He's never yelled at me or tried to intimidate me. He's never been disrespectful or let anyone else disrespect me. He's even been kind of protective of me." I smile shyly. "I once kicked out one of his conquests while he was in a meeting. She threatened me, and it was actually a little bit scary. It's one of the only women that came to the office that I actually told him about. I was pretty freaked out. He drove me to his house that night, and I slept in a guest room. He had someone check out my apartment and stay there for a little while to make sure she didn't show. The next morning, he took me home so I could get ready for work and we drove in together."

"That was me. He put me out there watching your apartment," Taylor says softly.

"Oh... I'm sorry. I didn't know."

"He also had me tail you for a couple of days and assign one of my guys to sit outside your apartment at night. Just to make sure."

"Oh... I didn't know that either." I can feel the heat creeping into my cheeks again, and I look away for a moment as I take a deep breath. "Um... Anyway. The more time I spend with him, getting to know him and everything, the more I like him. The little things he did and does for me... like telling me not to schedule meetings for Monday mornings so that I wouldn't have to stay late and help him prepare on Friday nights. He didn't want me to have to give up my weekends, and he felt really bad the one time he kept me from girl's night. It's the one time a week that me and two friends get to really talk and catch up after our week. The more times I had to deal with his woman of the week, the more hurt and upset I became. I didn't think he would ever see me as more than his assistant. And I suppose I didn't really see why he should. I'm nowhere near the gorgeous, tall, model type that he seems to like. So, I decided to put my heart out of its misery. It broke every time he looked at me, and I just couldn't do it anymore. I decided the best option was to give up the best job I've ever had and walk away from him."

"Wow. That's... a lot. Not what I was expecting."

I shrug. "I had planned on buying my own car and giving him the Camaro back. Even though I love that car. I didn't feel right keeping it. I didn't really feel right taking it in the first place, but I convinced myself it was a company car."

Taylor chuckles. "You, Breetana, are not what I thought you'd be."

I blush. "Is that a good thing or bad thing?"

"Good. It's a very good thing." Taylor looks over my head and nods. "Hey, Chase. How was your meeting?"

"Long. He wouldn't shut the fuck up." He leans over to kiss me. "Sorry, baby. I tried to get done early so we could get out of here, but he really wouldn't stop talking, and I want to keep his account. He's one of my biggest clients."

"It's okay. I understand."

"Was Taylor nice to you? I told him not to be too intimidating when he interrogates you. Didn't want you to run away." He smiles and winks at Taylor. Taylor and I both start laughing.

"She passed the test, man. You've got yourself a good one."

"Good to know you think so, but I already knew." He holds out his hand and pulls me up with him.

"Aren't we about to take off?" I ask, confused.

"Yes. But I want to give you a proper hello. I've missed you all day long, Bree." He pulls me close and kisses me deeply. I almost forget we have an audience, but it doesn't matter. When Chase pulls away and pulls me down into the seat next to him, Taylor isn't paying any attention to us at all. He's busy looking at something on his phone.

We all get seatbelted in and within moments, we're in the air. I really could get used to this private jet thing. Takeoff isn't terrible in the slightest. Pretty smooth sailing, actually.

After the plane levels out, Chase unbuckles his seatbelt and mine. He offers a hand to help me up. Taylor winks at me and smiles. I laugh and shake my head as Chase leads me to the back of the plane. When we get to the infamous bedroom, I stop dead in my tracks. Chase turns and looks at me.

"How is this possible? This room is huge. How did you fit it on a jet?"

Chase laughs. "I tend to get what I want, baby. People make it work for me because they like the paycheck."

"That is such a Chase Shaw thing to say." I smile. He pulls me to the bed and lays down. I crawl in next to him.

He wraps his arms around me and kisses the top of my head. "I had intended on showing you the room, then taking a nap. But now that I have you in this bed, the last thing I'm thinking about is a nap."

"Hmm... Really? What exactly are you thinking, Mr. Shaw?" I picked up on what calling him Mr. Shaw does to him and am rewarded with a deep growl as he shifts and kisses my neck.

He runs his hand down my back and cups my ass underneath my skirt. I really hate wearing skirts, but I might just keep doing it if it gives him such easy access. He squeezes my thigh. "You. With nothing on but your bra. Depending on how much you spill out of it."

I reach down and hike my skirt up to my waist. I don't really understand why, but I'm so comfortable with him. The flashbacks I had when I was first with him are lessening the longer he's near me.

He groans again as he moves his hand from my ass, across my hips, and to my stomach, just above my panty line. I catch his bottom lip between my teeth and gently bite. He gasps and lets his hand wander further down.

I've never ever wanted anyone to touch me as badly as I want him to right now. The pressure and tingling sensation building up is unbelievable. I've wanted him like this for so long. The fact that it happened once and he's still here wanting to do it again makes my head spin.

I spread my legs slightly. He takes the invite and cups me over my panties. I moan into his mouth as his tongue slips into mine. I can't help myself. My hands have a mind of their own as I reach down to touch him. He rubs his hand up and down against me. He's already hard, but my hand on his cock awakens him. He immediately grows harder and bigger. He takes his hand away from me, and I whimper.

He grins. "Just a second, baby. I'll give you what you want, but hard-ons fucking hurt if you're stuck in a pair of pants." He frees himself, and it springs into my hand. He's massive. He's not just long. He's thick. He's big in every sense of the word, and I can't help but stare.

"Wow. Shit. Wow, Chase."

"Like what you see?" He smirks as he watches me.

"Yes. I do," I say breathlessly.

"Good. It's all yours."

I hesitantly reach to touch it. He's like steel encased in satin. Or velvet. I gently rub him as he returns to teasing me. He rubs me over my panties again until I'm nearly panting. After a few moments, he presses his thumb against my clit, and I nearly jump on him. I keep up with his pace as I stroke him.

"More. Chase, please?"

"Are you sure?"

"Yes."

"Tell me, baby. Tell me what you're ready for."

"I want what you did in your office," I whisper with a blush. I'm not a virgin, but I feel like it with him.

"Absolutely, beautiful."

He smiles at me. I love how adoringly he looks at me as he leans down to kiss me. He gently, like I'm made of the finest porcelain, slips my panties down. I wiggle out of them, and he traces his fingers in light circles along my upper thigh while he deepens the kiss and groans into my mouth. I keep up my pace while I stroke him as he cups my core once more.

"Are you sure about this? Are you sure you want this again?"

"Yes, Chase. Really. I'm ready."

He teases my lips with his tongue as he runs the back of a finger down my folds. I shakily inhale and squeeze him a little tighter while I stroke him. "Mmm... Slow down a little, baby. I'm getting really close."

He kisses my smile, and I slow down my strokes. He pushes a finger against my tender bud, and I gasp. He slides a finger down, slips it inside, and starts thrusting. I nearly cry with pleasure. He knows just how to touch and where.

"Oh my…"

"Yeah? Feel good?"

"So good. So, so good, Chase." I begin moving with his finger as he flicks my clit with his thumb. The sensation shoots straight to my pussy, and I throw my head back. "Mmm... Chase…"

"My name on your lips is driving me crazy, Bree." He kisses my throat as he adds a second finger to the expertise of the first while he keeps pressure and light movement against my sensitive nub.

I'm not really all that experienced with getting guys off, but I've been paying attention, and Chase seems to really like long, slow strokes and a spot just below his tip played with. I keep doing that and revel in his soft sighs and whispered words of encouragement against my mouth as he kisses me.

"Right there, baby," he murmurs.

"Mmm... don't stop doing that." Every time he draws his fingers out, he hits a spot inside me that intensifies the pleasure coursing through me as he strokes my clit.

I buck my hips against him faster as his strokes inside me deepen and quicken. I've never had anyone give me this type of pleasure before. Other than myself or my trusty vibrator, but him? He's taking me beyond anything I've ever given myself. Certainly anything that was ever forced on me. I feel him tense and twitch beneath me, and a growl escapes his lips as he kisses my neck.

“There. Chase! Right there…” I arch into him. My pussy clenches and tightens erratically as I get closer and closer.

He gives more attention to my clit as he drags his fingers along the spot inside me. He continues his ministrations. My stomach tightens, and so do I. Seconds later, unable to stop myself, I’m careening off a cliff. My hips jerk into his fingers.

“Ah! Chase! Chase!”

Something warm and sticky covers my hand and hits my stomach as Chase monas. “Holy fuck, Bree,” Chase pants. He deepens our kiss once more and slows his thrusts as we both come down from our high.

“Oh… God…,” I whisper against his lips.

After a few moments of kissing and catching our breath, Chase reluctantly pulls away, sliding his fingers slowly out of me. “Mmm. That was amazing. Best hand job I've ever had. Including from myself.” He kisses me with a smirk.

I giggle. “You're just saying that,” I say shyly.

He shakes his head. “Nope. You're amazing, sexy girl. I mean that. You learn quick.”

“In that case… that was definitely better than anything I've ever done to myself, and I can't wait to do it again.” I kiss him.

He smiles and pulls away languidly. “I've honestly never wanted to just *be* with someone all the time like I do you. I can't get enough of you. I love the way you smile. I love the way your eyes light up when you laugh. How you blush when I compliment you. I miss you when you aren't near me. I can't stand not having you in my bed at night. It's so new for me to feel like this.”

“I feel the same way. I have for so long,” I whisper before clearing my throat and touching his chest. “I love how you're so respectful and protective of me. How you won't let anyone talk down to me. I love everything about you, and I hate when you aren't near me.”

He exhales slowly. “Goddamn, you have no idea how happy I am to hear you say that.”

I smile and softly kiss him. “Mmm... I feel like we should probably get up, and get cleaned up. It's not really a long flight.”

“I guess you're right. I don't really want to, though.” He kisses my nose, and then forces himself to get up. He gives me a hand and leads me to the bathroom in the room.

I hadn't noticed, but there's a dresser. Chase walks to it. He gives me a once over and raises an eyebrow as I'm putting my panties back on.

“What?” I ask as I pause, my panties at my feet.

“I just realized your skirt is really wrinkled.”

“Oh. Don't worry. It's okay. We're just going straight to the hotel anyway.” I pull my panties up.

“Are you sure? I love Taylor, but if he sees you like that, he won't drop it.”

“I can take it. It's okay. All of my stuff is packed anyway. I didn't bring anything on the plane. The staff took the bags.”

“I have a pair of sweats.”

I raise an eyebrow. “And Taylor wouldn't latch onto that?”

We both laugh. “Okay, okay. Good point.” I watch as Chase changes out of his suit into a pair of jeans and a long sleeve shirt.

“Holy…,” I breathe.

Chase laughs as I stare at him. “What, beautiful?”

“You should always wear jeans.” My eyes roam over his body, unashamed at ogling him. “Seriously. It's like they were made for you.”

“They were, baby. You pick my stuff up from my tailor. You know all of my stuff is tailored just for me.”

“I know, but I've only ever seen you in suits. And gym clothes. And sweats the other day. I’ve never, ever seen you in jeans.”

He stalks towards me until he’s close enough to pull me into him. I slip my arms around his waist and grab his ass as I smile up at him. He grins before leaning down to kiss me. “I told you to pack casual for me, right?”

“Yes.”

“And?”

“I did.”

“What did you pack?”

“Necessities. And everything I thought you would look amazing in... including jeans.”

“Good girl.” He leans down to kiss me again as a knock sounds on the door.

“Chase, it's time to land. Get your head out from between Breetana's thighs, and get your asses out here.”

Chase laughs, and I turn as red as my shirt. “Oh my God,” I groan.

He kisses me and hands me another long sleeve shirt. I look up at him, perplexed. He smiles and grabs the hem of my shirt. I look down and see white on it.

“I tried to get your shirt up before I came, but I wasn't quite quick enough. Sorry. I'll send it to the dry cleaners. Just put it on the bed with my suit. Staff will deal with it.” I strip off the shirt, and Chase's eyes become immediately darkly hooded. “Christ, you're beautiful, Bree.”

I giggle. Again. I never ever giggle. But here I am giggling like a schoolgirl. I change into his shirt and inhale its unique scent. “I love the smell of you. It's intoxicating and comforting at the same time.”

“I could say the same for you, you know.”

“You're never getting this back. You know that, right?” I smile as Chase laughs again. “At least not until it stops smelling like you.”

“Baby, if that's what you want, it's all yours. And when it stops smelling like me, I'll just spray some of my cologne on it.”

“Now you're really never getting it back.”

He smiles and takes my hand. We get seat-belted back into our seats and begin our descent as Taylor grins like an idiot.

I shake my head. “This is going to be a thing now, isn't it?” I say with a soft, amused smile.

“Oh yes,” Taylor says. “Big thing.”

“Be nice,” Chase chuckles.

“I'm always nice,” Taylor says, giving an innocent smile.

“I can think of a few people who are rotting in a jail cell who may disagree. Along with several broken-hearted women.”

“Not nearly as many as you,” Taylor quips. I laugh.

“Maybe, but I finally got what I wanted. She's worth all of them, times all of my billions. Makes her pretty damn priceless in my book. So don't be a dick.”

“I would never. I like her too much!” Taylor holds up his hands and winks at me.

I roll my eyes. “Oh boy. You two gonna start fighting over me?” I love how easily I can interject into their easy banter.

“I'd win. Hands down.” Taylor gives me a serious smile.

“I taught you everything you know,” Chase says cockily.

“Ha! Bullshit. The academy did!”

“Boys! Boys! I only have eyes for one of you.”

“See? I win. And I didn't even have to fight you. She knows instinctively whose tongue she prefers in her mouth... and between her thighs.” Chase winks at me. I swat his arm, and Taylor bellows with laughter. Chase sweetly kisses my hand.

It's not long before we’ve landed and are getting ready to get off the plane. I take a few deep breaths. I haven't set foot in Duluth since I left ten years ago. Duluth holds horrible memories but nothing like Silver Bay. Nothing. I'm terrified, but I force myself to stay strong for my sister. She doesn't need me to fall apart. She needs her older sister to be strong for her, and that is just what I intend to do.

Hopefully everything will go smoothly, and everyone will leave us alone. I don't want Chase or Taylor knowing what happened. I’m sure Chase would run. And Taylor? He's fiercely loyal and protective. I don't doubt he would know exactly how to dispose of my body.

I reach up and wipe a tear away as Taylor and Chase joke around with each other. I should tell him. But I don't want him to hate me. I don't want him to think I'm a whore or a bitch or slut like everyone else does. I love him. He may not know it, but I do. I’ve fallen so far in love with him over the past three years that him walking out of my life at this point would truly be my undoing.

I won't be able to come back from that.

Chapter Six

⚔ Chase ⚔

I take Breetana's hand as I open the door to the SUV I rented. She steps out, but she looks terrified. Taylor doesn't miss it. He glances at me, and I give him a slight shake of my head and shrug of my shoulder. Taylor nods, and the three of us walk into the hotel. Breetana cowers behind me. When I try to release her hand, she grips it tighter and stares up at me, wild-eyed.

"Baby, I don't know what's going on, but nothing is going to happen to you. Not with me and Taylor around, okay?" She nods, but she looks like she wants to flee. I look at Taylor.

He takes my hint and steps in. "Breetana. Chase is just going to check in. Do you trust me?" he asks.

She nods, but her breath is shaky. Her eyes dart around the lobby.

"Breetana. Look at me. Nothing else matters but me. Look at me, sweetheart." He keeps his voice even. Calm.

She looks at him, but I can tell how scared she is, and it nearly breaks me.

"Take my hand, sweetheart."

She takes his hand, and he allows her to grip it as tightly as she needs to. Her grip on mine loosens, and Taylor holds out his other hand.

"Come on, Breetana. I know you can do it. Trust me."

She closes her eyes and releases mine but quickly grabs his.

He looks at me then back at her. "We're going to go over by the elevators. Okay, Breetana? No one is over there. Just you and me."

"O-okay." She visibly takes deep breaths as he leads her away.

I take a second to compose myself before turning to the counter to check in. It only takes a few minutes, but every second away from her when I know she needs me is like torture.

Pure fucking torture.

I finally get the keys to our rooms and hurry across the lobby to get to her. When I round the corner at the elevators, Breetana is on her knees dry-heaving and coughing.

Taylor is hugging her and rubbing her back. He looks confused as hell. "Breetana? Chase is here, okay? Ready to stand up?" he asks in the most soothing voice I've ever heard him use. She nods but doesn't release the grip on his shirt. I punch the elevator button, and he gently guides her in as soon as the door opens.

"Bree. Baby, talk to me. What's happening right now?" I ask her. She shakes her head and stays hidden in Taylor's chest.

He keeps his grip on her waist as he looks at me. "I'm sorry, man. For the first time in my life, I don't think I know what to do."

"Step one is getting her to the room. We'll go from there." I hate that it's Taylor holding her. I wish it were me, but she feels safe, and that's all I care about.

As soon as we step off the elevator and find our room, I open the door and usher them both in. Breetana has calmed slightly, but her grip on Taylor's shirt is still prevalent. I close the door behind them, and before I have any time to react, Breetana runs from the room.

"Holy shit, man. Something really bad happened to her," Taylor says. His hand is shaking as he runs his hand through his hair and turns away. I've never seen him nervous. He doesn't show it. He's always been the most calm and collected person, in any situation, I've ever met.

"What? Did she tell you what happened?"

"No. But something happened. As soon as we rounded the corner, she fucking started crying. Hard. She dropped to her knees, and just started sobbing so hard she nearly threw up. Fuck. I've never seen anything like that, and I've seen a lot, Chase." He turns back towards me. "She fell apart."

"I know. I saw." I don't waste any more time. I take a deep breath and head towards the bedroom in the suite. I cautiously open the door and poke my head in. "Bree?" She doesn't answer. She's lying flat on her stomach on the bed. I walk into the room, closing the door behind me, and crossing to the bed. I crawl in next to her. "Baby? Please talk to me. I want to understand what's happening, but I don't. Tell me what happened here."

"I can't. I really can't. I'm scared." I put my arms around her and force her to look at me.

"Bree, what's going on? What are you afraid of?" I make sure there's not a single hint of CEO in my tone. It's my turn to be the calm and collected one.

"I'm afraid…" She burrows into my chest. "I've fallen for you, Chase. Really. I know you probably think I'm crazy, but I really did. I'm scared you're going to leave me."

"Baby, I won't. I won't. I just want to know what's going on here. I hate seeing you so scared. You scared the fuck out of Taylor. He isn't afraid of anything. And you're scaring me because I don't know what's happening."

"I promise I will tell you. But please don't make me right now. I really want to talk to Kiki. I've felt so bad she's been here alone all day." She tries to get up, but I hold her tighter. I know she's trying to be stronger than she feels.

"Please don't run again, Breetana."

"I'm not. I'm sorry I scared you. But I need to get to Kiki. She needs me." She takes several deep breaths to steady herself.

"Baby, I know. I know she needs you. Just…" I don't want to push her.

She said she had fallen for me. Fucking Christ, help me, but I'm a goner. I had fallen hard for her. I don't want to keep her from her sister. I don't want to push her, but I feel her shutting down. I feel her closing me off and pushing me away again.

I don't want that. I can't let her do that to me. To us. Not after how far we've come in such a short time. She was starting to trust me. If I push her, I know she'll run.

I sigh. "Just don't push me away, Breetana. I'm here. I dropped everything to be here for you. That has to count for something. I'm not going anywhere. No matter how hard you push me away, I'll still be here." I hug her tighter. She doesn't say anything, but she does hug me closer as she takes another deep breath. I kiss the top of her head as I release her and get up. "Go to your sister. I'll be here when you get back."

"Chase." She stands up and walks to me, stopping in front of me. She puts her hands on my shoulders and stands on her tiptoes, but she still can't quite reach my lips. I smile and lean down to kiss her. "Thank you. For understanding that I need to be with her. And for not pushing me. Even though I know how hard it is for you."

"Maybe it'll help you see that I'm not going anywhere. That I'll be right here despite everything."

"Thank you." She kisses me again and leaves the room. I don't walk out to the living room of the suite until I hear the door to the suite close. Steeling myself, I find Taylor. He's sitting on the balcony looking at Lake Superior. The breeze is cool, though the humidity is thick.

"Feels like Chicago," I say as I sit next to him.

"Way fucking worse. People go crazy in weather like this."

"With a cool breeze?"

"That's by the lake. I bet over that hill you could cut through the humidity with a knife. It's so thick I bet it stops bullets."

I laugh before turning serious once more. "She scared the fuck out of you. Didn't she?"

"I've seen a lot of shit, Chase. Scary shit. I've seen panic attacks. That? That was the worst fucking thing I've ever seen. That wasn't a panic attack. That was a scared fucking woman completely falling apart."

I swallow to steady myself. "I know."

"As soon as I kneeled down, she grabbed my waist. Her hand was close to my gun. I didn't know what the fuck was going on. And then she grabbed my shirt and wouldn't let go, Chase. Like she needed me to anchor her."

"I know. Believe me." I look at him before looking out at the lake again. "She still won't tell me."

"I'm going to research it. Do some investigating. Something happened to that girl. Something bad. Something that traumatized her."

I nod slowly. "I know."

Taylor is quiet for a little while. Finally, he clears his throat. "Chase, I need to know right now. Before I start digging. What's going on between you two has been going for a long time. It's not new. It might seem like it because the relationship is finally starting, but it's not brand new feelings. You've had them for a while. What are you looking for with her? Honestly?"

I don't hesitate for a second. "I love that girl, Taylor. I'm sorry I didn't tell her sooner, and I'm sorry for putting her through what I did. But none of that matters now. I love her."

Taylor breathes a sigh of relief. "I was really hoping you'd say that. I know you're fiercely loyal and protective of those you love."

"Why? What do you know right now about what happened?"

"Nothing. But I think that whatever happened to her is going to really test your relationship."

"I'm not going anywhere."

"I wasn't talking about you. I know you won't."

I take a deep breath. "You think she'll run."

"I think her being here and us going to Silver Bay tomorrow is going to be extremely hard. For her. For her sister. For us. It's going to be very difficult. You are going to have to prove you aren't going anywhere. I think this is going to be a very hard and very long road."

"Well, I'm up for it. I'm not fucking going anywhere. She thinks whatever happened is her fault. I don't like that she looks at herself as... I don't know. Not good enough. Not worth it. And it has to do with whatever happened."

"I could look into it. I want to. But I won't if you don't want me to. I strongly advise against that decision, though. Whatever happened is fucked up."

I want Breetana to tell me on her own. But I also know that I can't help her if she's afraid to tell me because she thinks I'll leave her. I sigh. "Fuck. Do it. Do what you do. But don't let Breetana know. I want her to come to me."

Taylor takes his phone out. "I have contacts all over the place. This particular one can get information without anyone knowing I was involved."

"Who?" I narrow my eyes slightly as I look at him.

"Probably better if you didn't know."

"Fuck you, Taylor. Breetana's involved. When it comes to my girl, I want to know everything."

"Fine," Taylor sighs. "But I promise you. You don't want to know." He dials a number, and I glare at him. "Hey! Ryan, it's Taylor... Yeah. I never got a chance to thank you for that. Listen. I need your help if you're willing…" He pauses, and then winks at me. I continue to glare. "I appreciate that. It's about a girl. Chase's girl, so this is... uh... well. It's personal. It's family. You know I wouldn't ask you for help otherwise."

I have to smile a bit at him calling me family. He isn't lying. We grew up together. We are like family. It always makes me smile when he says it. He didn't have anyone he could count on growing up except me and my mom.

"Well, there's some trouble. We think it has to do with her uncle, and Chase said something about college. She's really down on herself, and whatever the fuck happened, she's pretty fucking convinced it's her fault. And it had to have been bad. We're sitting here in Duluth, Minnesota, and as soon as we walked into the hotel, she had a fucking all out... I don't even know. It was far fucking worse than any panic attack I've ever seen." He pauses and listens for a moment. "Her name is Breetana Carter. She's from Silver Bay, Minnesota. But this could've happened in Duluth... Date of birth?" He looks at me.

I tell him then smile a little. She's turning thirty this year. He repeats the information as he paces and gives what information he knows to this Ryan guy. Finally he hangs up.

"Well?" I ask.

"He'll help us."

"Great. But you know what I meant. Who the fuck is he?"

Taylor sighs and sits down. "He's the brother of another billionaire. Owns some kind of a real estate company. Jason Crane."

"Property development. Very different. Jason and his wife Jessa invest with my company. He's a VIP client. I know who he is."

"His brother's name is Ryan Crane. He's the leader of one of the most powerful mafias in the entire world."

I nearly choke as I look at him incredulously when it hits me. I know who Ryan is, too. I also hold his accounts. I know he's clean, but fuck.

"What the fuck did you just do? You just got me and Breetana involved with the fucking mafia? Are you fucking crazy?" I'm seething. It's taking all of me not to throw him off the balcony. I jump up and start pacing.

"Chase. You have to trust me on this. Ryan is actually a good guy. He's helped me out on a lot of cases. Granted, taking down other gangs and mobs helps him out so it's a mutual thing, but he doesn't bother innocent people. He isn't into crime exactly."

"He's the fucking leader of the mafia, Taylor! I might hold his investment accounts and know of him. I know he's a good guy. But holy shit, Taylor! The mafia!"

"Fuck, Chase. Keep it the fuck down!" he hisses. I glare and reign in my temper. "I trust him. And if I trust him, you know you can. I don't fucking trust anyone."

"I trust you, but this is the mafia. He might be the greatest person in the world, but he has enemies. Fuck, if she gets hurt, Taylor…"

"She won't. Ryan is discreet, but he's also loyal to a fault. He's never betrayed my trust. He won't betray yours. He'll protect her."

I nod and lean on the balcony railing. I close my eyes and breathe in the fresh air from the lake. I've never not trusted Taylor, and I won't start now. I don't like that the mafia is getting involved, but I need to protect Breetana. From what exactly, I don't know., but I'll do it.

No matter what the cost.

Chapter Seven

⚔ Breetana ⚔

I've been sitting on the couch in my sister's suite with her head in my lap for nearly an hour now. She's barely said a word, but she's finally starting to relax. I can feel her breathing even out.

He hit her. The son of a bitch hit her. Her eye is bruised and swollen, and I was so angry when I saw it that all of my own fears of being here immediately went away. No one messes with my sister. No one. He'll pay for this. I'll make certain of it.

"I'm sorry I made you come here, Tana. I'm sorry I'm so stupid and can't deal with this on my own," Nicole whispers.

My heart breaks in two, and I nearly cry myself. "Stop it, Kiki. Right now. This isn't on you. This is on that stupid asshole Billy and Uncle Joe."

"I shouldn't have believed him. That he was sorry and wanted to work it out." She chokes back a sob. I force myself to be strong, even though all I want to do is cry for her. I hate when she calls herself stupid. I hate that she thinks that way about herself. I hate how broken my little sister is.

"You can't blame yourself. Billy never should've laid his hands on you. And Joe never should have let him."

"He egged him on, Tana. He told him I deserved it for being such an embarrassment."

I stroke her hair and lean down to kiss her head. "This isn't your fault. I promise I'll fix it. I promise." I don't know how, but they will pay for this. All of it.

She relaxes a little more and sighs. "Do you remember when we were kids, and you would make my day better by doing just this? Or brushing my hair? Or braiding it?"

"I do. I really miss this. I miss you."

"Well, I'll be with you now!" She laughs weakly.

I smile. "You will. I'm excited!" I say more cheerfully than I feel. I'm happy she'll be coming back to Chicago with me, but I hate that it's under these circumstances.

"I'm excited to meet this hot boss guy you won't shut up about," she teases.

I blush and laugh. "Would you like to meet him now? He's right next door. And his friend is in the room on the other side of you."

"So, I'm a Kiki sandwich?"

I laugh again as I look down at her. "Yes. I wanted you to feel safe. Taylor is a police officer. I didn't know he'd be coming, but I'm glad that he did."

"You're here. I feel safer now than I have in so long. You've always protected me."

"And I always will," I vow.

Nicole gets up and wipes her eyes. "Well? Let's go. I'm dying to meet the man who dropped everything to bring my sister to me when I needed her most."

I smile. "Chase really is a shockingly beautiful soul."

I stand and lead her to mine and Chase's suite. Chase and Taylor are sitting in the front room. They both look up at us when we enter, and they stand.

"Nicole, this is Chase. He's my... um…" I'm not really sure what to call him, but Chase smiles and swoops in to save me.

He walks closer and holds out a hand to Nicole. "Breetana's boyfriend." I beam at him as he shakes her hand. "And this is Taylor. He's my brother." Chase gestures to Taylor.

He's standing stock still, staring at my sister. My eyes widen as I see the look in his eyes. He clears his throat and shakes his head as I smile widely. "Hey. I'm... um... Taylor."

"Oh... um.... Hi. Hi…,Taylor." Nicole shakes his hand and looks down. I smile wider. Chase raises an eyebrow at the scene but says nothing.

Finally, I clear my throat and Taylor drops Nicole's hand. "Should I get us a drink?" I ask.

"Yes. Please. Whiskey. Neat," Taylor says with a confused and pained expression. He plops on the couch, and I laugh. Chase smiles as Nicole joins him. I head to the bar, and Chase heads to the fridge.

"Glad to see they put the juices I requested in here," Chase says.

"I made sure all of your demands were met," I smile.

"Just wanted to make sure your sister has something to drink since she's pregnant."

I look up at him as he puts the apple juice on the bar and slips his arms around my waist. "I really love that you think of everything."

"I pay attention, and I'm very detail-oriented." He kisses my neck as I pour whiskey for him and Taylor. He releases me and pours the juice into a cup for me and another for Nicole. "I also know you aren't a big drinker."

"Not usually. Unless I want to forget something," I joke.

"Like some jerk who makes you feel like another conquest?" His mouth turns up into a teasing smile.

I laugh. "Yes. Exactly."

"I hate that I made you feel that way, you know. I should've been fucking honest and told you years ago how I felt about you."

My breath catches. Has he really felt the same way about me for as long? I don't dare let myself believe that. "I never drank that night. I didn't even go out. I went home. Too depressed to -"

"Chase. Breetana. You guys need to read these. We have a problem," Taylor calls from the other room.

I glance at Chase. He grabs his drink and mine and heads into the other room while I grab Taylor's and Nicole's and follow. I hand them their drinks, and Taylor hands me Nicole's phone. I turn to Chase. He's sitting in an oversized chair, but the other one is kind of far away. We wouldn't be able to read together. I settle for the arm of the chair, but he pulls me into his lap.

He kisses my shoulder and slips his arms around my waist as we begin reading. "Shit," Chase breathes.

"Oh God," I whisper. All of the text messages are Billy calling Nicole stupid for running. He says he found her. That he knew she was in Duluth. But the last one... it sent chills up my spine.

Billy: If you think your bitch sister can do anything to save you, I guess I'll have to go through her, too. Shouldn't be too hard. She's a lying slut just like you are. Be there soon, baby. We can have a bunch of fun with that lake right outside.

"Oh, God, Kiki. Why? Why didn't you tell me he was texting you all day?" I can hear the panic that I'm trying to hold back in my voice.

"I had my GPS off. I didn't think he could find me. I thought he was bluffing. Until the last text. I just got it now." Nicole is shaking. Chase looks up at Taylor.

"Nicole," Taylor begins a little unsteadily. "I... don't think it's a good idea for you to stay in that suite."

"How does he know?" I ask. "I rented it under Chase's name. My name isn't associated. Neither is Nicole's. I'm so confused.

"I don't know, Breetana. But I really don't like what's going on here. Call it instinct," Taylor tells me.

"Well, she'll stay with us," I say decisively.

"We both can't fit on the couch, baby, and she's in no condition to sleep on the couch," Chase says.

"It's okay. I'll be fine," Nicole says.

"Not happening. You can sleep in my suite. I'll take the couch," Taylor cuts in.

"But that isn't fair to you!" Nicole exclaims.

"I'll be fine. Not the first time I've slept on the couch."

"I feel like I should at least get a say. I don't feel comfortable sleeping by myself, obviously, but what if he gets in and gets to me anyway?" Nicole's eyes dart around the room as she hugs herself.

"Maybe you should sleep with her, Taylor," I suggest. I know he likes her. The undeniable attraction between the two of them is hard to miss. Even with everything she just went through. Matters of the heart just can't be controlled. Nicole and Taylor both blush furiously, and I put a hand to my mouth realizing my mistake, but I giggle a little. "I just meant in the same bed."

"I agree. At the very least, in the same room," Chase says.

Taylor nods and smiles weakly. "I think I should call Ryan."

"Ryan?" I look at Chase.

"He's a... uh... a contact. Of Taylor's." Chase looks at Taylor. "You should call him. He's going to need all of the information."

"Nicole, is it okay if I take your phone and send these to him?" Taylor asks.

"Oh... um.... I guess it's okay. I... I'm sorry. I guess I don't understand what he's going to do."

Taylor takes Nicole's hand and looks at her. "Ryan is a friend. He's helped me out of a lot of sticky situations. I called him earlier after Breetana went to your room because I really think there's something bigger going on here. Call it a cop's instinct, but Ryan is the only person I trust other than the people in this room and mine and Chase's mom. I don't know how far up this guy goes, but if he can find you with no GPS, then I'd say far."

Nicole looks at him a moment and then nods. Taylor walks out to the balcony to make his call.

"I know you won't be in your suite tonight, but I think it might be a good idea if we leave the room connectors to our rooms open," I say to Nicole.

"Okay. I'm game. Why?" Chase asks, narrowing his eyes.

I shrug. "I know it's kind of dangerous. If he does show, and she's not in there, he may try to get into other rooms. But if he comes and starts pounding on the door, Taylor and Nicole could slip over here pretty easily."

"I don't know if Taylor will go for that, but I'll talk to him," Chase says.

"He's a cop, right? We don't have to leave the door open. I feel safe with him." Nicole smiles at me as reassuringly as she can. But all I can think about is her safety.

"It's up to you, Kiki. Of course. I just want you to feel safe," I say.

Taylor comes back in as I call Nicole 'Kiki.' "Why do you call her Kiki? I'm dying to know."

I smile. Nicole laughs. "When she was born, I couldn't say Nicole," I begin. "Or Nikki. So I started calling her Kiki. I just never really stopped."

"And I call her Tana because I couldn't say Breetana. I had trouble with my 'R's when I was a kid."

"That's adorable. Really." Taylor half smiles as he leans back on the couch.

Nicole looks at him. "Tana was wondering if we should keep the doors between the rooms open in case he does show, and we have to escape."

"I'd prefer them closed and locked. I can protect you better with less places for him to enter through," Taylor answers.

Chase chuckles. "I thought you'd say that."

"So did I. It was just an idea," I say softly.

Taylor can see the worry on my face as he stands. He walks over to me and kisses me on top of the head. "Get some sleep, Tana. I promise I'll keep your sister safe."

I groan as he offers Nicole a hand up and leads her to the door. "This is going to be another thing, isn't it? The nickname?"

"Fuck yes," he laughs. Nicole laughs with him as they leave our suite, hand in hand.

Chase gently pushes me off him and walks over to the adjoining door, making sure both sides are locked. After he's checked all the locks on all the doors, he takes my hand and pulls me to the bedroom.

As soon as we get there, he strips to his boxer briefs, and I smile at the sight. I change into a tank top and join him in bed. He pulls me close and kisses me.

"He hit her, Chase."

"I saw, baby. Taylor mentioned it to Ryan."

"Is this Ryan guy really going to help us?"

"Taylor doesn't trust anyone, baby. If he trusts him, then I do, too." I settle into his arms. "Go to sleep, Bree. We've got a long day ahead of us."

He kisses the top of my head again and again, and I sigh. He doesn't know the half of it. He has no idea how long it's going to be.

The next three days will never end.

Chapter Eight

⚔ Chase ⚔

Holy fuck. I stand next to Taylor and look up at the house in front of us. Breetana is in front of me with her back to me and my arms wrapped around her. Taylor is standing next to me, holding Nicole close to his side. I can tell he likes her, but I don't bring anything up. It's not the time.

I'm happy for him, though. Despite the situation. He deserves to feel the way I do about a woman who captures his heart like Breetana did with mine. Never thought I'd see the day, though I did expect that if it came, he'd fall fast and hard.

When Nicole left the house yesterday, only one window was broken. Today, three windows are broken, and the front of the house is spray painted in bright red. 'Slut.' 'Whore.' 'Bitch.' All words used in the graffiti.

But the one I don't get. 'Sweet Pussy Bakery.' I assume it has to do with her business, but I thought she closed it. It doesn't make sense to spray paint that on her house.

"Why? What is the purpose of this?" Breetana asks, tearfully.

"'Sweet Pussy Bakery?' I get everything else. But that?" I ask.

“My bakery was called Sweet Escapes Bakery. I focused on exotic flavors. My pineapple rose cupcake was one of my best sellers.” Nicole pauses and takes a deep breath. “Billy... he always told me I tasted so sweet. That I should make a signature flavor of myself.” She breaks down in tears and buries her head in Taylor's chest. He holds her close and runs his fingers through her long blonde hair.

Yeah. He’s a goner. He becomes a sucker when a woman cries. He can’t handle them.

I glance around and notice a few of the neighbors have taken notice of us. They’re glaring and whispering to each other. Taylor notices, as well, and clears his throat, but just as he's about to talk we both see a truck with supplies drive into the driveway. A guy gets out, and I feel Breetana stop breathing. He glances at her. Nicole breaks free from Taylor and grabs Breetana's hand, pulling her into the house. I narrow my eyes, even more confused than before. We will definitely be talking about that.

“Hey. One of you Chase Shaw? I'm Shaun Blithe.”

“Yeah. That's me. We spoke on the phone.” I shake his hand as Taylor joins me.

He shakes Shaun’s hand as well. “Hey. I'm Taylor.”

“I assume these are the supplies I ordered?” I gesture to his truck.

He turns and nods. “Yeah. Should be everything.” Taylor and I follow him to the truck. He drops the tailgate and jumps into the back. I can sense Taylor's uneasiness as he watches him. Shaun turns back to us. “Word of advice from a local. One man to another. Stay away from those two. They thrive on ruining people's lives.”

I cross my arms over my chest and glance over at the house. “Looks to me like it's the opposite here. Like someone's trying to ruin theirs.”

“That?” He nods to the house. Taylor is more tense as the moments pass. “I did bring you more supplies than you ordered when I found out there was more damage. But that right there is just someone finally getting revenge. Been a long time coming.”

“There's nothing right about what happened here,” Taylor growls, glaring at him.

“I didn't say it was right. I said it was revenge. Those two started ruining lives years ago.”

“Oh yeah? What did they do that was so bad?” I ask.

He starts unloading the truck, handing Taylor and I supplies as he talks. “The older one. Breetana? She got knocked up in college at a party. But she'd been with so many different guys that night that her boyfriend didn't know if it was his or not. He broke up with her, and she obsessively stalked him. He finally had to get the police involved. She fled to some big city to escape charges being filed.”

Taylor glances at me and narrows his eyes. No fucking way either of us are believing a word that comes out of this asshole's mouth.

“Pretty shitty. What about the other chick?” Taylor asks. We can tell this guy likes to talk. And that he thinks we believe him.

“Nikki? She's power hungry. Always wants more. She's slept around this town to get what she wants. She didn't have to pay a damn thing for the licensing or for the permits for her bakery. She just gave out a few favors to a few high people. Where she fucked up was when she was caught with the Mayor. By his son, who was supposed to have been her boyfriend. He was pretty heartbroken.” He finishes the unload and jumps down. “Anyway. I'd steer clear of those two if I were the two of you. They bring trouble wherever they go. Not sure what either of them promised you.” He looks both of us up and down. It takes everything in me not to throat punch him. “Or what they've done already. But they're not worth it.” He nods and gets back in his truck. We watch as he drives away.

“What the fuck just happened?” Taylor asks as Shuan’s truck disappears.

“No fucking idea. I need to check on Bree.”

We both turn towards the house when Taylor's phone goes off. He puts a hand on my arm, stopping me as he answers. “Ryan! Hey. What'd you find out?” His eyes go wide as he glances at me. “Hang on. Hang on. Chase is with me. I'm gonna put you on speaker.” Taylor heads towards the SUV and jumps in. I reluctantly follow. I want to know what Ryan found out, but I want to get to Breetana. I jump in next to Taylor, and he puts it on speaker. “Alright. You're good. Chase is listening.”

“Okay. First thing first. You asked what happened to Breetana. It's not good, bro,” Ryan says.

“Just tell him,” Taylor orders.

“When she was fifteen and her sister was thirteen, their parents died. It was suspicious as hell. They died in a fire that was suspected arson, but ultimately ruled accidental. I did some digging and found reports. The original reports were buried. Police who were first on scene said that witnesses saw someone running from the scene before they heard an explosion. Official reports make no mention of the witnesses or the person running."

"So a cover-up," I say.

"For certain," Ryan agrees. "But that isn't all. The original arson investigator said there was evidence of an accelerant, and that it looked as if someone tampered with the gas stove. He found small cuts in the line going to the stove. He believed someone cut slits in the line to cause a gas leak, and then used the accelerant to give him time to get out before the explosion. Officer's even had a suspect."

"Let me guess." Everything is so obvious to me now. Fuck. "I bet it was their uncle."

"Yep," Ryan confirms. "Joseph Carter. Older brother of their father."

"Did they arrest him?" Taylor asks.

"They did," Ryan continues. "But he never went to trial. The arson investigator was fired shortly after on allegations of corruption. His report was thrown out and another investigator was used. The issue is that the new one said he was there during the original investigation, which the original one vehemently denies. He had his own report, but since he wasn't lead, he said his report never came to light. He said the original investigator told him this case was above his pay grade. Leave it alone or he'll get hurt."

"Threatened him?" I ask incredulously.

"That's what he said. His report, the official report used, said there was a gas leak, but there was nothing suspicious. It was an unfortunate accident," Ryan says.

"What about the cops who showed up?" Taylor questions.

"Their reports were changed," Ryan answers. "Said the house was fully engulfed on arrival, and no one had seen shit."

"Sounds to me like they were paid off." I shake my head and rub my temple

"You're right. They probably were. They were fired around the same time as the arson investigator for drug charges, though, so it didn't matter. The entire case against Joe was thrown out."

"Jesus Christ," I say.

"That's not even the worst part," Ryan continues. I stare at the phone. It can't possibly get worse. "After his arrest, there are several reports of sexual and physical abuse allegations all made by, or on behalf, of Breetana. They started coming in after Joe was released and continued for years. None of them saw the light of day. He made it seem like she was crazy. That she was troubled. She was having issues dealing with the tragic deaths of her parents. She was acting out. A horny teenager who came on to him."

"What the fuck?" I'm getting more and more angry the more Ryan talks. I can't fucking believe what I'm hearing. How could someone do what's been done to her and still be fucking breathing?

"So, no one listened to her." Taylor closes his eyes as he leans his head back on the seat.

"Her story never changed. It was always that she was protecting her little sister from him. He left her little sister alone and took out all of his wrath and sick fucking fantasies on her instead. The cops finally removed her sister from the situation when she was sixteen and showed up to school with bruises all over her body. Doctors did an exam and said there was significant evidence of sexual abuse. Joe went to jail for ten years."

"You mean he just got out." My stomach drops. Fuck this can't be happening.

"Last year," Ryan confirms.

"Holy shit," Taylor whispers.

"In college, Breetana went to the University of Minnesota in Duluth. At a party, she was pretty wasted and had sex with her long-time high school sweetheart. When she woke up the next morning, her boyfriend had called her uncle to pick her up. Joe was shaking her awake, according to the report Campus PD filed and her statement. Someone called them because they heard screaming. When Campus PD showed up, he was gone, but he'd beat her up pretty badly."

"Let me guess," Taylor interrupts. "Never charged."

"Never fucking arrested. He had an alibi. Said he went to breakfast with her boyfriend while she slept it off. Said her boyfriend was upset because he walked into her room, and she was with five different guys. And they were all taking turns with her. She dealt with so much harassment after that, she dropped the semester. Transferred to the -"

"University of Illinois in Chicago," I finish for him.

"Yes," Ryan confirms.

My heart is one hundred percent broken for her, and what she went through. "Fuck."

"What about Nicole?" Taylor's eyes are on the house, but he looks just as fucked up as I feel about all of this.

"After the cops questioned him for beating up Breetana, he went home and took out all of his aggression on Nicole. He was arrested for that the next day. Nicole was lucky enough to get placed with a foster family that really wanted to help her. They didn't adopt her officially, but she was family. They put her through college. Helped her open her bakery."

"Where are they now?" Taylor asks.

"Moved to Florida last year. They live in a retirement community in Kissimmee. She had a pretty great life until about a year ago."

"When fucking Uncle Joe was released," Taylor growls dangerously.

"You're catching on. It was a little while after his release. She was dating the Mayor's son for many years. They were planning to get married. She got pregnant. Everything was great. Until rumors started spreading about her sleeping around. The Mayor didn't like the press and scandal. Especially when one of the rumors involved her sleeping with him to get lower taxes on her bakery"

"Why the fuck would anyone believe this shit?" I can't fucking believe any of this.

"Because his son came out with a statement saying it was true. The city called for his daddy's resignation and a boycott of any business the two of them had any part of. Nicole was forced to close because of the number of customers lost."

"What about the Mayor?" Taylor questions.

"He was re-elected by a fucking landslide. Even though most of the city was calling for his head."

"Voter tampering?" I throw out with certainty.

Ryan chuckles. "No doubt in my mind."

"There's still something missing," Taylor says. "Something doesn't make sense."

"Well, maybe this will make sense. I'm flying in right now with some guys because you guys are in way over your fucking heads."

Taylor and I look at each other. My stomach drops. Taylor clears his throat. “Care to elaborate?”

“There’s a huge fucking drug train that spans from Mexico to Canada. It goes up I-35. Right through the heart of Minnesota.”

“Fuck!” Taylor grips the headrest of the seat in front of him tight enough that his knuckles turn white.

“Joe Carter is involved with the cartel.” Ryan confirms my worst suspicions. “He's high ranking. Has some guys working for him.”

“Who? Tell me fucking who?” I glare at the house.

“The mayor's son, for one. Billy is the name. I checked into that ex-boyfriend of Breetana's, since he was such a big fucking part of her uncle's alibi. He's Joe's second in command.”

Taylor punches the seat in front of him. “Fucking get here, Ryan. If he's paid off all these people to stay out of prison, there's no telling who's involved. I have no contacts here, and those girls are sitting ducks.”

“We should just leave. Go back to Chicago right now,” I say.

“They'll just follow,” Ryan says. “You want to know how they found Nicole? They've had a tail on her. Chicago is the worst place you can go right now. That city is run by the cartel.”

“Why not make a move before we got here?” Taylor is obviously trying to make sense of everything. I commend him. I don’t fucking understand any of this shit.

“Think about that, Taylor. Come on.” Ryan sounds like he can’t believe Taylor would ask such a thing.

Taylor looks at me and punches the seat again. “The son of a bitch wants Breetana, too.”

I suck in a breath as I begin to understand. “He wasn't counting on us showing up with her.”

“I'm two hours away. Get back to the hotel. Stay out of Silver Bay until I get there,” Ryan commands.

“We're at Nicole's house right now,” Taylor says.

“Leave. Now. I'll meet you at the hotel.” Ryan hangs up, and Taylor and I jump out of the SUV.

“Why haven't they made a move yet?” I ask.

“They did.”

“What?” I look at him, confused as hell as we walk to the house. I try hard not to run, picking up on Taylor's actions and sensing I need to remain calm.

“He sent Breetana's ex.”

“What?” I stop dead in my tracks.

Taylor turns to me and lowers his voice. “You saw Breetana's reaction when Shaun showed up. And you saw Nicole nearly run to her and pull her inside… away from him.”

“You think Shaun is her ex?”

“Yep. No doubt in my mind.” He turns back to the house, and I follow him in.

My heart is completely shattered for both of them. I feel bad for going behind Breetana's back and not waiting for her to talk to me, but right now, I’m glad as hell that I did. We need to get the fuck out of here. No one will ever hurt her again. Either of them. Not so long as I’m around. And I’m not going any-fucking-where.

Chapter Nine

⚔ Breetana ⚔

Nicole pulls me into the house, and I collapse onto the couch. I put my head between my knees to stop my racing heart.

Nicole sits next me and rubs my back. "Talk to me, Tana."

"Why him? Why did he have to be the one Chase called for supplies?" I'm trying not to cry, but I can't stop the tears. My body is racked with sobs. All I want is Chase to tell me it's going to be okay. That he isn't going to leave me. But he's out there right now with my ex. And I'm sure Shaun is filling his head with lies.

"Tana. You know his company is the only construction and hardware company in the area."

"But he has employees! Why would he come here? Hasn't he done enough to me?" I lean back against the couch and draw my knees up to my chest. I bury my face in my arms. "He's going to tell Chase all the lies he spread."

"Chase won't believe them. He's smarter than that."

"I should've told him. I should've told Chase everything. I was just so scared." My mind is racing faster than my heart.

"I'm sure he'll understand."

I vigorously shake my head. "No. Our relationship is all new. He has no reason to believe me." I feel my heart actually break at the thought of losing Chase. It shatters in my chest. I feel the pain and know I deserve everything that's happening. I should've trusted him. Now it's too late.

"Tana? Tana, look at me," Nicole says softly.

I have to be strong. I can't fall apart. Not in front of my little sister. Nicole needs me. She needs me to keep her safe. From everyone. I take a deep breath and wipe my eyes. "I'm sorry. It was just a shock seeing him. I'm okay."

"I know you better than that."

"The concern here is you, Kiki. Not my stupidity with Chase. I'm here to protect you."

"You've protected me my whole life."

I turn away. "Not your whole life." I whisper it, and the tears start again.

Nicole takes my face in her hands and forces me to look at her. "Tana. Don't. What Joe did wasn't your fault."

"Yes, it was. I wasn't here to deflect his attention away from you."

"You were in the hospital because he attacked you! How could you have done anything to help me?" Her eyes glisten with tears.

"I shouldn't have gone to the party. I should've been home. With you. He wouldn't have touched you then. He wouldn't have beat you. He wouldn't have raped you like he did so many times to me."

"It's over now. Until yesterday, I hadn't seen him."

"It should've been me. Not you. I'm the one who deserves all of this."

"Oh my God! Are you crazy?" She puts her hands on my shoulders and turns me to look at her. "Breetana Marie Carter. Stop it! You didn't deserve what Shaun did to you. You trusted him, and he betrayed you! He took advantage of you. He drugged you! You didn't even remember what happened until days later! And what Joe did to you? Breetana, you have never ever deserved anything that he did to you. Neither of us deserved it. He did what he did to us because he's fucking sick! He killed our parents just so he could have us!"

I know she's right, but I can't convince myself. I can't convince my heart that had I been here instead of running away, Nicole would be okay. Everything that happened to her wouldn't have. I would've stopped it.

"I'm sorry for running away. I am so, so sorry I didn't protect you." I start sobbing once again.

Nicole pulls me into a fierce hug. "It's not your job to protect me."

"Yes, it is, Nicole. It's always been my job."

"Tana. No. Listen to me. It's not your fault. It's not. You can't blame yourself for other people's actions. *You* taught me that. You didn't do any of this to me. Or to yourself. We didn't do this. But our job now is to be here for each other and get through it. Support each other. That's our job."

I nod as my tears soak her shirt. I lay on the couch with my head on her chest for what seems like hours before I finally work up the strength to talk again. "I feel so selfish. Being like this when I'm supposed to be here for you."

"When was the last time you ever let me be here for you?" she asks softly. I'm quiet for a moment as she looks at me. I fight my battles on my own. I always have. "Never, Tana. The answer is never. Let me be here for you now."

I sigh. "I'm scared."

"I know you are."

"I'm scared Chase is going to hate me."

"He won't. I saw the way he looked at you last night. And even today at breakfast. That man loves you."

"You don't know that. We've only actually been together as a couple since Monday. That was only three days ago."

"And he's already given up everything to fly out here with you. You didn't even ask him to. He just did it. He loves you, Breetana. You have to trust that. Even after what Billy has done to me, I could never close myself off to true love. You can't either. You've found that. I know it."

"I'm still so scared. I should've told him. He's going to be so mad at me. And I would deserve it."

"He won't be mad at you."

Before I can say anything, Taylor walks through the door. I watch as Chase follows. He looks angrier than I have ever seen him.

"I know you guys have a lot to talk about, and I want to give you time, but we're out of that. We need to move," Taylor says before anyone has a chance to say anything.

"What's going on? Why do we need to leave?" I ask.

Chase looks pained as he helps me up. "I'll explain on the way, but he's right. We have to leave, baby." He kisses me. "I know what you're thinking, but I'm not going anywhere, Breetana. I don't think any of what happened was your fault. And I'm not upset with you. I don't know why you think I would be, but I'm not." He gives my hand a squeeze.

I follow him in shock. "You can't know everything."

"I don't, baby. But I know enough. I promise we'll talk on the way, but we have to leave."

Taylor guides Nicole to the door and takes his gun from his holster. "While we were out there talking to my contact, I've seen the same car drive by twice. I don't like it. We're leaving, but we need to do it my way."

"Just tell me what you need," Chase says.

Taylor hands Chase a second gun that he takes from his ankle. My mouth just drops. I didn't know he was carrying two of them. "We're putting your Sunday night practice to use. You and I go out first. The girls stay behind us. Nikki to the front of the SUV. Tana to the back. Got it?"

"Got it," Chase says with a nod.

Taylor glances at us before back at Chase. "On my six as we walk out the door. Breetana behind you. Nicole behind her. As soon as we're out, Chase at my nine. Breetana, I want you behind him. As close as you can. I want your hand on his back at all times. Nikki. Same with you. Behind me. Hand on my back. Understand?"

His eyes meet ours. They're dominant and hard. No nonsense. All serious. Nicole and I both nod, but we're terrified. It's obvious that whatever's happening is serious, and we don't understand just how much.

Taylor senses our fear. "Listen to me. Nothing is going to happen. I'm a cop. I'm overly cautious by nature. But there are things going on right now that neither of you guys are aware of. We'll explain when we get the fuck out of here, but right now, we need to go. Okay?"

"Okay. We trust you," Nicole says softly.

Taylor smiles and nods to Chase. We all take up our positions and walk out of the house. I watch as Chase puts a hand on Taylor's shoulder. I follow his lead and put my hand on his back. Nicole puts hers on my back, and we all walk out together. As soon as we're out, Chase moves to Taylor's side, and Nicole and I follow, moving behind them as they told us to.

When we get to the SUV, Taylor quickly guides Nicole inside. “Get down as low as you can, beautiful. I know it’ll be hard, but I’ll help you back up.”

“Okay,” she says quietly, her voice shaking. He closes the door as Nicole slides down into the seat until she’s nearly on the floor.

Chase opens my door as Taylor covers us. “Same thing, baby. Duck down. Stay down.” I get down on the floor. Chase and Taylor quickly walk around to the other side and jump in the vehicle, Chase with me and Taylor driving.

“Both of you stay down. I'm getting us out of here, and it'll be fast. I'm not taking chances. If I see a tail or a squad, we're losing them and losing them quickly. That means both of you stay on the floor until I say. Hang on tight if I give the command.”

“Okay,” I nervously whisper. Taylor backs out quickly and takes off. My head is in Chase's lap, and his hand is firmly on my shoulder. “Is Kiki okay?”

“She's fine, baby. She's on the floor, and Taylor is holding her hand.” He runs his fingers through my hair. “I know you're scared, but Taylor lives for this shit. He'll get us out of here safely.”

“She's pregnant. I don't care about anything else. I’m worried about her.” I grip Chase’s thigh as I stay on the floor.

“Breetana. I'll get us out of here. I won't let anyone hurt either one of you,” Taylor tells me.

“I'm okay, Tana. It hurts a little being on the floor like this, but Taylor is looking out for me.”

I nearly cry. “I just want to hold your hand right now. I'm so scared.”

“I know. Me, too. Let's just get out of here first, okay? I'm sure they'll explain when we're safe.” She tries to keep her voice calm and strong.

“Just relax, Bree. I've got you, okay? I know it's hard to relax at a time like this, but you've got me, and you've got Taylor. You're safe. You both are.”

I nod and squeeze my eyes shut as I reach for Chase's other hand. He holds it tightly as Taylor speeds through the streets towards the relative safety of Duluth.

I take a deep breath and breathe him in. In order to keep my sanity, I decide to tell him everything. "I'm sorry I haven't told you. I'm scared you won't believe me. Or that you'll hate me."

Chase tangles his fingers in my hair. "I don't. I could never hate you. How could you think that?"

"Whatever Shaun told you, Chase, please, please don't believe it." I squeeze my eyes closed, and the rest comes out in a whisper. "I don't want to lose you."

"Baby, look at me." He takes my face gently in his hands and lifts my face so that I'm looking in his eyes. "I know you're going to be upset with me for going behind your back, but Taylor's contact found out a lot of shit. I know about everything, baby. And I'm not going anywhere. I'm right here."

I don't know what to say. Part of me is relieved, but the other part of me knows he can't know everything. If he did, he wouldn't be here. I take a deep breath and pray I don't lose him. "My parents. They died in a fire that my uncle started. He was investigated, but never convicted. He became our legal guardian. He was perfect up until that paperwork was signed. Then he told Kiki and me that he did it because he wanted kids."

Chase lets out a breath and keeps running his fingers through my hair. "Sounds like lies."

I take another deep breath and nod slowly. "He started getting really... handsy with Kiki. You could tell how uncomfortable she was around him. So, I started sleeping in her room with her. One night, he came into her room. I wouldn't let him near her. So, he took me."

Chase's grip tightens. He lets out a low growl. I can feel him slightly shaking. "Baby," he whispers.

"He touched me. Made me touch him. He… raped… me. Over and over. He hated that I wouldn't let him touch Nikki. He hated that I had gone to the police about what he'd done to me. He hated that some of my teachers even reported the abuse. He would hit me. He would shove me. He broke my wrist once when I hit him back. He would kick me. But I wouldn't leave my sister. I stayed with her. I went with her wherever she went. I took her with me whenever I went."

"Fuck…" He runs a thumb across my lower lip.

"Except one night. Shaun invited me to a party. Nicole had just started dating Billy. I had talked to Billy's parents and made arrangements for her for the night. She was supposed to go to his house after school and stay the night there. In a guest room. Joe was at work. She thought it would be okay to go home and grab a book she forgot. But when she was leaving, Joe came home. He was early. He knew I wasn't there, and he wouldn't let her leave. When she didn't show up at Billy's, he called me." I close my eyes. Chase rubs the back of my neck soothingly. Nicole sniffles. Taylor lets out a long sigh. I plunge ahead. "I didn't answer. I didn't hear my phone. The music was loud. And I was with Shaun. He knew everything that was happening, and all he wanted to do was save me. Or so I thought. He brought me a drink, and we talked for a while. I started not feeling well, so he took me back to my room. He said he didn't care about the party. He was happy just being with me. I remember we kissed. We made out. And then I don't remember a lot until I woke up."

"Your uncle was in the room," Taylor says.

I nod with another sigh and take another breath. "I guess I don't know what you know, but yes. He was in the room. He was shaking me awake. I was dizzy. Really disoriented. He slapped me really hard. I screamed and fell out of the bed. I woke up in the hospital three days later."

"Fuck. Three days?" Chase's grip inadvertently tightens. It's still the most soothing touch I've ever felt.

"Yeah. I had been drugged by Shaun. Beaten into unconsciousness by Joe. Nicole was at my bedside when I woke up. She was bruised, and I knew. He had gotten to her, and it was my fault. I left her."

"Baby…, no…," Chase whispers. He leans down and kisses the back of my head.

"He raped her Saturday night. Beat the hell out of her while he was doing it. And then tied her up so she couldn't leave when he left to deal with me. When he was done with me, he did it all over again with her on Sunday. He let her go to school Monday. Stupid and cocky of him, but he thought that since they hadn't done anything to him when it came to me, he could get away with it with her. Billy took one look at her and called the police. She was placed with a good family that very night. And he was arrested, convicted, and sent to prison."

"Breetana -"

I plunge ahead. "After I was released from the hospital, I went back to school. I couldn't get a hold of Shaun, and he never visited me when I was in the hospital. I went to his room, and his roommate opened the door. He smirked at me and tried to grab my boobs. Said I looked like shit, but he'd still fuck me. I slapped him. Shaun heard and pulled his roommate away. Then he broke up with me. After that, I couldn't even walk across campus without people calling me names. My room was vandalized daily. People would pass me notes calling me a slut. I got death threats. Guys walking by would slap my ass or grab my pussy. Feel me up. I found out that it was Shaun. He told everyone I had gotten pregnant at that party. That he walked into my room and saw me fucking a ton of guys at the same time. He told people that I had tried to seduce my uncle."

"Jesus Christ. Baby, I'm so sorry."

I take a breath and continue. There's no point in quitting now. "The hospital had run a drug test, and during the exam, they saw semen. So they ran a rape kit and had a DNA test done. The doctor, after I came to, told me I had been drugged with a significant amount of the date rape drug. Usually, it's out of your system pretty quickly, but I had so much that not only did I test positive, but it's the reason I was still so incredibly out of it when my uncle showed up."

"He raped you? Shaun?"

"I honestly don't know." I shrug and bite my lip. I feel numb. "I had started to remember some things. I know I was willingly making out with Shaun. It's after that I don't remember."

"He drugged you, and you don't remember the sex. He fucking raped you, Tana," Taylor says, his voice low. Nicole whimpers.

I sniffle and wipe my eyes. "Well, it doesn't matter. I asked the hospital for my test results, and they couldn't find them. I asked the police for my rape kit, and they said it had been compromised. I had nothing on Shaun. And he was ruining me. I dropped out of college, but he had even turned Silver Bay against me. Kiki begged me to transfer schools. She knew my love for Chicago and convinced me to go. I made sure she was okay after the trial and everything, and I left." I bury my head in his thigh. "I left her alone. I had vowed never to leave her again, but I did it. For my own selfish reasons."

"Baby. You didn't do anything wrong," Chase says.

"I abandoned my sister," I retort.

"Breetana. It's so obvious to me that you love your sister. That you would do anything for her. You made sure she was okay before you left. You had no reason to think this was going to happen."

"And I asked you to leave, Tana," Nicole says quietly. "I told you that it was for the best. That I was okay. He was gone. I had Billy. I had my adopted family. Nothing bad was happening until last year."

I sniffle and nod. It's going to take time to convince myself that she's right. That the blame needs to be placed solely on the shoulders of those responsible. Joe and Billy. They ruined her life. They're going to pay.

I just don't know how.

Chapter Ten

⚔ Chase ⚔

Taylor pulls up to the hotel we're staying in and parks. "Remember what I said. Stay close. We weren't tailed, but that doesn't mean we aren't being watched." Breetana is shivering and Nicole is fighting to take deep breaths. "Chase? Ready? We cover them as much as possible."

"Just say the word." We both get out at the same time and walk to the other side of the SUV. Both of our eyes are scanning everywhere. "Maybe we should've waited for your contact. Extra cover."

"More conspicuous."

I suppose he's right. Never thought I'd say it, but I'm missing the extra cover the mafia could provide right now. We both open the doors for Breetana and Nicole at the same time and usher them as quickly as possible into the hotel. No one says anything until we get inside the elevator.

"Holy shit," Breetana whispers, but we all heard it.

Nicole takes Breetana's hand. "Almost there," Nicole says. I kiss Breetana's head and give her a hug.

"Same deal as when we left the house," Taylor says. "This elevator opens, me first followed by Chase. We do a sweep of the floor before either of you come out. As soon as I tell you it's okay, Breetana on Chase's back, Nikki on mine."

Nicole nods. "Okay."

Taylor and I position ourselves in front of the girls and pray no one else wants to get on the elevator. We both ready our Glocks as soon as we're close to the top floor, and I wait for Taylor's lead. I hate this. I hate Breetana is so fucking scared.

The elevator stops on our floor, and the doors open. Taylor immediately jumps into action, scanning the right side of the hallway while I scan the left. We use the elevator as cover in case we need to jump back into it.

"I'm clear, Taylor," I say after a moment.

"Yeah, me too."

Breetana and Nicole do exactly as Taylor said, and as soon as I feel her hand on my back, we start moving. I want to get in the room as quickly as possible. "Got a key card out?" I ask.

"Yes," she whispers. I pull her in front of me as soon as I reach the door, and she quickly opens it. Taylor goes in first to sweep the room while I keep the two of them in the hall, scanning for any movement at all the entire time.

"It's clear. Everyone in," Taylor rumbles. We all nearly run into the room. Taylor closes and locks the door behind us. Breetana and Nicole are huddled together.

I let out the breath I've been holding. "Fuck, Taylor. There's a reason you're the cop here. Not me." I hand him back his extra gun.

"Keep that. You know this isn't over. Ryan has an extra holster, I'm sure. And if he doesn't, we'll get you one."

I sigh. "Taylor, I hire people to protect me."

"The fuck you do. Why the fuck do you think I've spent so much fucking time training you to protect yourself? For the hell of it?" He glares at me. I glare right back. "You're the most stubborn man I know. You've never hired a security detail, even though you're one of the richest fucking men in the world. You're going to give me a damn heart attack one of these days. I have no idea how you've lasted this long without one."

"I've never fucking needed one!" I yell.

"Can you guys please stop yelling at each other?" Breetana looks like she's about to cry and drop from exhaustion.

I instantaneously feel like an asshole. “I'm sorry, baby.” I walk to her, and she nearly falls into my arms.

“Thank God. I was barely holding her up.” Nicole slumps against Taylor. He leads her to the couch as I sweep Breetana in my arms.

“How long until Ryan gets here?” I ask Taylor.

“Plane lands in thirty minutes.”

“These two need rest. Take care of Nikki. Come get us when they get here.”

“Done.”

I carry her to our bedroom and gently lay her down as she looks up at me. “I just feel so cold. I don't know why. It's not really cold outside.” She crawls under the covers, and I crawl in after her. She burrows in my arms. “I'm sorry.”

“For what?”

“Dragging you into whatever this is.”

“There is no way I would leave you to deal with this on your own. No way. It wouldn't matter if you and I weren't even dating. I'd still be right by your side, Breetana. I just wish there was something I could do to make you trust me enough to believe that.”

“I trust you, Chase. I do. I'm sorry I didn't tell you sooner. I was truly scared. I didn't want you to look at me differently. I didn't want you to think I'm crazy. Like everyone else did.”

“I didn't. I don't. I won't. You went through fucking hell, Breetana. And look at you. Look how far you've come since then. You put yourself through college. You worked in some pretty dodgy places. And now you have a high paying job at one of the biggest financial investment companies in the world. You lead meetings with VIP clients on your own. Your boyfriend is a billionaire. You got where you are by yourself. Despite everything that happened to you. You're pretty fucking incredible, baby.” I feel her smile against my chest. “What do I need to do to make you realize that none of this is your fault?”

“It's hard, Chase. I spent years blaming myself. I hid it from Nicole for so long. I loved hearing about how well she was doing, so I never brought anything else up.”

“Did you ever go to counseling? Because if that's what you need, I'll do it. I'll get it set up. I'll do anything to make you understand how incredible you are. And that everything that happened was not because of you. You didn't deserve any of that."

"No one has taken the time to listen to my side. What you did for me today, just listening, that was the most incredible thing anyone has ever done for me. No one has ever just listened to me. And believed me. No one's ever just been here for me. Besides Nicole and Reese, I mean. I've never let anyone else other than them in. So many people didn't believe me before. What was the point of opening up, you know?"

"I know, Bree. But you never have to worry about that with me. Okay? I promise you that I will never leave you. You can always trust me. I'll never turn you away. You can always talk to me. About anything. I'll always be here for you, baby. Always." She nods into my chest and kisses my chin. I smile down at her and kiss her forehead while I hold her close.

"No more secrets."

I smile. "No more secrets. Just be honest with me. Your honesty is one of the things I love so much about you."

"No more being scared to open up to you," she whispers.

"No more not trusting me."

"No more shutting you out."

"No more running away from me."

"And no more blaming myself."

I smile and rest my hand on her hip, squeezing gently. "No more blaming yourself." I lift her face so her eyes meet mine, and I kiss her before wrapping my arms back around her.

"Thank you for not leaving me. For protecting me. For everything, Chase."

"Always, baby. You always have me. I'm not going anywhere." We stay in each other's arms for a long while when we hear some commotion in the suite. Breetana jumps and holds onto me tightly.

"Shh... it's okay. It's probably just Ryan. If it wasn't, Taylor would be shooting right now."

"Okay... okay. I'm okay." She takes a few deep breaths.

"Ready?"

She nods. "Ready." We get out of the bed, and I take her hand in mine, leading her out of the room. Before I open the door, she stops me. "Wait."

"You okay?"

She reaches around my neck and pulls me down to her lips. I smile before returning her kiss. It's long. I can feel her put everything she is into the kiss, and I can't help but groan as I pull her flush against my body and turn to pin her against the door. I try to hold back, but my cock has a mind of its own. It helps me none when she reaches down and grabs me.

"Breetana, you're gonna be the fucking death of me."

She laughs as I grab her hand from my cock and kiss it. "Aww… not fair."

"Not fair, huh?" I reach down between her legs, over her jeans, and rub my hand over her before cupping her and squeezing and then pulling away.

"Chase…," she breathes.

"Later. And I'm not complaining at all, but I have no idea how you can be that wet for me after the day you've had."

"You can't possibly know how wet I am. You were over my jeans." She smirks. I give her a dangerous smile before sticking my hand down her jeans, pushing aside her panties, and sticking my middle finger inside her. I give her a couple of strokes as I kiss her neck. "Oh God. Chase... mmm…"

I kiss up her jaw to her mouth as I unbutton her jeans. I know she's been through a lot today, and I know we have a lot to deal with, but I don't care. I know my girl, and I know she needs this. Just as much as I need to touch her. I push her jeans down while I kiss her and give her another finger.

So much for teasing. I'm going to make her come. I need to feel her.

"You have no idea how good you look in jeans," I say against her neck.

"Neither do you."

There's a light knock on the door. Breetana jumps, but her pussy is still pulsing around my fingers. I grin and nip her lower lip while continuing to slowly push and pull my fingers inside of her and out.

"Give us a couple minutes, Taylor," I say, giving nothing away to what I'm doing against the door.

"Take your time."

I listen to Taylor walk away as I bend to kiss Breetana. Her breathing has quickened, and her soft sighs are driving me crazy. She's somehow managed to unbutton my pants and is stroking my cock. She's so wet for me. The sounds of her pussy make me so much harder.

"Fuck, Breetana. Holy fuck." I thrust my hips so my cock slides into her hand. She kicks off her jeans, and I lift her, bringing her back to the bed and dropping her. I pull off my jeans and lay on my back. "You know what the sixty-nine position is?"

"Yes. But I've never done it." She bites her lip, and I growl.

"Get the fuck up here. I need to taste you." She stares at me wide-eyed before she straddles me and gives me what I want. "Lean down like you're on your hands and knees so you can touch me."

"Aren't I supposed to give you a blowjob from this position?" I can hear the smirk in her voice.

"Fuck, baby. Yes. But I don't want to push you too fa-." I groan. My eyes roll back in my head as she takes me in her mouth, cutting off whatever I was about to say. "God… damn, baby. You're mouth..."

I run a hand up her back and down to her perfect ass before I move the thin lace fabric aside once more. I pull her down to me and lick her sweet pussy. She tastes even better than I thought. She pushes down on my tongue slightly as she takes me as deeply as she can in her mouth.

She bobs her head up and down as she sucks. My cock hits the back of her throat again and again. She strokes me as she swirls her tongue around my tip. I take her bud in my mouth as I put two fingers back inside her.

"Chase! More. Please, more." Her hips rock against me as she sucks me harder. Faster.

I push deeply inside her as my tongue plays with her bundle of nerves. It's my mission to send every single one of them into ecstasy, so I pull her closer to me. Her hips to my rhythm, and she sucks just as fast.

"That's it, baby. Good girl. Does that feel good?" I rumble against her pussy.

"God yes. Yes, Chase. So good… mmm… so, so damn good." She runs her teeth along my length, moaning against my dick, and then licks along the path her teeth made. She takes my tip in her mouth again and starts sucking hard and fast.

"Christ, Breetana. It's a good thing you're about to come because I can't hold back anymore."

"How do you… oh!" Her pussy clenches hard around my fingers. Her thighs tremble. She pulses uncontrollably.

I lick, and then gently suck on her bud. "That's it, baby. Come for me."

"Chase…"

I grab her hair and try to pull her back, but she sucks me deeper into her mouth. "Fuck, Bree. I'm about to come." She sucks on my tip before taking me back to her throat. I can't hold back. Hot liquid spills from me just as she comes for me. I keep licking her as she swallows everything I give her. "Oh my God. Fucking Christ, Bree, you're perfect."

"Oh! Chase!" Her hips jerk hard against my tongue as I finger fuck her and suck on her clit, flicking it with my tongue.

Breetana swallows everything I give as I slow my thrust to help her come down. She gives me a last lick and slowly gets off of me. She tries to stand up, but I grab her and pull her back to me so I can kiss her.

"Babe. We really should get out there."

I pinch her nipple, and she moans. I'm not ready to let her up. "I needed this."

"Me, too, honestly."

She leans in to kiss me again. I reluctantly let her up because she is right. We do need to get up. If we didn't, I'd still be licking her clean.

We both get dressed and head out to join everyone else. The light in Breetana's eyes has returned, and I can't help but feel happy about that. She's going to make it through this.

We.

We're going to make it through this.

Together.

Chapter Eleven

⚔ Taylor ⚔

(Before Ryan's Arrival)

I sit down on the couch in Chase's suite and rub my temple's. I've had a headache ever since I got off the phone with Ryan earlier. And it's only gotten worse and worse as the day has gone on.

"Are you okay?" Nicole scoots a little bit closer to me and puts her hand on my leg. She smells like honey. The scent is so uniquely her, and I've come to love it. In one fucking day I can't get this girl out of my head.

"I'm okay," I tell her after a few moments. She sits there with her hand on my leg and looks at me. One fucking day, and she can see through my shit already. "I just have a hell of a headache, sweetheart. That's all."

She smiles and gently squeezes my leg before she stands up and grabs Breetana's purse. I cock an eyebrow as I watch her. She grabs something out, and then fills a glass with water. She walks back to me and sits next to me on the couch, handing me the pills and water.

"Tana gets really bad headaches. Migraines. She always has Excedrin in her purse." She smiles as I take the pills. I swallow them down and put the glass on the table next to me before leaning back and closing my eyes. "So, what do we do now?"

I leave my eyes closed. "We wait for Ryan and his crew, beautiful."

"I love when you do that," she says softly after a long pause.

I open one eye and look at her. She's sitting next to me, but is on the edge of the couch. "Do what?"

"Call me things like beautiful, sweetheart, gorgeous, and baby." She shrugs, keeping her eyes forward. "I don't know if you're doing it because you don't remember my name or what, but I know that I've never felt so... special."

I open both eyes and bite my lip, fighting back a laugh. She's so fucking adorable. I reach up and wrap a piece of her silky blonde hair around my finger. She shivers and smiles.

"Come lean back. Get comfortable. Rest for a bit before Ryan gets here. It's going to be a long night." She leans back, but doesn't look comfortable at all. "Nikki. Come on. Get comfortable." She scoots back and leans into me. I put my arm over her shoulders, and she rests her head on me. "I absolutely have not forgotten your name. I will admit I'm quite a player. I'm guessing you sensed that. But I also know the real deal when I see it. You're the real deal, Nicole."

"Things like that. No one has ever said that to me before."

I'm kind of surprised. "So this ex of yours. You were together for how long? And he never made you feel special?"

"It was usually all about him. I guess I never realized that it was supposed to be different than that. I convinced myself I was happy, and that everything was fine. Billy had been there for me through everything that happened with my uncle. When Breetana left, Billy and I were inseparable."

"When did that change?"

"Honestly? A long time ago. But I had never known anything other than him. I didn't want to let go."

I rub my hand up and down her arm fighting every single urge I have to kiss her. "You are special. And I really have no issues being the one to make you feel the way you deserve to feel."

She shifts and puts her arm around my waist. I have to force myself to take deep breaths and hope to God she doesn't notice the fact that she's making me hard. I haven't had sex in a couple of months, but I'm usually a lot better at controlling my urges.

Except around her, I guess. I have an immediate reaction to her. I haven't felt it with any other woman I've ever been with.

She was scared to death last night and begged me to hold her until she fell asleep. I did put my arm around her, but I kept my cock away from her. I knew if I felt her against me, it would be embarrassing for me.

She chuckles, and I know she's seen it.

I groan. "Sorry."

"You don't need to be. It's nice I have that effect on someone. It's been awhile."

"I get the feeling your ex made you feel like you aren't attractive. I don't know why because you absolutely are."

"Before he got me pregnant, we hadn't had sex in a year. And after I got pregnant? Not once."

I watch her cross her legs, and it makes my mouth water. She tries to hide it by rubbing her legs together, and I smile. "Nice to know I have the same effect," I say with a grin. She looks up at me, mouth agape, and I laugh. "You have no idea how much I want to relieve that pressure between your legs, darlin'."

She closes her eyes and squeezes her legs tighter. "Oh God... Lord help me, but I wouldn't stop you." She looks down at her hands. I look at my watch. We still have fifteen minutes until Ryan's plane lands. I'm sure Chase and Breetana are doing everything I want to do with Nicole right now, so the chance of being interrupted is slim. "Honestly…, I could probably use the distraction. And just saying that makes me feel like such a slut."

"You were with one guy for eleven years. How the fuck does that make you a slut?" I ask in complete shock. She shrugs and leans forward, struggling a little bit with her very full stomach. I touch her back, letting my hand fall as I sit up next to her. "Nikki. You aren't. Not even close."

"I just want to feel wanted. It's been so long. And I feel so stupid."

I rub her lower back. "For wanting to be wanted?"

She takes a deep breath and shakes her head. "For wanting to be wanted by a man I just met."

I nod. “There it is. Now we're getting somewhere. You want me. You want me to want you. But we barely know each other, and you feel like that's crazy. Your reaction to me is crazy. Right?”

She lets out a breath. “The fact that you can read me so well. It’s scary.”

“Reading people is my job. You, however, are not hard to read.” I lean back again and shift so that I’m more on my side and facing her. “Nicole. Come here.”

She scoots back on the couch next to me. I reach up to turn her face with one hand so she's looking at me while the other plays with her hair. I love her eyes. They're golden and reflect the soft light in the room.

I smile and lean forward to kiss her. I start with her neck. She leans to the side, giving me easier access. I let my hand trail down to her collarbone and slightly lower. Her breath hitches as I kiss up her neck to her jaw line. I drop my hand lower, and she arches into my touch.

I kiss the side of her mouth and, finally, her lips as I slide my hand down to her very, very full breast. She moans into my mouth as I slide my tongue inside to dance with hers. I pinch her nipple and rub it before moving onto her other one.

“Wow…” It comes out as a whisper as I pull away. She rubs her legs together harder with a deep red blush.

I smile. “There's a lot I can do about that, you know. Just say the word.”

“I really, really want you to touch me.” She reaches down and pushes her pants down far enough for me to get to the part of her craving my attention. Then blushes even more when she realizes her hormones have gotten the best of her.

My mouth goes dry as I watch her. “You sure? I don't want to push you.”

She nods. “I'm sure, Taylor. I am.” She crushes her mouth to mine, losing all of her resolve, and grabs my hand, pushing it down where she wants it.

I laugh. “You really have missed a man's touch, haven't you?”

She shakes her head, biting her lip. “Not really. I just crave you. I feel so stupid, but I can't help it.”

“You're going to have to stop calling yourself stupid, gorgeous.” I push her soft satin panties aside and dip one finger inside her. She gasps, and I kiss her to drown out her moans. “It's just not going to fly with me.”

She nods her agreement as her eyes roll back in her head. “Mmm… so good…”

“You're so fucking wet. Tight as hell.” I keep my pace as I move my finger inside her and continue kissing her. I kiss her neck, and then her perfect mounds. She lifts up her shirt. I nearly stop breathing. She's spilling out of her bra. Everything about her is perfect. “Damn.” I lean down to kiss each of her nipples over her bra as I add a second finger.

“Oh! Taylor. Taylor, I'm close. So close. Already.” She's trying to stay quiet, and I grin as I set my thumb against her clit. She nearly screams as she arches into my touch and moves with my rhythm as I stroke her.

I feel her tighten around my fingers. Her pussy clenches erratically. I quicken my pace on her clit. I kiss her throat and up to her lips.

“I'm gonna come…, Taylor…”

“I can't wait to feel it.” I kiss her again and again as I continue thrusting inside her. Faster. Harder. Deeper. She quivers against me as she rocks against my fingers. I swallow her moan as she shatters.

I slow my thrusts as her hips jerk into me. Her tongue darts into my mouth again and again. I suck lightly on hers, slowly twisting my fingers until I finally stop. She pants as I pull away from her lips with a grin. Her eyes are closed. She looks blissed out.

After she comes down a few moments later, she looks up at me. “Do we have time for me to get you off? You deserve it after everything you've done today.”

I smile and kiss her softly as I remove my fingers from her perfect pussy. “Later. This was about you this time. You needed that.” I suck her off my fingers with a low moan.

She pulls her pants up, and then takes my hand, looking at my watch. “He should be landing now. But it takes time to get here.” She maneuvers herself to her knees. “And I’m feeling brave.”

I look at her. God she’s fucking sexy as hell. I unbutton my jeans. She pulls them and my boxer briefs down, freeing my erection. “You don't have to do this, Nikki.”

“You said this was about me.”

"It is."

"This is what I want. I want you." She takes me in her mouth, and I dig my fingers into her hair.

"Shit." My stomach tightens. She deep-throats me and starts sucking on my tip as she uses her tongue on the sensitive place below it. "Holy shit. You're good at this."

She strokes me, sucks me, and licks me until I'm weak in the knees. Over and over she bobs her head up and down on my cock. She scrapes her teeth along my length and tugs gently on my balls. I moan, getting dizzy off her and the pleasure she's shooting through me.

With no warning at all, my dick thickens for her. She moans, sending vibrations through my cock. My hips jerk into her mouth. She stays still and lets me thrust into it. Every time I hit the back of her throat, she swallows around me.

My spine stiffens. A jolt slams through it straight to my dick. I pull her back just as I start spilling my hot liquid onto her chest and all over myself. "Holy fuck. Nikki," I pant as she continues stroking me. "Goddamn."

She leans back, clearly pleased with herself. After taking a second to catch my breath, I stand. I help her up and get her situated on the couch. I walk to the kitchen to grab a washcloth. I wet it down and return to her to clean her up and myself. When I'm done, I rinse out the cloth and hang it in the bathroom to dry. I come back to her and flop on the couch, pulling her to my side.

"I hope you liked it," she whispers shyly.

"Baby, it's the best blowjob I've ever had." I close my eyes with a grin. She kisses my neck as my phone goes off. I quickly look at the text.

Ryan: On my way.

I sigh and turn to kiss her.

"Looks like it's back to work," she says softly against my lips.

"We got time. Relax for a bit."

She smiles and closes her eyes. I didn't expect that to just happen, but fuck. It was so worth it. No woman has ever made me feel anything like Nicole does. With just a look or a touch, she brings me to my knees. It's a place I've never let another woman bring me to. A place no woman has ever come close to bringing me anyway.

Just her.

I can't believe that in a matter of one single day, all I want is this girl.

Chapter Twelve

⚔ Nicole ⚔

Ryan Crane is obviously a very powerful man. When he arrived, it was almost like he completely took over the entire floor. He has twelve men with him, and they are all scattered around Chase's suite. The suite is large, but with everyone inside, it makes everything seem so much smaller.

More intimidating.

Ryan has spent the past twenty minutes explaining the cartel and Joe's, Billy's, and Shaun's involvement. The cartel. It's astounding that we're a part of this now. I don't know what to think, but the fact that my life has changed drastically and so fast is scary.

Breetana has pretty much withdrawn into herself as she sits on Chase's lap. He holds her close. Tightly. He hasn't let her go this whole time. He's even swaying gently with her and rubbing her arm and back soothingly.

I choke back a sob. I want that. That kind of love. I thought I had it. I can't believe how wrong I was to believe such a foolish thing about a man who so very obviously never loved me at all.

"Given what we find ourselves up against, I think it's important to up security on the girls. All of you, actually. I'm sure they know who

Chase is by now. And I have no doubt they know you're a cop, Taylor. Puts you both in just as much danger."

"What do you mean upping security?" I ask softly. Ryan looks at me and sighs. I avert my gaze feeling like an idiot. I'm really new to this, but I'm sure I can figure out what he means. "Sorry. I guess that was a dumb question."

"I mean my guys don't leave your side," Ryan answers gently.

I nod and wipe a tear away. I hate embarrassing myself like that. I glance at Taylor, who is sitting on the other side of the couch. Knowing Billy and my uncle are part of a drug cartel is terrifying to me. I could really use some comfort right now, but I don't want to bother Breetana. She needs Chase. I don't know if it would be right to curl up to Taylor. Even though it's all I want to do.

Instead, I get up and walk to the bedroom in the suite. I just need to get away. Be alone. I wish I could run and never come back. I sniffle as I sit down on the bed and fight the urge to start sobbing uncontrollably. It doesn't work.

I vigorously wipe away my tears as my baby kicks. He hates when I'm upset. He vigorously kicks at me until I start rubbing my stomach. Today is no different. I have to smile as I rub my tummy until he calms. At least I got something good out of this entire situation. Even if I'm raising him on my own. He'll never face what I did. I'll make sure of it.

"You disappeared." His deep voice reverberates through me and sends shivers down my spine.

Taylor.

He's leaning against the door frame with his arms crossed over his chest. He's stunning, and I have to take a second to catch my breath as he starts walking towards me. He smiles as he kneels in front of me.

"You okay?"

I can't help but laugh. "What part of any of this is okay? I'm terrified, Taylor. Breetana is the strongest person I know, and even she's falling apart. At least she has Chase. I'm doing all of this pregnant and alone." Tears threaten to fall.

Something like anger crosses his piercing blue eyes. I flinch and instinctively cross my arms protectively over my stomach. I pissed him off. I said something dumb and made him angry. He quickly stands, and I brace myself for the hit.

"Jesus Christ." He turns and strides to the door. I take a shaky breath.

Ryan appears just as Taylor is shutting it. "She okay?" he asks.

"We'll be a while. Just get set up. Chase can show you the other two rooms." He closes the door and turns back to me. He leans back against the door and rubs his forehead. "Nicole. Let's get one thing straight. Right now." He slowly walks towards me and kneels in front of me again, taking my hands in his. "I would never ever hurt you, and you are not alone in this." His voice is calming and soothing. He puts a hand on my stomach. "I'd never hurt your baby."

The baby flutters and seems to cuddle into Taylor's touch. Tears sting my eyes again. Taylor feels the movement and smiles widely as he looks down at his hand on my stomach.

"I think that means he likes you." I whisper because I don't trust my voice to not crack and betray my feelings, but it doesn't last.

Taylor kisses my stomach, and I lose it. I try to cover my face but he doesn't let me. Instead, he sits next to me on the bed and pulls me close to him. I bury my head in his chest.

"You can trust me, Nikki. I'm not going to let anything happen to you," he says quietly.

All I can do is nod as he lets me cry. After a couple of minutes, I've composed myself enough to pull away. I reach up to wipe my tears away, but he beats me to it. His touch is like anything I've ever experienced. It's soothing and electrifying all at the same time.

He gently pulls me up and leads me to the bathroom after he wipes my tears away. He runs the water in the sink until it's warm, then steps back, leaning against the counter so I can clean up.

"So? What happened there? Why did you leave?"

I glance at him as I dab at my eyes. "Just overwhelmed. I saw Breetana felt the same way, but she has Chase to help get her through it, and I didn't want to pull her away from him for my own selfish reasons." He watches me as I clean my face, and I sigh. He can read me like a book, and it's unnerving. "I didn't know if we were at the point I could turn to you in that way."

"For comfort?"

I nod and shrug slightly. "I know what we just did, but… I didn't know if I could…" I trail off. " You know. In front of everyone."

I raise an eyebrow. "Do you think you're an embarrassment to me or something? That I wouldn't want people to know I like you? A single and pregnant woman with bruises on her face?"

God, it's unnerving. It's something I didn't even want to admit to myself, but leave it to him to pull it out of me. "I don't know if I hate that you can read me so well, or if I really like it." I put the washcloth down and turn the water off. Taylor turns me towards him, reaches down to grip me under my thighs, and lifts me. My eyes widen at his strength. I'm not that light right now. "Holy shit."

He grins as he sets me gently on the counter and settles between my legs. "What?"

I look up at him as he slides me closer to the edge and to him, keeping his hands on my hips. "You didn't strain yourself, did you?" I bite my lip, genuinely concerned that he hurt himself lifting me.

"By doing what? Lifting you?"

I nod and run my hands up his chest and to his arms. He's massive compared to me. I could never leave his arms again and be happy forever. I can't resist touching him. He's perfect. He's like walking sex.

Taylor leans down to kiss me as he pulls my hips against his. I feel him straining against his jeans, and I whimper. Stupid, stupid pregnancy hormones. He moves himself against me, giving me the friction I need. He runs his hands under my shirt and takes both of my breasts in them as he continues letting me grind myself against him.

"Holy shit. Taylor. Oh God…"

"Need more?" he asks against my neck as he licks and sucks it.

"Please. Please, more. More," I beg. My body is completely betraying me, but I need it. I need him more than I need to breathe.

I'm practically panting when he pulls my pants down and slides two fingers inside me. He muffles my moans with his kisses as I move my hips with his incessant, hard, and deep strokes. After a couple of minutes, Taylor gets on his knees, fingers still moving inside me.

My eyes widen. "Oh God…"

"Think you can stay quiet?"

I nod, and he winks at me. I bite my lip and throw my head back when his tongue touches my clit. "Mmm... Oh my God…"

"Feel good?" His tongue flicks me again and my body jerks.

"Yes... yes," I moan. His fingers are insistent in their pursuit to please me, and his tongue has found a rhythm that's driving me to near madness. "Taylor... I'm... gonna…"

"Good girl. Come, baby. Let me taste you." He nips me and crooks his fingers inside me as he thrusts.

I break. I cover my mouth with both hands to muffle the scream. He licks up everything I give him before slowly standing. I'm still covering my mouth as I watch him. He's grinning arrogantly, but it's so sexy. He licks his lips and wipes the corner of his mouth before he leans down and kisses the side of my head.

"I can't resist you, beautiful." His breath is warm against my ear, and I sigh in contentment. He kneels once more to pull both my panties and my jeans up. He lifts me off the counter and sets me gently on the floor.

"Damn my pregnancy hormones."

He chuckles, and I smile. "Why?"

I feel my cheeks turn scarlet, and I try to cover it by burying my face in his chest. He wraps me inside of his arms. "Because one minute, I'm bawling my eyes out, and the next I'm... a horny teenager. For lack of a better description."

His laugh rumbles his chest as he hugs me tightly. "I'm happy to be the person to help you out with that."

"Holy God. Where the hell did you even come from?" I ask him. He laughs again before leaning down to kiss me, and then bending to kiss my stomach. I blush even more. "Your sweetness is going to make me fall in love with you."

He takes my hand and leads me out of the bathroom. "Good. You deserve to know what it feels like. For real. Not whatever bullshit you went through with your ex." He stops before he exits the room and turns to me. "I don't play games, Nikki. I've never liked anyone the way I do you."

"You said yourself you're a player…"

"More so because I've never found anyone I actually want to spend time with. Until you. So…, if you need me to hug you out there, like Chase is with your sister, I have no problem with it. I want you to be able to come to me. And feel comfortable with it." He leans down to kiss me again. "And there is no fucking way I would ever be embarrassed to be with you. Or seen with you."

I smile at him as he laces his fingers with mine and leads me back to the group. He sits and pulls me into his lap. I've never felt so safe. So protected... so… happy. So… in love? That can't be it. I just met him.

But I already want him to stay.

Chapter Thirteen

⚔ Breetana ⚔

I meet Nicole's eyes when Taylor returns with her and pulls her into his lap. I smile at her, and she smiles back. I was right. Something is happening between those two. Nicole deserves to be treated like a Queen. I don't want to see her get hurt. I don't think she could take it after all of this. But I think Taylor just might be what she needs.

"So, Nicole. While you were away, we came up with a plan for you." Ryan sits down in the chair next to Taylor. Chase and I had shown him the other two rooms, and many of the guys Ryan brought with him are now getting settled in the suite Chase rented for Nicole.

"For... me?" She looks at Taylor, and then Chase and me uneasily. Taylor tightens his grip a little and kisses her shoulder.

"Yes. For you. The plan was to keep the four of you here while my crew and I dealt with this mess. But…" Ryan glances at me before continuing. "After some... persuasion... from your sister, we came up with something different."

"Persuasion. That's what we're going with here?" Chase whispers in my ear as he kisses it.

I giggle softly. I stood my ground and told him that there were things Nicole needed to do so we could leave here and head for Chicago. It was something I felt was important and needed to be taken into account. He was discussing just leaving everything here, but we can't do that. We're not made of money, and I know Nicole would refuse handouts.

She's a lot like me.

"Sexy as hell. That's what it was." He kisses my shoulder. I wiggle against him, but make it look like I'm just shifting. "Fuck me, Bree. You're killing me here. Stay still." He's whispering still as Ryan talks, but I can feel him against me. I love the way he feels against me.

"Breetana mentioned that you guys are boarding up the windows so there's no damage to the house before you can get it sold. And that Chase hired movers to deal with everything else."

"I still have things to pack. Important things," Nicole says softly and super hesitantly.

"Chase mentioned that," Ryan continues. "So, here's what we're going to do. Cancel the movers. For now. We'll all head up to Silver Bay tomorrow to deal with your property and belongings. Three of my guys stay here to guard the rooms. When we get to your house, me, Chase, Breetana, and Taylor as well as two of my guys will be inside with you. Three of them will head to investigate Shaun, Billy, and your uncle while the other four remain at the house. They'll deal with boarding up the windows. I think we have time before shit really goes South, but when it gets to that point, we need to get out. I don't care what's left to deal with. We go."

"What about the graffiti?" Taylor asks.

"We'll deal with that, too. We'll rent a power washer to deal with it. The focus is getting the house boarded up and getting the things you need, Nicole. Clothing. Important things. We'll box up the things you want moved, clean out the rest of the house, and then call in the movers and a company to deal with any repairs the house needs."

"My house is foreclosed. It goes to the bank," she says dejectedly.

"I'll deal with that. Don't worry about it," Ryan assures her.

"After it gets fixed, what's to stop anyone from just vandalizing it again?" I ask.

"It doesn't," Ryan shrugs. "Which is why I have a few more people flying in tomorrow to stay there until it's sold."

"You're coming in with a lot of forces here, Ry," Taylor observes.

Ryan nods. "That's the point. We want to show force."

"Why? You're just going to piss off the cartel," Taylor retorts.

"Again. The point. I want them to see we're moving in on their territory."

"So, you can start a fucking turf war? I won't let either one of them get hurt," Taylor growls protectively.

"Taylor," Chase warns.

"I want your guys guarding them until we get Nikki packed up. Then we leave."

"Taylor. They'll just come after us in Chicago," I say softly. It's an argument we already had with Ryan. Taylor glares at me, but I can see he knows, too.

"I never thought I'd be the one to say this, but we need to trust him," Chase says. "This shit is his life. He knows how to deal with it."

"Fuck," Taylor sighs.

"You deal with gangs and organized crime, right?" I ask. He nods and rubs his temple.

"This is not gangs and organized crime, Taylor," Ryan says as he watches him. "You aren't going after your usual criminals. This isn't me feeding you tips, and you taking out the bad guys. This is a fucked up situation."

"I know. Fuck, I know. Okay? I just don't want anything to happen to Nikki or the baby. Or anyone." He puts a protective hand on Nicole's stomach, and my mouth drops. I quickly regain my composure before anyone notices, but I'm shocked at how natural that just came to him.

"This is what I do, Taylor. I show up. I take over. I do it with force if I need to." Ryan's voice leaves no room for argument, but it's still calm. Like he's talking to his family. It makes me wonder just how close Taylor and Ryan really are.

"What's the rest of this plan? Because this is my family we're talking about. The people in this room. They mean everything to me, Ry."

"The rest of the plan hinges on the intel my guys gather. We'll figure it out tomorrow. Tonight, each of you have two of my guys in your suites. I'll be staying in Nicole's suite with a couple of others. The rest of my guys are in suites on this floor. The doors connecting the rooms remain unlocked and open at all times. We need easy access to each room."

Taylor sighs. His hand hasn't moved from Nicole's stomach. "Okay. Your show."

"I know this isn't how anyone wants to see this play out. The truth is, I need intel." Ryan smiles a little and nods at Nicole's stomach. "You look like you're about ready to be done with pregnancy. Any day now, huh?"

Nicole bites her lip and starts to immediately cry. Before I can stop her, she darts from Taylor's lap and flees the room. The doors between the three rooms are open, and she runs through them to Taylor's suite.

Taylor blinks, astonished. "Nikki! Honey, get back here." Taylor immediately gets up to follow her, but I jump to my feet.

"Let me." I look up at him. "Please? I think…" I look after her. "I think she took that wrong." I look at Ryan with a soft smile. "Like you just called her fat."

Ryan's eyes widen. "Fuck. No. No!" He puts his hands up in a gesture of surrender. "Not at all. I was just commenting that I think -" He cuts himself off. "Oh shit. I get it." He nods. "I get it. I should apologize." He starts to get up.

I shake my head. "I think this might be a sister thing."

I smile again at each of them and follow Nicole. I haven't seen her face to face in a while, but I have talked to her on the phone. She's extremely sensitive. It might have a little to do with the pregnancy, but I think it has a lot more to do with Billy. He was awful to her. He called her so many names, and I'm sure I don't even know half of it.

I slip into Taylor's bedroom and find Nicole sobbing. She's clutching her stomach, and I immediately rush to her. "Oh my God! Kiki, are you okay?"

She nods, but continues sobbing hysterically. "He... doesn't like... when I cry." She hiccups and takes a deep breath, trying to control her sobs. "He... kicks until... I stop."

I lay next to her and hug her. "Honey, it's okay." I run my fingers through her hair and massage her scalp just like I did when we were kids. It has always soothed her. If I'm being honest, I've missed it as much as she has.

After a little while, she's calmed down enough to talk. "I'll never be good enough for him," she whispers.

"Oh, Kiki. That isn't it. That's not what happened out there. Your mind is just running away with you."

"I tried to convince myself of that. But with Ryan's words… I just spiraled. I keep thinking of Billy."

"Oh, Kiki. Ryan didn't mean that the way it came out. He realized right away what happened. He was just saying that with all the stress and you being so close to giving birth, you have to be ready."

She chuckles softly. "I am."

"As for Taylor. He's not Billy, Kiki. I don't know him well, but I can tell he's a good man. He has to be. I know Chase. Taylor is like Chase's brother. They grew up together. Seeing the way he is with you, watching how protective he is of you, and watching him put his hand on your stomach like he was ready to defend your baby from the world? Kiki. He called you his family. All of us. It's so obvious how he feels about you."

She sniffles again. "Stupid pregnancy hormones." She smiles softly. "I hate that I can't control my emotions. I feel so stupid for running."

I smile. "You were upset. Everyone understands. The stress is so high. For all of us. It's okay to have a breakdown." I stay hugging her for a long while, running my hands through her hair.

"Thank you, Tana. I love you."

"I love you, too, Kiki. Go to sleep. It has been a hard and exhausting day. We all need sleep."

She nods and snuggles into me. "Stay." Her voice is heavy with sleep.

I don't even have a chance to answer before I feel her breathing even out as she falls into a deep slumber. My eyelids are heavy, and it's not long before I myself am asleep.

Chapter Fourteen

⚔ Taylor ⚔

I keep glancing towards the suite where Nicole and Breetana ran. "Fuck," I grumble and rub my eyes. "The fuck is wrong with me? How is this a thing after one day? It's not like me."

Chase chuckles. "I knew it, bro. I've been saying it for years. I knew when a woman caught your eye, that'd be it for you."

Ryan nods towards the suite. "She gonna be okay? I feel like shit for saying that."

"I'm sure she'll be fine. I admittedly don't know everything, but I know her ex talked down to her and made her feel unworthy. She doesn't think she's pretty. And she's at the stage in her pregnancy where her hormones are fucked." I shake my head. "I don't really know much about that either. Just going off observation. One second she wants my tongue. The next she's in tears."

"You got your work cut out for you," Chase says with a grin.

I can't help the smile. He's right, but I don't care. I'm already falling for her. I guess he was right about that, too. All these years later after me telling him I'd never fall in love, here I am. I wasn't lying to Nicole when I told her I'd never found someone I wanted to spend time with. And I was honest when I said I don't fuck around when I find what I want. I just never thought I'd see the day. I've never been the type of man who sat around envisioning the perfect woman and how many kids I wanted.

"You know, I've been thinking about this cartel," Ryan begins as he leans back.

I raise an eyebrow. "Yeah?"

"I have suspicions it's attached to the same branch I took out with Alex a few years ago."

I nod as I glance over my shoulder at the door to the suite once more. Nicole and Breetana still haven't come back. I sigh and try to stay focused.

Alex.

Alex Lucinio is one of Ryan's closest friends. He's like family to him. Which means he's like family to me, too. His brother, Josh, went through a lot of fucked up shit over the past several years. Poisoning or some shit. A lot of brainwashing. All from his very own father.

He prevailed, though. Took over the Lucinio Mafia and allied with Ryan fucking Crane himself. Ryan is ruthless. People say he has no soul. He'll kill without a second thought. There are a lot of dark rumors about him. When people see him, they either flock to him or run. People on his bad side know damn well he's about to fuck them up.

Ryan isn't about taking over territories like most mafias, though. He doesn't shake people down. He doesn't do anything most would think a mafia leader would do. In fact, everywhere Ryan has expanded has been cleaned up. Drug deals and crimes in his areas are down. In Chicago, I've gotten the credit for it because the takedown was all mine.

Truthfully, the guy got me where I am. I wouldn't have the successful career I have if not for him. Besides my task force and Chase, there isn't another person I would trust with my life. Hell, I wouldn't even be alive if not for him.

"You think you've gone up against them before?" Chase asks, breaking my thoughts.

"Not them, exactly," Ryan answers. "I want to look into them more, but I have Josh on standby. Might need his help."

I smile a little. "How is he? Haven't heard from him in a while."

Ryan smiles. "Not bad. He's been making a lot of trips to Gainesville, Florida. He says it's nothing, but we all know it's a woman. He hasn't brought her around yet, though. He said he's keeping her to himself for a while."

I chuckle. "Don't blame him." I glance towards the suite again and sigh for the millionth time.

"Taylor, just go," Chase says with a soft smile. "It's late anyway. That girl is probably exhausted."

I nod and nearly jump up. I stride through the middle suite into mine and hurry into the bedroom. My girl wrapped in Breetana's arms, and my heart constricts as I stop dead in my tracks. She really has no idea how beautiful she is. After I compose myself seeing such a touching sight, I silently walk to the bed and gently wake Breetana.

She turns her head to me and smiles softly. "She's okay," she whispers. "She realized pretty quickly that no one meant to hurt her."

"No one did. But I get why her mind took that in another direction," I whisper back.

She smiles softly. "Don't hurt my sister."

"Not a chance."

"Promise?"

"On my mother's soul."

She nods and gently extracts herself from her sister's grip. She gives me a soft squeeze on my arm and kiss on my cheek before she leaves and closes the door. I find one of my t-shirts and kneel on the bed.

Nicole jumps at my sudden weight next to her. "Taylor?"

"Yeah, baby. It's me. I was just trying to get you into something more comfortable to sleep in," I say raspily. She shifts onto her back and sits up. She takes her shirt off, and then reaches around to unhook her bra. The shade in the window is open, and the moon reflecting off Lake Superior lights up the room enough so that I can see everything she's doing. I groan as I watch her spill from the bra. "My God...You're beautiful."

She laughs. "Being pregnant has made them a lot bigger. I'm usually only a C."

"So what are you now?" I say, biting my lip with a grin. She reaches up and squeezes both of them. My eyes widen. "Oh my fuck. You're so hot."

"Maybe… this is a hint for you," she says teasingly, looking up at me. I waste no time leaning her back on the bed and stripping her of her jeans, leaving her sexy satin panties on. I lay next to her and lean down to kiss her as I rest my hand on her stomach, rubbing my hand softly back and forth across it.

"I think you should take off your shirt." She bites her lip as she watches me.

"You do, huh?" I smile as I kiss her again. I love the way she tastes. Something sweet mixed with her, and I can't get enough.

"I do. And maybe your jeans, too."

I chuckle. "Oh yeah?"

"Mmhmm."

I take my shirt off, then my jeans, leaving my boxer briefs on. I throw the jeans and shirt on the floor. I reach down next to her and grab my t-shirt I found for her. I put it on my pillow and then return my hand to her stomach. Nicole unabashedly stares at my body.

"You're so…" She pauses, and I'm actually nervous at what she's about to say. "Well-sculpted? Completely... gorgeous."

I smile and lean down to kiss her. "You're absolutely gorgeous, as well." I run my hand up and cup her breast. She moans at my touch and reaches up to put her hand over mine. "So… what size?" I rub my thumb back and forth across her nipple as I gently squeeze it. I lean down and flick my tongue across her other one. She sighs and pushes into me, running her fingers through my hair.

"A triple D."

"Shit…" I take her nipple in my mouth and roll it between my tongue and teeth, scraping my teeth over it ever so gently.

"I won't be this size forever." Her breath hitches as I continue my assault on her tits.

"It doesn't really matter to me what size you are. I just want you to be mine."

She gasps. "Really?"

"I don't mean to scare you by moving too fast." I pull back and look up at her.

She smiles and cups my cheek in her small hand. "Would it be too bold of me to say I just want to be yours? And that I want you to be mine?"

"Maybe if it was anyone else. But I don't like to waste time when I know what I want."

"And it's really me that you want?"

"Nikki. Haven't I made that obvious?"

"I... I guess. I... guess I am just really surprised."

"Why?"

I grab the t-shirt and hand it to her when she starts to shiver. She sits up to put it on, and I pull the covers back so she can climb under with me. She does and curls into me, lying on her side to face me as I wrap the covers around us and my arms around her.

"You kissed my stomach. Twice. You lit up when you felt him move. You put your hand on my stomach when we were on the couch. And you kept it there. Like you were trying to say you'll protect both of us."

"Nicole. Sweetie, I really, really like you. I've never felt like this before. It's like I got hit with a sledgehammer. I want to be with you. All the time. I'm crazy for you. It's nothing like me. At all. And then when I felt the baby kick and gravitate to my touch, that was it for me. Right then I decided there's no point fighting this. I'm falling pretty fucking hard and fast for both of you here."

"Taylor..."

I lean down to kiss her. She pulls away with a sharp intake of breath and reaches to her side. My heart stops beating. "You okay?"

"I'm fine. He doesn't like when I lay on my right side."

"Well, get comfortable." I breathe a sigh of relief that it wasn't anything major. She rolls to her left side so her back is against my chest, and her ass is pressed against my cock. I groan.

She laughs. "I'm really tired, but if you hold me all night long, I'll do something about that hard-on in the morning."

"Deal," I growl into her ear as I kiss it. I kiss the back of her head, and she takes my hand. She puts it under the t-shirt she's wearing and on her stomach.

I can't believe how much she's changed my life. How she's made me want to settle down with her and raise her baby as my own. I don't understand any of this, but I don't bother trying. I'm old enough to know that there isn't any point trying to stop it. Love makes no sense. There's no rhyme or reason to it. It just is.

I fall asleep to the subtle movements of the life she carries inside her. I fall asleep to her breathing. Despite wanting no part of love for most of my life, all I want now is for both of them to be mine.

Chapter Fifteen

✗ Chase ✗

I'm lying on my back staring pensively at the ceiling as Breetana lays next to me, her head on my chest. The sun is just rising over the horizon, bathing the room in an orange glow. Breetana's hair shines around her as the light hits it. She's so beautiful. So perfect. She's sleeping so peacefully, and I have to thank whatever God exists for that. She needs it. I can see how exhausted she is. I know her. She holds everyone up even when she's falling.

My biggest fucking regret is that I was part of dragging her down. For three years. She was the one keeping me together and dealing with all of *my* shit. Covering for *me* when I couldn't be bothered enough to show up after a night out. Dealing with all the other women, even though it was only her I wanted. It's always been her.

She's been doing it all on her own. With no one. Except her sister who was miles away and dealing with her own demons.

Every time I think of what I've done to her, how I've added to all of her stress and fears, my heart hurts. Literally hurts. And since I can't stop thinking about it, I feel like I'm having a constant heart attack.

I look down at Breetana and gently move her off me so I can get up. I don't want to wake her.

Actually, I don't want her to wake up until this entire fucking nightmare is over. I want to protect her from all of this. Shield her. She's the most amazing, kind, beautiful, selfless person I've ever met. She doesn't deserve this. She deserves the best of everything. The best the entire universe has to offer. Every being in the entire galaxy and beyond should be falling at her feet and treating her like the Goddess she fucking is.

I stand and throw a pair of sweats on before I sneak out of the room, making sure to leave the bedroom door open a little so I can hear if she calls for me.

I walk out into the kitchen in the suite and raise my eyebrow at the coffee already made.

"Sorry if I woke you." I turn to see one of Ryan's guys walking in from the other room. "I don't do well without coffee in the morning."

I chuckle. "Yeah. Same here. Although, my girl spoils me. Usually when I show up at the office, there's a Vanilla Latte on my desk within ten minutes."

"Vanilla Latte, huh?"

I laugh softly. "It's a vice."

"We all got 'em. Mine's Ryan's chicken marsala. Sometimes when something good happens, we all get a celebration, and he makes that for us."

I pour my coffee and turn back to him after taking a sip. "Rico. Right?"

"Yeah. That's me."

"And you'll be one of the two with Breetana?"

"Yes, sir. Me and Pete. Greg and Miguel will be with Nicole."

I nod. "Nothing gets by you guys when it comes to them. I don't care what happens to me as long as those two are safe. Understand?"

"Yes, sir. I understand, but with all due respect, my orders include you and Taylor. From what I understand, Taylor is like a brother to Ryan, and he doesn't let anyone in his circle. Ryan protects his family and those close to him. Fiercely and viciously if he needs to. You're part of Taylor's family which makes you part of Ryan's. We protect our own, Mr. Shaw.

And we do it at all costs." He smiles and nods before he turns and settles on the couch with his coffee.

I have no idea what the fuck I've gotten myself into, but I won't let Breetana do this without me. No fucking way she's doing anything without me again. Thank fucking God I have Ryan on my side.

I head out to the balcony to finish watching the sunrise over the lake. There is really nothing better than watching a sunrise. It's peaceful. Serene.

"Can't sleep?" Ryan's deep baritone comes from behind me.

I lean on the balcony. "I don't think I've slept since Monday night." I don't look at him, but I do take a deep and incredibly shaky breath. Ryan leans on the balcony next to me, looking over the lake. "I've messed up a lot in my life. Especially with Breetana. But now that everything with us is out in the open, and she's truly, finally mine…, I'm scared. I don't want to lose her. I can't."

Ryan puts his hand on my shoulder for a moment before letting go. "There are very few people I've let in my life. I have my parents and my brothers, Nick and Jason. Jason's wife, Jess. She's like the little sister I've never had. I have a good friend named Alex. He's like a brother to me. His brother Josh. Same thing. And then there's Taylor."

This does get me to look at him. "How long have you known him?"

"Years. It started out with me giving him tips, him taking people down for me. Over the years, though, Taylor has become far more. He's become one of the very few people I know I can count on. He's become family." He looks at me. "I protect my family, Chase. If you and Breetana are like his, then it makes you just as much mine. I'll protect you both just as fiercely as I will him, his girl, and that baby. You won't lose her, Chase. Not on my watch." He pats my back and walks back into the suite.

I sigh and stay outside a few minutes longer before deciding on a shower. The hottest shower I can stand. Maybe it'll relax me a little bit.

I walk back into the bedroom and see Breetana is still sleeping soundly. I want to let her sleep, but I can't help pressing a soft kiss to her forehead. I'm grateful she doesn't wake up, but I have to smile when she smiles in her sleep.

A few minutes later, I'm standing in the shower under a hot and hard spray when a realization slams into me.

I love her. It's probably something I've known for longer than I care to admit, but I really love her. I fell in love with her a long time ago. It's more than just wanting her. More than just intense attraction. More than just wanting to spend time with her or feeling an obligation to protect her.

I sigh and rest my head against the shower wall as the water beats against my back.

"Chase?" Breetana's voice is soft, and I look at her. She's wearing my long sleeve shirt from the plane, and my heart beats a little faster. I open the shower door and pull her into the shower with me. "Babe! Your shirt is getting soaked!"

"I don't care." I pull her close and bury my face in her hair. I take a deep breath and kiss her neck as tears sting my eyes. The water runs over the both of us, soaking her, but I don't give a shit. I just need her in my arms. "I love you. I love you so damn much, Bree. I'm sorry for everything I've put you through. I'm sorry for being the cause of so much stress to you. For not being someone you could count on like I did you. For -"

"Chase. Baby, stop. Stop." She reaches behind me and turns off the water before stripping off the soaked shirt and dropping it on the shower floor. She takes my hand, pulls me out of the shower, and hands me a towel.

"Bree -" I stop talking as she shakes her head and dries off. I gulp air as I slowly start drying off while I watch her. "I... feel like I just pissed you off."

She smiles and steps towards me, taking my face in her hands. "You didn't."

"Then -"

"Don't. Just finish drying off, and come back to bed. Okay?" She strips off her soaked panties and throws them on top of the shirt in the shower.

"Holy fuck." I can't take my eyes off her as she leaves the bathroom drying her hair.

I quickly finish drying off and wrap another towel around my waist, following her out of the bathroom. She climbs into the bed completely naked. I can't speak. She motions for me with a single finger, and my body moves on its own. She lifts the covers, and I strip the towel and crawl in next to her.

"Bree -"

"Chase. Shh." She pulls herself closer, and I wrap her in my arms. I take a couple more shaky breaths. "Why do you think you've been the cause of my stress?"

"Holy shit, Breetana. Are you kidding? The last three years I've done nothing but put you through hell. I've given you impossible to-do lists. I know the hours you put in making sure it was all done. You covered for me with several clients. And not once did you complain. Even with all of the women. You never complained. You took it all. You've put me in my place a few times, but you never complained. You just shouldered it all and did what I asked."

"Because doing what you ask is my job."

"No, baby. Your job is to make sure I'm where I'm supposed to be. Your job is not to run my meetings when I don't show up. Or get my dry cleaning, or make sure my maid cleans up after me when I drink myself into a fucking stupor."

"Chase, what's wrong? What's going on in your head? You know I love my job. You know I don't mind doing anything you need me to if it helps you. The only thing I have ever had an issue with is the women. You know that. So what's happening right now?"

I bury my face in her hair once more. It's still damp, but still smells like her. Coconut. "I love you. I'm sorry it took me this long to realize it. I just…" I trail off. She reaches up and runs her fingers soothingly through my hair. "I'm sorry it took this whole situation for me to finally realize that I've treated you like shit."

"Chase. No. You didn't."

"How can you say that? Look at everything I put you through. With the women. Undue stress preparing for meetings I should've been in. Dealing with women at my house that stayed over that I didn't want to deal with. And all of that on top of all of this? Everything you've dealt with you've done by yourself. I didn't help. I fucking should have been there for you. I've loved you ever since you walked into my office. I never should have let you go on this long believing I didn't." I let out a frustrated sigh. She hugs me and kisses my neck. "I never should have let you think for one second that I didn't care about you. I should've been the one that you felt like you could talk to if you needed to." I'm surprised at the tears falling from my eyes, soaking her neck. Even more surprised that I'm shaking.

"Babe. I never felt like you treated me badly. I hated the women, but how could I say anything about them? I never told you how I felt either." She's caressing my back with the most amazingly comforting touch I have ever felt. I'm never letting her go. Never letting this go. "You bought me a car when mine broke down."

"You were driving a death trap. I was terrified I'd get a call that you wouldn't be in because your car blew up."

"You make me eat lunch."

"Because you starve yourself."

"You didn't fire me when I was late after my car broke down."

"I was waiting for it to break down after seeing what the hell you were driving around in."

"You make me go home when I get my migraines. Or lay in your office on your couch with the lights out and the shades drawn."

"What the fuck kind of person would I be if I made you work through pain like that? I've seen you nearly pass out from those."

"You send me soup. You've sent me dinner on so many occasions."

"Because I know you. Sometimes, I'm pretty convinced you never eat anything. If I didn't make sure you do it, you would probably waste away." I feel her smiling into my neck before she chuckles and kisses my shoulder. "What could you possibly be happy about right now?"

"Did you just hear anything you just said to me? Chase. You've cared for me more than anyone in my life has. Other than my parents. And Kiki and Reese. But ever since I moved away, it's been just me."

"Baby, that's my whole point. It -"

"I love you. More than anything. And the reason is because despite everything with the women, I knew the entire time that you cared for me. That's why I stayed. Not because I loved my job. Which I do. I really do love my job. I love doing things for you and being able to help you. But that's never been the entire reason. The reason I stayed, Chase, the reason I *stay…* is *you.*"

I pull back so I can look at her. "You love me?"

She wipes a tear away from the corner of my eye. "How could I not? How could I not fall head over heels in love with someone like you? You're insanely hot." She smiles and winks.

I laugh. "Of course that's the only reason, right?"

“Nope. You look great in jeans,” she teases as she kisses me. “And when you're all wet? All I want to do is lick the droplets off your abs.”

I laugh again as she smiles at me and reaches up to touch my cheek. “I really do love you. And I'm really sorry I never told you sooner.”

“And I really do love you, Chase. So much. And I’m also really sorry I never told you sooner either.

I kiss her, giving her everything I possibly can in the kiss to show her how much she means to me. When I pull back, her eyes are sparkling with unshed tears. I kiss each of her eyelids. “What do you say we finish that shower? Be alone to just... enjoy each other until we have to head up to Silver Bay.”

“I love that idea.”

I get out of the bed and take her hand to pull her up. Not letting go of her hand for a second, I lead her to the shower. She's perfect. She's everything to me. She holds my heart.

Hell.

She *is* my heart.

Chapter Sixteen

✗ Nicole ✗

The scene unfolding in front of us is something out of a movie. Ryan, along with mine and Taylor's new security detail, are all driving in a black SUV with tinted windows in front of us. Behind us is Breetana's and Chase's security detail. And behind them are two other vehicles. They are all black. All SUVs. And all carry heavily armed men. When Taylor follows Ryan into the driveway and parks next to him, the security detail behind us pulls in behind us, and I can't help but laugh.

"What's so funny, baby?" Taylor asks.

"This." I gesture at the entire scene. "All of it. It's like a scene out of... I don't know. A mafia movie."

The other two SUV's pull up on the street in front of my house, and I shake my head as I begin opening the door to step out of the car.

Taylor grabs my arm, and I involuntarily wince. "Wait. Remember? Ryan and his guys need to do a sweep. Make sure it's safe."

"Right. Sorry." I look down at my hands in my lap, feeling like an idiot for forgetting the entire reason they're here. Even briefly.

Taylor leans across the center console and kisses my cheek before reaching down to squeeze my thigh. "How many times are you going to make me say that you aren't stupid, and to stop thinking that way about yourself?"

Unnerving. He is so unnerving. The way he just knows what I'm thinking. Knows what I need. From him and otherwise. It's crazy.

Breetana reaches out to touch my hair and squeeze my shoulder before she lets her hand fall. "It's going to take time to get used to, Kiki. That's all."

"If it makes you feel better, I almost just did the same thing," Chase says with a chuckle.

I look back at Chase. "Really?"

"Yeah. I stopped myself when Taylor told you to stop."

"See? Chase is the smartest man I know, and he just did the same thing," Taylor says. I smile at him, and he presses a soft kiss to my lips. I'm falling for him. So hard.

After a few minutes, Ryan walks out to our vehicle and opens my door. He leans in and gives me a soft smile. "Ready to go?"

"Yep," I say softly.

"Taylor will stay with you. Chase with Tana. Me in front with Rico. The others behind. Taylor and Chase. Use the vehicles for cover and come around the front while we get the girls out. We walk into the house. No stopping."

"Yes, sir." Taylor gives a wry smile.

Ryan laughs. "Let's move."

We all do exactly as Ryan says. As soon as Taylor meets me in the front of the vehicle, he puts a protective arm around me. Chase does the same for Breetana, and we all hurry into the house. I don't dare let out a breath until the door is closed firmly behind us.

"You okay, sweetheart?" Taylor asks.

I nod and smile a shaky smile. "I just want to get this over with and get out of here."

"I know, baby. What first? What do you need from us? You're the boss."

"Honestly, I'm overwhelmed. I don't know where to start." I bury my face in my hands, and Taylor puts his arms around me.

"Hey. Hey, look at me, baby," he whispers in my ear. I take a deep breath and look up at him. He smiles and runs the back of his hand along my cheek. "One step at a time."

"It's kind of dumb -"

"Nicole," His voice drops to a dominant level that makes me shiver as he shakes his head. "No. We talked about that shit. Start over."

I blush. We did talk about that. Right before he gave me the best orgasm of my life. I shake my head. "I like lists. It helps me organize my thoughts and what needs to be done. But it'll take time. I don't want everyone to be bored."

"Ma'am, we're here for you. Don't worry about us," Miguel, one of Ryan's guards, says.

I smile and nod as I head to the kitchen and find my notebook. Taylor follows and leans up against the counter. "I need the nursery packed up. Baby clothes and toys. The crib is brand new, and I really love it. Everything in the nursery comes with. I worked hard on that. It's the only thing here that's really mine. Other than a few sentimental things."

Taylor chuckles. "Okay. Nursery."

"And then there's things in the bedroom I need. Clothes and necessities. And paperwork that I keep in a safe." I'm writing quickly, trying to keep up with my thoughts as Taylor watches me. He turns and leans forward, resting his elbows on the counter next to me, watching as I write. "China and China cabinet... Hmm. Dishes, pots and pans. Guest bedroom. Couches, chairs."

"You think you're really going to need all of this stuff?" Taylor asks, raising an eyebrow as he looks at me.

"I'm essentially starting over." I glance at him and continue writing.

He puts a hand over mine. "Where are you going to live?"

"Obviously Chicago." I look at him. "Why?"

"So, you move in with Tana. Why would you need your entire guest bedroom, living room, dishes, and…" He glances at my list and smiles. His eyes light up, and I'm lost. "Pink shower curtain and matching bathroom things?"

I shrug. "I could put them in storage."

"You know how I feel about you. Right?"

"Yes."

"You know I want you in my life. I don't know what the future holds, but I know I'm all in. You. Me. And the baby."

I swallow. "Are you about to ask me what I think you are?" I whisper and bite my lip.

He smiles and sweetly kisses me. "Maybe you could move in with me. Breetana is probably going to move in with Chase. Which means you would be alone at her apartment, and as your boyfriend, I hate that idea. Especially with you so close to giving birth. My house is pretty large. Chase insisted." For the first time ever... Taylor seems to not know what to say. I smile at him and put a hand on his cheek. "I'm just saying there's a lot of room. If you get mad at me, there's places you can be alone. I have enough room for a large nursery, and to raise a baby."

"Babe, are you actually nervous?" I smile teasingly at him.

He lets out a breath. "Fuck yes."

"The great Taylor Reddick. Big bad Chicago cop with his ridiculously, sexy, large muscles is actually nervous?"

"You're fucking enjoying this." He smirks and licks his lips.

I'm instantly wet. "Absolutely. Every moment. And... yes. I will move in with you."

"Really? I thought you'd fight me on that."

"Maybe old Nicole. New Nicole just wants to be with you."

He kisses me again, teasing me with his tongue. I moan. "The kitchen at home isn't closed-in like this one. It's an open floor plan. We'll be alone so I won't have to worry about it when I take you on the counter unless we have company. So, I should probably take advantage of the privacy we have here, huh?"

He reaches over and trails his hand up my bare leg and under my dress. I don't really like dresses, but they're the most comfortable thing I have right now. And right now, I'm thankful I'm wearing one.

My eyes go wide, and I grab his hand. "Taylor!" I nervously glance towards the door. "There's like ten people out there!"

"So?" He only smiles as his eyes grow lustful.

Holy shit, this man. He leaves his hand on my leg as he moves the other around to my back, lifting my hair and kissing my neck. I lean into him. He slides his hand down and rubs my tits with one hand while the other teases my entrance over my panties.

"Taylor…," I breathe as I softly moan. "What if someone walks in?"

He's pressed against me and is swaying side to side with me. His hard length and his hands make it hard to think as my eyes flutter closed.

"You really want me to stop?" His breath is hot against my ear as he kisses my neck to my cheek before moving to the other side and starting all over at my neck.

"You know the answer to that."

"Mmhmm. I do. I know exactly what you need right now." He slips his hand under my dress and bra, cupping my breast at the same time he moves my panties aside and slowly rubs a finger between my folds to my center. He dips just his fingertip inside before he runs it back up to make the rest of me wet.

"Mmm... Taylor…"

"Yeah?" He circles my clit, and then slips back into my center, a little deeper than before.

"Oh... So good." I reach up, wrapping my arms around his shoulders, and give in to him completely.

"Mmm... you like that, beautiful? You like when I tease you like this?"

"Yes... yes."

He pulls back out and circles my sensitive bud once more. "God, you're so fucking incredible." He's moving slowly, but the pressure he's building inside me is unlike anything I've ever felt. I push against him, feeling his hard cock against my ass as he starts rubbing my clit. I moan and gasp. "Shh…," he whispers.

"Taylor…" I whisper his name as I start to tighten. "Taylor... Oh God…"

"There is nothing in the world sexier than you right now with my name on your lips."

"I'm gonna come. Mmm…" I rub my ass against him, and he pushes into me. He finally pushes two fingers inside me and gives me slow, deep strokes while he presses his thumb against my clit harder. I bend slightly and put my hands on the counter in front of me to steady myself. "Shit. Oh... don't stop. Right there. Oh…"

He lets go of my breast and puts his hand over my mouth. "Someone's gonna hear, baby."

"Mmm… fuck. Taylor!" I scream. His hand muffles my cries of pleasure. He knows in such a short time where to touch me. How to drive me crazy.

"Come on, baby. Give me what I want. Or are you gonna make me use my tongue to get it from you?"

His breath is hot against my neck as he continues his deep strokes and pressure on my clit. I'm so close, but oh my God. His tongue. I nod my head up and down and Taylor growls. He slowly takes his fingers out of me and spins me to face him. He teasingly runs his hand down my ass to my thighs and lifts me.

He puts me on the counter and kisses me. "Promise to be quiet?"

I shake my head no and give him a sexy, pouty smile. He kisses me and pulls me to the edge of the counter before he dips his head down between my legs. With one hand, he slides two fingers back inside me, and I gasp. He puts his other hand over my mouth and his tongue against my clit. He licks and sucks on it while he strokes me. His hand muffles my scream as he rips my orgasm from me. It takes less than ten seconds.

When he's done lapping everything I gave him up, he lets my mouth go and stands with a super cocky smirk.

"Oh my God. You're so, so good at that," I say with a blush.

"You taste so good, honey." He leans forward to kiss me, and I taste myself on his tongue.

I hug him for a moment. He pulls me close to him. When I let him go, he leans down to kiss my stomach. The baby flutters and curls into his touch. "Wow. He really, really likes you. He doesn't even do that for me."

He grins like a little boy who got everything he wanted for Christmas. My heart melts, and I reach out to run a hand through his hair as he starts talking to the baby. "Does this mean you aren't going to be a mama's boy?" The baby shifts again, and I wince a little bit. Taylor's eyes widen almost impossibly, and I laugh as he steps back. "Holy shit! What was that? Was that his head? It was like your stomach just grew a fucking bump!"

"That was probably his elbow. Or his knee. He just shifted when you were talking to him." I smile. He's so happy and smiling so widely that I can't help but reach for his hand and pull him back, placing it back on my stomach. "Talk to him. Feel how he reacts to your voice."

"Hey there, little one. I don't know what all of this means. I'm new to it all. But I'm sure happy your mama fell into my life."

"Taylor…" Tears sting my eyes. He bends to kiss my stomach, looks up, and winks at me before turning his attention back to the baby. I cover my mouth with my other hand to stop the sob as Ryan walks into the room. He stops short and grins like an idiot.

"Pretty sure you and I are going to get along great. What do you think?" The baby moves under his hand and pushes. The sob escapes. Taylor looks up at me and straightens, cupping my face in his hands. He notices Ryan and smiles softly before focusing all of his attention on me. "What's going on in that beautiful head of yours?"

I sniffle before kissing him. "When you asked what he thinks... his hand pushed up. Like he wanted to hold yours. I know it was his hand. I felt it."

Taylor smiles and uses the pads on each of his thumbs to wipe away my tears. "Your pregnancy hormones are going to be my complete demise, honey," he whispers. I laugh and hug him.

Ryan leans against the counter next to us. "We were starting to wonder if you two ran away," he jokes.

"Not a bad fucking idea. Pretty sure Chase would be game to take us all away from here." Taylor gives him a weak smile.

"Fuck. I'd take you all away from here." Ryan gazes pensively at the wall.

"We can't run, though. Tana was right, and so were you. They'll keep coming for them."

"Which is why we need to end this once and for all. Hopefully the peaceful way."

"You mean the legal way," I tease.

"Sure. The legal way." Ryan gives a dangerous smile, and Taylor shakes his head, but he's smiling.

I sigh, and they both look at me. "Can you get me down? We should probably get started."

Taylor kisses my forehead and lifts me down. I've never been good at hiding my emotions, and today is no different.

Ryan puts an arm over my shoulders and pulls me to his side. Taylor smiles. "You know. Taylor. He's like a brother to me," Ryan says.

"I gathered." I take a deep breath and let it out.

"There isn't anything he could ask of me that I wouldn't do for him."

I gesture across the entire room. "Considering where we are, I gathered that, too."

"What I'm trying to say here is I know you're scared. And I understand you don't know me or really anything about me except that I'm some big, scary mafia boss from New York. But Taylor is my family."

"Which makes you his family, baby. Other than me, Chase and Tana, there isn't another person in this world other than Ryan that you'd want on your side," Taylor says.

"I won't let anything happen to you," Ryan vows.

I look down at the floor. I want to believe nothing is going to happen to me or Breetana, but I just don't think they know how cruel Billy and Shaun can be. How heartless they really are.

Even I know that people who have no empathy are dangerous.

Chapter Seventeen

✗ Breetana ✗

Chase and I are in Nicole's guest bedroom going through boxes and boxes of memorabilia looking for two particular photo albums. I sigh as I sit up on my knees. I look around the bedroom at the mess we've made from my spot in the closet.

"I love my sister, but I think she has pregnancy brain."

Chase laughs as he surveys the damage we've made while he moves to his knees next to me. "Your sister is great, but you may be right. I haven't seen any photo albums in this mess." He looks above us.

"Maybe I should ask her where it is."

"Wait a sec. Didn't she say they're both in a big white box?"

I try to follow his gaze but see nothing. "Yeah. But I don't see any other white boxes anywhere other than the ones we've already gone through." I lean forward to peer up on the shelves above me but still see nothing. Chase grins cockily and kisses me. One of his hands comes to a rest on my ass. I give him a teasing wide-eyed smile. "Oh no. It's gotten to you. All of the stuff in this room. You're losing your mind, too. Chase! Come back to me!" I reach up to take his face in my hands and stare into his eyes in all mock seriousness. He laughs a maniacal laugh, and I burst into a fit of giggles.

"Seriously, babe. How much do you love me?" He moves in front of me and turns, still on his knees. Both of his hands come to a rest on my ass.

"Hmm... The answer to that is greatly dependent on how quickly you can get me out of this madhouse."

He leans down to kiss me. "I think the answer then is about to be something like 'more than life itself'." He leans down to kiss me once more, and then stands. I watch him curiously as he reaches above him and slides a box across the very top shelf. He lifts it down.

My mouth falls open. "How? How did you even see that from here?"

"I have an unfair advantage."

"And what is that exactly? Your rippling muscles? The fact that you didn't even break a sweat, and it looks like that box weighs a ton?"

He grins and puts the box down in front of us. "All of that. But in this case, my height. I'm a foot taller than you. Even on my knees I'm bigger. I saw a glimpse of it. Thought we got all those boxes down. Looks like it was stuck behind one." He starts opening the box, but closes it quickly before I have a chance to see what's in it. He smirks.

I laugh. "What?"

"Remember a minute ago when I asked how much you love me?"

"Of course. How could I not?" I try to open the box, but he holds the flaps down. "Chase! Come on. What's in there?"

"How much do you love me?"

I grin at his playfulness. "You're so incredibly sexy when you're like this."

"You bring it out of me. Now…" He leans on the box. "How... much... do... you... love... me?"

I sigh dramatically. He laughs. "More than anything in the entire world. No. Universe. No! More than anything in the entire everything!"

Chase smiles widely at me. "If those photo albums are in here, I get you…" He nods towards the bedroom and grins. His eyes never leave mine. "...over there on that bed."

My eyes widen. "Chase!" I laugh, and then quickly jump up to close the door and lock it. I'm really liking this game of his. I sashay back to him and the box. He watches my every move, a twinkle in his eyes. "What if... I don't agree to your terms?"

"Agree, or we stay in this room going through every single box in that closet. Never… touching… this… one."

"You wouldn't torture me like that." I pout.

He laughs. "Is that a dare?"

I laugh. "Okay! Okay! Terms agreed to. What's in the box?" I'm almost jumping up and down. He gives me a sly smile as he slowly opens it. On top are two photo albums and a jewelry box, but that's not what grabs my attention. "Oh my God!"

I nearly dive into the box as I pull out a long, flowing wedding dress. Immediately tears sting my eyes. "Oh my God! I can't believe she kept this." I catch Chase watching me, a soft smile on his face, as I twirl around the room. I stop. I still hold the dress against my body, but I reach up to wipe a tear away. "What?"

"Nothing. Just thinking about how beautiful you would look walking down the aisle to meet me at the altar wearing that."

I blush furiously and look down at the ground. I smile as I walk back to him and the box. "Do you... really think about that? About us?"

He smiles as he stands and puts a hand on my cheek. "I don't want to scare you off, but yes. I've never wanted to be with anyone like I do you. I've never been in love with anyone but you. I can't see my future without you in it, baby. I love you. And now that I've told you that, you aren't getting rid of me."

I feel like my face could split apart, but I don't care. Hearing him say those words to me is everything I've ever wanted. He gently takes the dress from my hands and sets it back in the box before he leads me to the bed.

He sits down and pulls me next to him. "Do you think of me? Of marrying me?"

"Chase…, I've been planning my wedding to you since you hired me."

He surprises me with a loud, hearty laugh. "Pretty damn honest, aren't you?"

"I think we've wasted more than enough time beating around the bush with each other, don't you?"

“Fuck yes.” He pushes me back on the bed and crawls on top of me, kissing my neck the entire time.

“I really do love you.” I wrap my arms around him and kiss his cheek and shoulder. “I can't stop saying it.”

“I hope you never stop saying it.” His hand snakes its way under my shirt.

“Chase…” I groan as he cups my breast over my bra. He straddles me and pulls me up to him. He ravishes my mouth as we both take off each other's shirts. He flicks the hooks on my bra, and I spill out against him with a gasp. “God. You're really good at that.”

“Years and years of practice.” He smirks.

I swat him. “No more. I hate all of them.”

“There's only you, baby. I'm all yours.” He sits on the bed and grabs my hips. He pulls me down on top of him. He's straining against his jeans, and I moan as I press against him. He unbuttons my jean cut-off shorts, and I kick them off. “Christ, Bree. You're beautiful.”

His hands roam over my body and his eyes follow. I press myself harder against him, needing to relieve the pressure he's building between my legs just by being him. It isn't until his hands reach my hips that he realizes I'm not wearing any underwear.

“Fuck me. Are you really not wearing panties?” He can't take his eyes off me, and my smooth center.

“I forgot to pack panties.” I bite my lip and hold back a smile. He coughs. “You've seen me naked.”

“Yeah, but when you're clothed, I expect panties as part of that. Now, all I'm going to be thinking about for the rest of the day is how you aren't wearing any, and how much I want to fuck you.”

“Maybe that's the point.” I rub myself against his jeans, and the sensation against my naked core is nearly too much to bear.

Chase moans and pushes up into me as he grabs both tits in his hands. “I’m not fucking you. Not here, baby.” He grabs my hips and flips me onto my back. “But I will make this pretty pussy come for me.” Seconds later, his head is nestled between my thighs, and his tongue is on my clit.

I arch off the bed. “Chase! Shit! Oh my God, that feels so good.”

“You taste like Heaven.” He slips a finger inside me.

I grip the blanket underneath me. “Oh... God… Oh my God.”

"My name, baby. I want my name coming out of your sexy as fuck mouth." He swirls his tongue around my clit as he moves his finger in a circle inside me.

"Chase. Mmm! What are you doing? What is that?"

"Just my finger," he chuckles.

"You're so… oh…" My eyes fall closed, and I meet each thrust. He adds a second finger and repeats the same slow circular motion as he takes my swollen clit in his mouth and sucks. "Oh! I don't care what you're doing. Just don't stop." I throw my head back on the pillow and arch into his mouth. His fingers slide deeper. "Chase… Mmm... I love when you do that."

"You think I don't know what you like by now?" His breath is warm against me, and his deep voice sends vibrations through me.

"You're a fast learner."

"Observant. I know if I do this…" He scrapes his teeth along my sensitive pussy, and then follows with his tongue. I push up into him, and his fingers slip deeper. "You do exactly that. And... if I do this…" He bites my clit and crooks his fingers inside me, scraping his nail gently along my walls. I instantly tighten for him. "You immediately tighten around my fingers."

"Chase…"

"Then if I do this…" He flicks my clit a few times with his tongue.

"Oh, Chase... I'm gonna come. Don't stop."

He slides his fingers inside me deeply and harder as he thrusts faster. My legs get weak. My stomach tightens. Seconds later, my release is rocking my body, and I'm spilling onto his tongue as I moan incoherently.

He licks me a few more times, and then smiles very smugly up at me. "You almost instantaneously come for me."

"You're so incredibly cocky that it's sexy." I smile as I ride the waves of bliss.

"What's sexy is you coming for me like that." He kisses his way to my mouth, stopping to lavish each breast on the way. As soon as he reaches my lips, he slips his tongue inside and wages a war with mine. The kiss is deep and as hot as it is sweet. When he pulls away, he smiles the sweetest smile. "You know what I really love?"

"What?"

"Being able to say that I love you and knowing you'll say it back to me. Every time."

"I love that, too," I say shyly. He wraps me in his arms and rolls over to his side, pulling me close to him. We're both quiet for a little while, our hands contentedly roaming each other's bodies. After a little while, I sigh. "We should probably see what else Kiki needs."

"Yeah... I guess you're right." He kisses me, and I close my eyes once more. I love the way he kisses me. It's like he's trying to show me exactly how he feels through his kiss. I can't get enough.

"I love you, Chase."

"I love you, too, Bree."

We both get up and get dressed. I grab the photo albums and take a last lingering look at the dress. Chase, of course, catches me.

I smile softly as I run my fingers along the fabric. "This is going to sound really silly, but... when I was twelve, I got my first period. My mom helped me with everything. I was kind of upset about it. And I didn't feel good. I had cramps. They were bad. My mom, being the amazing person she was, told me that I had become a woman, and she wanted to show me something." Chase gently takes the photo albums from my hand and tucks my hair behind my ear. "She took out her wedding dress and showed it to me. She even let me put it on."

"This dress?" He points to the dress in the box that I'm staring lovingly at.

I smile. "She said one day, when I met the right person, this dress would belong to me. With a few alterations." I look back up at Chase. "But we have more important things to do than reminisce." I turn to leave, leaving the dress in the box.

"Baby. If you don't take the dress, I will."

"It's okay. Really. I'm sure Kiki kept it because she wants it. We'll get it packed up for her, but I want to get her these first."

"Breetana."

"Chase."

"Take the dress. It's not like you both can't use it. Unless you get married at the same time. Which won't happen. Taylor may be my brother, but no fucking way I'm sharing our day with anyone else," he says possessively. I stare up at him and blink. He smiles. "What?"

"You just... you did it again. You hinted at marrying me."

"Does this surprise you? Babe, there's no way I'm letting you go after finally having you. I don't want anyone else. Just you."

"Chase…" I throw my arms around him, and he pulls me close to him with his free hand.

"I'll get you a ring and make it official, but I do want to marry you, baby. Waiting so long to tell you how I felt and trying to deny it was stupid on my part. I don't want to waste any more time."

"Me either." I bury my head in his chest.

"Take your dress. We'll talk to Nikki and figure it out."

I smile and happily take the dress. I'm giddy at him calling it mine. I practically bounce down the stairs. "Nikki! Look what I found!" I round the corner and run into Taylor. Chase isn't quite close enough to catch me, and I fall on my ass. "Ow…"

"Shit. Baby, you okay?" Chase asks.

Taylor grins down at me and pulls me up. "Sorry, sweetheart."

I rub my ass. "What the hell? What is it with you two? Are you constructed of steel?"

"Chase and I work out every morning," Taylor says as he steadies me.

"You know I'm in the gym every day." Chase kisses the back of my head as Taylor lets me go.

"You both hurt," I say, shaking my head.

"I'm sure you ain't the only woman to say that." He winks. Chase laughs. Taylor leans down to pick up the dress.

"You found it." Nicole smiles at the dress, then me. "I made sure it was one of the things I packed after mom and dad... you know."

"Kiki…, that's so... It's so sweet of you." Tears sting my eyes as I look at Taylor dusting the dress off.

Nicole smiles even wider. "I know how much you love that dress. And you didn't think of yourself when we were packing our things. You were only thinking of me."

"Because I'm your big sister. It's my job to take care of you."

"And it's my job to make sure you also take care of yourself." She hugs me. "Mom always said that dress belongs to you. I wanted to make sure you had it."

"Thank you. For the dress. For everything." I take the dress from Taylor and hug it to my chest. It's one of the only things I have of my mother's.

"I love you, Tana."

"I love you too, Kiki."

Chapter Eighteen

✗ Chase ✗

I love watching Breetana. Anything she does is sexy as fuck. She's standing by the mirror admiring the new panties I bought her on the way back to the hotel. My mouth is practically watering. She wasn't kidding when she said she had forgotten them. She only packed one pair, so she had two pairs of panties. One of them is the one she was wearing this morning when I soaked her by pulling her in the shower. The other is the ones she was wearing on the plane.

"Breetana, you're driving me fucking crazy." She stops and looks at me ridiculously shyly. She has no idea. Really. None. At all.

She bites her lip. "Sorry. I always do this when I get new stuff. Especially bras and panties. Just to make sure they... hold everything in." She looks down at the ground. I reach down to adjust myself.

No.

Fucking.

Idea.

"If you're going to torture me, at least give me a show."

Her eyes widen, and she looks up at me in shock. "Like… you want me to model for you?"

"Damn right."

She swallows. Hard. I love her, but one of my favorite things in the world is making her blush like she is right now. She's so fucking hot when she does.

I've been doing it ever since I met her. Just telling her she looks nice makes her blush, but I've always taken it one step further. It's never just been 'she looks nice'. It's more 'that shirt makes you look hot.' I love when she wears clothing that's just a little too big and falls off her shoulder so I can see the color bra she's wearing and call her out on it. The deep shade of red she turns is hot as hell.

"Breetana, seriously. Put my t-shirt or something on. If you don't, I'm not going to be able to control what I do to you."

She raises her head up just enough to look at me through her long lashes. "Maybe I want that…"

It's my turn to swallow. Hard. I quickly recover and drop my hand to my cock. "Then give me a show." I squeeze a little. She watches my movements as I stroke myself over my boxer briefs. I grin and let my eyes travel over her body. "You like that?"

"Holy shit, Chase. I totally understand why everyone wants you."

I laugh as she slowly and sexily walks towards me. "Stop. Right where you are." My voice is commanding. A little deeper. Raspy. She does and smiles shyly. "Give me a show, baby."

She looks at me through her lashes. "What do you want me to do?"

"I want you to keep walking like you are. Except slower and run your hands over your body."

She takes a few slow steps and starts with running her hands through her hair. She slowly reaches her neck and continues down her collarbone to her breasts. I groan as I take my cock out of my underwear, giving it a few strokes.

"Oh God, Chase," she whispers.

I smile wickedly. "Don't stop, beautiful."

She takes a shaky breath as she continues running her hands down her stomach and to her hips. She reaches the bed and climbs on top of me. She straddles me, and my hands automatically find her ass and pull her down so she can feel me. She slowly starts moving herself on top of my cock. The feel of the lace panties she's wearing against my naked dick makes me growl as she kisses me. I'd stop if she told me to, but fuck. I want her.

I flick the hooks on her bra and take it off her. She throws it on the ground. Her. Naked. Against my chest. I love the feeling. I love the feel of her nipples hard against my skin.

“Breetana. Fuck. If you keep rocking against me like that, I'm gonna come all over your panties.”

“I want you, Chase. This. More than anything in the world. I want you.”

“Are you ready? Because I don't want to pressure you, Bree. If this right here is what you need, and you can't give me more right now, I'm really okay with that.” Her flashbacks play in my mind. I don’t want to send her into one. Especially since I know why they happen now. What caused them.

“No. I'm ready. I trust you. I want to be with you. I love you, Chase.”

God, I feel like I've waited my entire life to hear those words. I slow everything down. I hold her still on top of me, denying her the movement she's begging for. She whimpers, but if I'm doing this, I'm doing it right. No rushing. Just me and her.

“I'm going to cherish you. Every part of you. I want you to love every second of this. We're taking this slow. So, if you get uncomfortable, we can slow down or stop. Okay?”

“Okay.” She nods. Her smile is brave, but I know she’s scared.

I nudge her off me and lay her on her back. I position myself on top of her and start by kissing her. She allows her hands to roam across my chest and shoulders. I move down her jaw and her neck, making sure I kiss the part between her neck and shoulder that she loves feeling me kiss. She grips my arms as I move down her collarbone and chest until I reach her soft mounds.

“I love kissing you. Tasting you,” I whisper.

She runs her fingers through my hair as I take one of her hard peaks in my mouth. I scrape my teeth along it, and then soothe it with my tongue before sucking. My hand plays with her other one. I squeeze her nipple between my fingers and pull. She moans as I switch sides, lavishing her other one with my teeth and tongue while I play with one my mouth just left. I'm hard as hell, but this is about her tonight.

"Chase…," she whispers.

I smile as my dick gets harder. "I love when you whisper my name like that." I kiss down her stomach to her panty line and run the back of my hand up and down her core outside her panties. "I love lace."

"I assumed. When you bought me lace panties."

I grin. "I've never stepped foot in a Walmart until today. I can't believe we bought eight pairs of these things for ten dollars."

She laughs, and then gasps when I put pressure on her clit, still over her panties. She pulls my hair slightly when I kiss her, still over her panties. "Oh... Chase. I totally forgot what I was going to say."

"When you forget your name, I'll know I've done my job." I hook my fingers into her panties and slip them down. I toss them and my own onto the floor before settling between her legs for the second time today. I slide two fingers inside her at the same time as my tongue touches her clit. She arches into me. "Fuck, Bree. I love when you arch into me like that."

"I can't help it. It's like my body sings for you. You feel so good. Your tongue… Oh!" She moans when I nip her. "Chase! Chase…" I take her clit in my mouth and both deepen and quicken my pace. Her hips are moving in time to my fingers. My tongue is insistent against her until, finally, I feel her tighten around me. I pull out and stop licking.

"Chase! Don't stop. What are you doing?" She scrambles for me.

"Patience, gorgeous." I kiss my way back up to her lips, stopping on each of her perfect peaks once more. When I reach her mouth, I kiss her deeply, passionately, giving her all of me. Giving her everything I am. Her hands run up and down my back. I pull back, gently biting her lip, and then looking in her gorgeous eyes. "Ready?" I damn near whisper. She nods. I position myself at her entrance and slowly push myself inside her wetness. She closes her eyes on a sigh. "You okay? Too much?"

"You're just... really big. And thick." She blushes. She's so tight around me. I've never felt anything like her. "I guess I didn't realize how small I am compared to you."

I slowly draw out of her and then back in, giving her a little bit more of me and coating myself in her, helping me slide in easier. I'm already almost ready to come just by how good she feels. After a few thrusts, I'm buried inside of her.

"My God, you feel better than I imagined. So tight."

"Not tight. You're just so fucking big," she moans as she pulses around me.

I chuckle and lean down to kiss her neck as I continue my slow pace, drawing out of her and back in. "You're perfect. Do you know that?"

"You tell me every day."

"Maybe it'll help you believe it." She wraps her legs around my waist, and I growl.

"Oh… wow. Holy shit, Chase. There. Right there."

Every time I draw out, I'm hitting a place on Breetana inside her that drives her crazy. The elusive G-spot men can never find. They just don't fucking try hard enough. "Baby, I can't believe how good you feel."

She starts to quicken her pace, thrusting up into me, and I'm a goner. I give her what she wants. I give her everything. I don't hold back. It's obvious she doesn't want me to. She gives me the sexiest moan I've ever heard with each and every thrust. Her body jerks against me.

I lose control. "Fuck, Bree," I moan. I slam into her again and again. "I need to feel you come. Fuck, baby." I bury my face in her hair.

"Chase... Yes! Yes. Yes... Yes!" She comes hard for me. Her pussy tightens. She bucks into me.

Her coming apart like this underneath me.

Her giving herself to me.

Her digging her nails into my arms and back.

Her scent surrounding me.

She's all I need.

I need her.

Just her.

"Bree. Baby." My dick thickens inside her. She tightens around me, making it impossible to move my cock. So, I bury myself inside her. "Shit. Baby. Oh…"

"Chase… Chase, I'm…"

"I know, Bree. Come for me. All over me."

"Ah! Chase! Chase!" She holds on for dear life as she falls apart. She slams her hips into mine and comes so hard that I wouldn't be able to hold back if I wanted to.

"Bree!" I yell as a familiar jolt shoots down my spine and straight to my dick. I come hard inside her, filling her pussy with jet after jet of my release.

Breetana collapses against the bed as I slowly pull out of her, panting. I fall on the bed next to her and pull her to my side. She sexily whimpers and wraps her arms around me.

This.

Right here. It's all I've ever wanted. A woman who loves me despite my flaws. A woman who I want to spend time with. My life with. A woman I want to be mine. Only mine.

Chapter Nineteen

⚔ Breetana ⚔

I finish taping a box of Nicole's China and marking it as fragile. I'm sitting in her living room with Chase, Rico and Pete. All three of them are armed. At both Ryan's and Taylor's insistence, Chase has one in a holster at his hip, and the sight of it makes everything so real for me.

I know how crazy it is, but I had done all I could to convince myself that I would wake up in Chicago. I would be with Chase in his bedroom. His arms would be wrapped around me, and we would be starting our lives together. Nicole and Taylor would be a happy little family, and we wouldn't have a care in the world.

It was the perfect fantasy.

Unfortunately, my fantasy's bubble keeps getting popped. I get reminded over and over again that I'm not just going to wake up in a perfect life. Like right now. There are six men in this house with guns, including Chase and Taylor, but I'm missing the presence of one.

Ryan Crane.

I've only known him for a brief time, but when he's around, I feel all four of us are safe. I trust his men to keep all of us safe, but I trust Ryan more. His protective persona isn't an act. He isn't doing this because he's being ordered to. He's doing this because he cares.

It isn't that I don't feel safe with Chase and Taylor. I do. But I want them to be safe, too. Ryan ensures that. I huff and blow my hair out of my eyes.

Chase reaches over to push it behind my ear, and he smiles. "You okay?"

"Just…" I sigh and stand up, grabbing another box to put together for the rest of Nicole's China, her inheritance from our grandmother. She's cherished it since we were little girls. There's no way we're leaving without it. Chase stands next to me. "I'm uneasy," I admit. "Without Ryan here. I don't know why."

"I am, too, Tana," Nicole says quietly. "I think it's because he's become part of our lives so quickly. We don't like him out there alone."

"He isn't alone, baby," Taylor says, smiling softly. "He's got a couple guys with him. He'll be okay."

"I just don't like us being apart. That's all," I tell them. Chase puts an arm around my waist and kisses my forehead.

"I don't think he'll be gone much longer," Chase says.

"I hope not."

"Ugh. This heat. I think I need some water." Nicole starts to get up from the chair she's in, but Taylor stops her.

"I got it, babe. Finish what you're doing."

She smiles up at him adoringly and my heart melts. I don't know Taylor well, but I can see how much he cares about her and the baby. She deserves someone to love her more than anything. Like Chase loves me. Like I love him.

I lean into Chase a moment, then start putting the box together again when, suddenly, the door flies open. Chase's grip on me tightens as I jump.

"It's just Ryan, baby. Sorry. I should've told you I saw him pulling up." Chase's words barely register as my eyes meet the eyes of the man behind him. A strangled sob escapes my throat, and I turn to flee. Chase senses my sudden discomfort and holds me closer to him, but I break free in my need to escape.

Tears stream down my face.

I run.

Chase grabs my hand. “Bree? What the fuck?”

The kitchen.

There's a door in the kitchen leading outside.

“Tana? What's happening?” I see Nicole reach for me as I break away from Chase’s grasp.

I’m propelled by fear.

I have to get out of here.

Run.

“Babe, I put ice -”

I run into Taylor.

Hard.

The water splashes from the cup, but he keeps most of it from hitting me or the floor.

With one arm, he lifts me slightly off the ground and holds me close to his chest. “Whoa, whoa, Tana. What the hell? What's going on, sweetheart?” He rumbles into my ear. I feel Chase's presence behind me as Taylor's other arm comes around my back. I cry and shake my head into his chest. “Chase?”

“I don't know, dude. She saw Ryan walk through the door and bolted.” Chase's hand finds my hair, and he starts running his fingers soothingly through it. “Baby, talk to me. What's going on?”

I’m shaking uncontrollably, and my grip around Taylor's waist tightens. “No. No. No. No, no, no.” I try to calm down, but I can't.

“Jesus. She's fucking terrified. Like she was that first night we got here,” Taylor says to Chase.

“No... No. No.” I'm still shaking my head, and I squeeze Taylor as hard as I can. I want to let him go. I want to fling myself into Chase's arms, but I can't. I'm scared that if I let him go, something bad will happen. That the entire world will crumble around me.

“Tana? Look at me.” Nicole softly touches my cheek. “Please?”

I can't look at her. I try. I really do. But I can’t “I have to get out of here. Please.”

I feel broken.

“Okay,” Taylor squeezes me tightly. “Okay. I'll get you out of here. Can you let me go so I can pick you up?”

I shake my head. “I can't. I can't let go.” I’m trying so hard to, but my body won’t respond.

"Okay. I'm gonna walk backwards. We're going to the kitchen," he says.

"Please don't let me go. Please," I beg.

"I got you, Breetana. It's just me and you, okay? I won't let go." He takes a step backwards, and I follow. He takes another, and I keep following.

"That's it, baby. One step at a time," Chase whispers. Thank God he's still near.

"You're doing great, Tana," Nicole says in my ear.

I hear the kitchen door swing shut, but I keep my eyes tightly closed. I'm trying to center myself. Anchor myself. I can't. I can't do it. I'm that girl again. The one everyone thought was lying. The one everyone thought was trying to seduce my uncle.

"Oh my God. He's... I... can't…"

"Sweetie, you aren't making sense. Please talk to me," Chase whispers a little bit shakily. I'm scaring him.

"Let me try," Ryan's deep, bass voice reverberates from somewhere behind me.

"What? Fuck no!" Chase says possessively, but it's more the fear. I can hear it. Feel it. He doesn't want to move from my side. He doesn't want anyone else around me.

"Chase, my brother's wife, Jessa, has panic attacks. Tana's going through the same thing. See how she's holding Taylor? Gripping him? Afraid to let go?" Ryan asks. I know my nails are digging into Taylor's back, but I can't stop it. "I can help. I have experience getting Jessa through." Ryan's voice is calming, yet strong. Soft, yet commanding.

"I can't do this." I'm shivering and shaking.

"Breetana? Can you feel Taylor breathing?" Ryan asks. I nod. "I need you to push everything out of your mind and focus on him. Okay? Focus on Taylor's breathing."

I feel Taylor start to take deep breaths, and I follow his steady, deep breathing. I keep my eyes closed and focus on his heart. His scent. Strong. Just like him. His heart is steady. Just like he is.

Chase is close. I can sense him. He's running his fingers through my hair. Rubbing my back. Nicole, always steady for me, is rubbing my arm and softly humming.

After a few moments I start to relax and slowly let go of Taylor. It's like I'm coming back into myself from a thick fog.

"I'm so sorry, Taylor," I whisper.

"Don't be. Scared me a little. Well, scared all of us, but it isn't anything to feel sorry about." He starts to slowly let me go.

"I... I just suddenly felt like this... pressure… in my chest and my head. All I could think about was getting away. I was just... just overwhelmed with fear. Like it was crushing me." I sniffle. Chase takes me in his arms. He's slightly shaking as he buries his face in my hair and kisses my neck. "I'm so sorry I scared you."

"Don't. Just tell me what the fuck happened," Chase whispers into my hair.

"Breetana? You saw me, then you fled. What's going on?" Ryan asks. Everyone's confused and speaking softly, afraid I'll run. I take a deep breath.

Chase.

His scent cuts through the rest of my fear.

"It wasn't you," I say after several moments.

"Then what? Who? What did you see?" Ryan questions. I try to pull back, but Chase holds me closer.

"Forget it. I'm not letting you go.'

"Something triggered you to panic, sweetheart. I really wish you would tell us." Ryan puts his hand on my shoulder, and I bury my face in Chase's chest. He runs his fingers through my hair.

"Tana. I'm so scared. Please tell us." Nicole hugs me from the side as best she can with Chase's arms around me. He releases me long enough to pull her close to us. I breathe Chase's comforting scent in once more before I turn in Chase's arms. Everyone is staring at me, concerned.

I take another breath and focus on Ryan. "The cop. The one who followed you in here, Ryan. He's... he's one of the ones who didn't believe me. Who accused me of seducing Joe. He sent me back to him. Chastised me for putting my uncle through such heartache."

"Oh, sweetie," Ryan says. "I really didn't know. I brought him here because he wants to help. I vetted him. He's on our side. He can help. But if you don't want him here, I'll send him away. No questions asked."

I look at Ryan. The sincerity and honesty in his eyes makes me sigh. "Do you trust him?"

"I questioned him. I looked into his bank accounts, his past. I have my ways. There are a lot of dirty cops in this town, but he isn't one of them. I believe he wants to help. I trust that. Trusting him completely, like I do others I work with, will take time."

I look at him a moment before deciding that I don't have the strength to make the decision. If Ryan trusts him enough to believe that he wants to help, then I will. "Then he can stay. But I want answers. I want to know why he treated me the way he did. Why he helped my uncle drag my name through the mud. And why he let him keep hurting me."

Ryan nods. "Fair. I'll be next to you the entire time." He glances at Chase. "And Chase will, too. Doesn't look like he has plans to let you go."

"Damn fucking right," Chase agrees dangerously.

"I don't want to be alone. Not for a second," I whisper. "He brings up too many memories."

"Not a fucking chance in hell," Taylor growls. "You'll have all four of us by your side. Nikki, too."

I nod, and take Chase's hand. He pulls me behind him and leads me out to Nikki's living room. I take a deep breath. Officer Appleton is sitting on the couch between Rico and Greg. "Officer Appleton." I try keeping my voice strong and even, though I don't feel any of those things. It betrays me and cracks.

"Actually, I'm a Sergeant now, but you can call me Ben, Breetana."

I just look at him. Chase has his arm around my waist. Taylor is standing on the other side of me. Nicole is next to Taylor and Ryan moves to Chase's side. This. This is my team.

"I just want to know why, Sergeant," I almost whisper.

He blows out a breath and nods, scrubbing his hands over his face. "Somehow I knew this day would come. Why don't you have a seat?"

I shake my head. "I'll stand. Thanks."

He smiles softly. "I understand. You're guarded. But really. It's a long story."

I glare at him, but let Chase lead me to a chair. I push him down, and then sit on his lap. He grins and holds me close to him. Taylor pulls Nikki onto his lap in another chair close to us. Ryan sits on the arm of the one Chase and I are in.

“So? Why?” I question angrily, but still quietly. I can’t bring myself to speak any louder. I’m terrified of him because he had to have been working with Joe back then. There’s no other explanation.

Ben takes a deep breath. “I became a cop when I was 28. I had been on the force exactly four months when you came in to file a report against your uncle. I believed every word that came out of your mouth. But I was still training, and my training officer didn't believe you at all. I don't know if you knew, but he was good friends with Joe.”

I narrow my eyes. “You certainly didn't seem like you believed me.”

“I was trying to keep my emotions out of it. Get the information. Do you remember when I left you in the interview room that first day?”

“Yes. It was like an hour. I was scared to death.”

“It took so long because I spent that entire time fighting for you. I was trying to convince my FTO to listen to you. In the end, I lost the battle. He called your uncle.”

“You guys called my uncle every time. Even when my teachers filed on my behalf.”

“I never did, Breetana. It was the other officers. My FTO in particular.”

I look at him incredulously. “You flat out told me you thought I was lying!”

He looks at me with watery eyes, and I’m slightly taken aback. “Breetana. Who else was in the room when I said that to you? That was, what? Your fourth report?”

“What does it matter who else was there?” I yell. My anger is overcoming the fear. I’m slowly losing control of my emotions. Furious, hot tears threaten to fall as I glare at him. “You told me that you thought I wanted it. That I was seducing him!” I scream. Chase tightens his grip around me. I don’t know if it’s a warning or for comfort.

“I know. I know. I'm truly sorry. But if you remember, my FTO and the Chief were in that interview. They both had threatened my job if I didn't cooperate. Most people would've shut up. Me? Fuck no. I wanted to know what they were hiding. I wanted to know why the hell they weren't doing anything with so many reports against him. I watched you, Breetana. Every single time you came in. Your demeanor.” His voice is still so calm, but I can hear a tremor. I sniffle and look away from him as I choke down the sobs threatening to escape. "I watched how you went from this strong, brave girl to this scared and jumpy girl. You went from telling me everything, to withdrawn and quiet as hell. I knew something was wrong. I pushed and pushed, but after they threatened me, they pulled me from your case. I kept investigating. I found out your uncle and my FTO both paid off the Chief and convinced him you were trouble. Remember when I showed up at your school and interviewed you? Just us?"

"Y-yes. I thought you believed me again," I nearly whisper.

"I never stopped believing you. I just had to be careful in my investigation. After that interview, I was pulled into the Chief's office. Joe and my FTO were there. Remember at the end before I left, you were crying?"

"You hugged me, and then I never saw you again."

"I was confronted with pictures. Pictures of me hugging you. And pushing your hair behind your ear. Chief accused me of an inappropriate relationship with a minor. He gave Joe the option of pressing charges against me on your behalf. Joe said he didn't want to ruin my life, so he was willing to let it go as long as I stayed away from you."

"So, you dropped the investigation," Chase says as he glares at him.

"Fuck no. I never dropped it. I kept at it. I took down my FTO and the Chief for corruption. I had enough to put Joe away and was on my way to arrest him on your behalf when the call came out for you, Nicole." He looks over at Nicole.

Her eyes widen. "Oh my God! You. You were the officer that showed up at the school!"

He smiles and nods. "I recognized the name and took the call myself. I rushed to the school. I took one look at you. That was it. I knew I could put him in prison for a lot longer with your case then with Breetana's. So, I focused on that. It wasn't until after you left, Breetana, that I knew how badly I had fucked up with protecting you. Everything he did to both of you came out in court, but the damage had already been done by Shaun to your reputation. It didn't matter what I did at that point."

"After you left," Ryan continues. "Ben started investigating Shaun and Billy."

I perk up, and my eyes widen. "And?"

“Well. I knew they were getting money from somewhere. The problem is I couldn't track it. I spent years trying to figure it out. I didn’t have the resources or programs to do it. Finally, I asked for help. I went to another department. I gave them all I had. The officers in Duluth did what they do best. They tracked everything. I found out the cartel was involved. But they’re slippery motherfuckers. I haven't been able to actually catch them, and I have nothing to pin on Shaun or Billy.”

“What about Joe?” Taylor asks.

“I knew right away that he was involved with everything that happened with Nicole recently as soon as he was released. But again, slippery. I can't catch them,” he says. I turn and bury my face in Chase's neck. He kisses me. “Look. Breetana. Nicole. Everyone. I know everything that goes on in this town. I know Ryan is mafia. Just the little bit of research I've done, I know every area Ryan has a faction has a remarkably lower crime rate. I approached him when I found out he was here because I want them out of my damn town. Now. But I can't do it on my own. I need help. And I can't count on very many people to help me. I think most of the department has been paid, bribed, or blackmailed. I know most of the council has been. And our Mayor.”

“This town needs a major clean up,” Ryan agrees.

I shiver and look around uneasily. I’ve had such a horrible unexplainable feeling all day. Finally, I put my hand on Ryan's arm, drawing his attention to me. “Can we leave? Go back to the hotel? I just have a weird feeling. I’ve had it all day.”

Ryan raises an eyebrow. “About Ben?”

I shake my head. “No. I'll explain later. Please? I just want to leave.”

“I actually second that,” Nicole whispers. I meet Nicole's eyes and can tell she's feeling the same way.

“I really am sorry,” Ben says to me.

“I forgive you. That… probably seems fast, but now that I heard the explanation, literally everything else makes sense. I understand you were trying to protect us. And I don’t want it to look like we’re fleeing, but I’ve honestly felt strange this whole time we’ve been here. I’ve been so on edge. I think that might have been the biggest factor in me fleeing.”

“I understand, Breetana,” Ben says. “No offense taken. You need to listen to your instincts.”

There's a flurry of activity as everyone gets everything ready to go. Ryan tells Ben to come tomorrow to talk. But it isn't until we're safely miles away from Silver Bay that I start to calm down. The feeling was far more prevalent when Ben was there.

I know someone was watching us at the house.

I felt it.

Chapter Twenty

⚔ Chase ⚔

Breetana is completely exhausted. I can see it. But giving up and falling asleep isn't happening. Not my girl. I have to smile at her strength. Her resilience. How far she's come in the few days we've been here.

She's standing in the middle of the room in our suite waiting for everyone to settle. I watched her go from scared to death to fucking Warrior Queen in a matter of minutes today, and it was the sexiest most inspired thing I've ever seen. I'm proud as hell. I wouldn't be able to wipe this stupid smirk off my face if I tried.

"Okay. I'll be up front," Breetana begins as she paces. I'm not even sure she's talking to us. "I was transported back to a really uncomfortable time today, and it scared me. A lot. But seeing Sergeant Appleton, Ben, today, wasn't really what triggered it. I'm positive of that now. Yes. He was part of it. He wasn't everything. Today I felt like…" She pauses and looks around at us. "Like we were being watched."

"Watched?" Pete, one of Ryan's guards, raises an eyebrow and looks at her a little confused.

"Yes," she confirms.

“We've got guys all over that place. If we were being watched, we'd know about it,” Greg, another guard says.

“I know there are a lot of people up there. But I felt it.” She shrugs.

Greg holds up his hands. “Look. I get you're nervous. We all do. But no one makes a move in that town without us knowing about it.”

Breetana shoots him a glare. “I won't ignore the feeling. And I am not the only person feeling it.” Breetana looks at Nicole.

“I felt it, too. Today,” she says quietly.

“She felt something. She wouldn't go to the bathroom today without me standing outside the door,” Taylor says hugging Nicole.

“I think if they felt something, maybe we need to look into it,” Rico says. Ryan nods.

“Come on. We have seven guys outside!” Greg argues.

“Enough. Everyone,” Ryan commands. “We of all people know to trust our fucking instincts. Or have you all forgotten Jessa?”

“None of us were on Jessa's detail,” Miquel says. He strikes me as a new guy.

Ryan snaps his intense eyes to Miguel. “Fucking lucky, huh? You'd all be dead.”

Breetana clears her throat. “What happened with Jessa? You've brought her up a few times.”

I smile and give her hip a squeeze. Good girl. They told me about it while she was comforting Nicole, but I’m glad she asked. It shows how smart she is.

Ryan sighs. “Jessa was being stalked by her ex for many years. Or that's who she thought was stalking her. When she met Jason, my brother, she was on the run. She applied at his company as a project manager, and he hired her almost on the spot. She worked for him for a year before her stalker found her.”

Breetana’s eyes widen. “Shit.”

Taylor nods. “Jessa didn't show up at the office the next day. She's a creature of habit. She was never ever late.”

“Jason was nervous,” Ryan continues. “He'd seen her in the elevator the night before, and she was acting strange. He didn't follow his instincts.”

Taylor sighs. "He went after her the next day. After she didn't show up for work. He and Nick, his head of security and other brother, went to her house and found her. She'd been beat up pretty badly."

"He didn't rape her, but he did a lot of damage. She had bruises and scratches everywhere," Ryan continues.

"Oh my God," Breetana sinks against me and covers her mouth.

Ryan nods. "Thing was, it wasn't her ex at all. It was his twin. Jessa didn't know he had a twin. She didn't even know his true last name. His dad was the leader of the Lucinio mafia in L.A. He was obsessed with Jessa. Alex, her ex, was trying to do everything he could to protect her. Originally, we thought his father and twin had concocted this sick, twisted plan for Josh, the twin, to marry Jessa, get her pregnant, and then he would become leader after his dad stepped down."

Taylor continues. "They would have an heir to take over after Josh. Their mafia would be set for years."

Breetana shakes her head. "Wait. This happened in New York? Or was it L.A.? Taylor, how were you involved? You're a cop in Chicago."

Taylor smiles softly. "Good question. Ryan called me when they were trying to figure out what the hell Josh's motive was."

"There's a reason Taylor works organized crime. His instincts are unparalleled," Ryan says.

Taylor shrugs. "I got a hold of some contacts and put the story together."

"You said originally. What… does… that mean?" Nicole asks.

"Good question. I'll get to that," Ryan says. "We put more security on Jessa and Jason when we figured it out, but Lucinio got to her anyway because some of my people didn't follow their instincts."

"They let her go for a walk by herself," Taylor says.

"Oh no…," Nicole says as she bites her lip.

Taylor tucks a strand of hair behind her ear as he continues. "She was on Jason's property but pretty far from the guards. Some of Lucinio's guys got to her."

"Long story short, we got her back, but Jason was fucking pissed it had happened in the first place. He walked away from the mafia long ago. He's never been able to deal with that life, but he still has the ruthless side that I do when he's pushed and his family or those he loves are in danger or being threatened. Two of the guys we had guarding her betrayed us.

They were working with Lucinio. They didn't make it to sunrise, and I wasn't the one who pulled the trigger."

Breetana nearly chokes. I feel her heart quicken as she realizes what he means. "You mean…," Breetana trails off. I smile. Thank fucking Christ this guy is on our side. I know Ryan and Jason as businessmen. But they're pretty fucking ruthless away from the boardroom, too.

Ryan nods. "Yeah. That's what I mean."

Breetana sinks into my embrace, and I hug her tighter. I kiss the back of her neck as she watches Ryan.

"That's not even the end of it." Taylor kisses the back of Nicole's shoulder like he's trying to compose his thoughts. "It got fucked up. We found out Josh was being controlled and manipulated. His father was giving him some kind of fucking serum that weakened his mind. It made it easier for him to control Josh's thoughts and actions. Lucinio convinced Josh that Jessa was his ticket out. It got to the point that Josh didn't know who the fuck he was anymore."

Ryan takes a breath. "In the end, Josh came out of it. He fought off the serum being used on him and Lucinio's manipulation and control over him. He helped lead us in taking Lucinio down and now Jessa is safe. She talks to both Alex and Josh every day. She's gotten close to both of them. I don't know which one she's closer with, but the three of them are all insanely tight. And Lucinio is fucking gone. Josh has a girl. He took her to meet his mom, but he's keeping her far from the rest of us."

"So this Alex. He was the ex?" Breetana asks, tilting her head and trying to follow.

Ryan nods. "Alex is like my brother. Like Taylor, we became thick as thieves quickly. Alex and I met during a battle between my family and his. His coward father left him to lead the battle against us. His father ran. Alex made his brother run and hide to protect him. My guys won the battle. I could have killed him, but there was something about him. We talked. We got to be good friends. Brothers, a close-knit family. I helped him in protecting and keeping Jessa hidden after she moved to Manhattan, though Jessa didn't know that until this whole thing with her went down."

"Ryan and Alex have been close for years. He knew of Jessa long before he met her."

"And that wasn't until she started working for Jason."

I can't help but chuckle a little. "Seems like you have your hand in just about everything."

Ryan smiles. "Can't get to where I am without that little talent. You should know. Seems like you know just about everyone."

I smile. "Not nearly as many or as diverse a group of people as you."

"How did you and Alex get so close if he was… well, your enemy, I guess," Nicole asks, looking shyly up at Ryan. "I don't understand how you were so close to someone from a rival mafia."

"Well, his father wanted *him* to lead. Not his brother. He forced both of them to lead battles and missions. Alex and his twin were only teenagers. His father shot my father, but Alex thought it was one of his guards. I only told him years later when we joined up to take down his father in order to protect Jess that it was his father, not a guard. My brother, Nick, had seen the entire thing. When we met, Alex was already dealing with a lot. I didn't want to add to that. I wanted him to learn how to lead and focus on leading and missions so he didn't get himself killed. He reminded me a lot of myself. Still does. Had he known that, he would've been distracted. And his goals were never what his father's were. He wanted his brother to take control. And Josh wanted to run it like me."

"Josh eventually became just as close to Ryan as Alex was. Probably because of Jessa." Taylor chuckles.

"Maybe a little." Ryan smiles.

Taylor rubs his eyes. "The point is, if Breetana and Nicole are feeling something is off, we won't be ignoring that."

"Fuck no," Ryan agrees. "We won't be ignoring instincts again. We almost lost my little sister because of that bullshit. That won't be happening here. Consequences will be just as severe, I can assure you."

Breetana shivers slightly, and I kiss the back of her neck again. She takes a deep breath and hugs my arms closer to her body. Ryan picks up on the subtle motion. Dude is observant as fuck. I like him more and more.

Ryan smiles and kneels in front of Breetana. He softens his voice. "If you feel like you're being watched, I can have more guys out here by the morning. Just say the word, and it's done."

Breetana bites her lip. "I think it would be a good idea. I really have a terrible feeling. After talking to Ben today and knowing how many people are being paid for silence and cooperation, I just... I think we're in over our heads."

"I honestly do, too. Being up against the cartel," Nicole chips in.

"How many more guys can you spare, Ry?" Taylor asks.

Ryan pats Breetana on the knee and stands, turning to Taylor. "I'll bring as many people up here as you think we need, but I'll be honest. For something like this, we may actually have a better chance in Chicago. One of my biggest factions is there, but so is Josh's. I can pull him up here, but we're stronger there."

"Isn't the cartel bigger there?" Breetana asks.

"They definitely have more resources," Ryan confirms.

"They aren't nearly as big as Ryan," Taylor says.

"What about... what you said about cleaning up Silver Bay?" Nicole asks.

"Oh, trust me. I'll still clean it up. But I'd prefer you guys not be there when I do that. I think we need to finish up with your house and get to Chicago. I know they'll follow, but I really do have a lot more people. Like I said. I'll pull Josh, too. That doubles us up."

"We'll have the department, too," Taylor says.

"And Chase's security at the office. Reese would help," Breetana said. "I don't know if you'll need them or not…"

"Reese is a good guy," I agree. "You can count on him to help however you need him."

"He's also my best friend," Breetana says. "He'll help if we ask."

Taylor nods. "I'll take what we can get. Anything to keep you guys safe and surround you with trusted people."

"Just be aware." Ryan looks at me, then at Taylor. I already know what he's about to say. "This could get really bad. Really bloody."

Taylor looks down at Nicole. "I'll do whatever I need to do to keep you and the baby safe, Nikki, but Ryan will cross lines that I can't. Lines I would cross if I needed to but would lose my job over."

"I won't let that happen," Ryan says. "That's what you have me for. That's what both of you have me for." He looks at me and Breetana before he looks back at Nicole. "To protect you, and to protect both Chase and Taylor from crossing lines they can't come back from."

"I think I do want more people up here. Until we leave," Breetana says decisively. "It's for the best. We don't have much left to do."

"I'll take care of it," Ryan says to her.

"I still don't think it's necessary. There's only three of them. Against all of us." Greg gestures throughout the room.

Ryan glares and growls. "Question me again, Greg. I'm begging you. I'm in a piss poor mood today. I want the challenge."

I chuckle quietly, using Breetana's body to shield me. Ryan reminds me of Taylor. And myself. Neither of us take shit from anyone.

Breetana stands and waits for me. I give her a questioning look, and her eyes flick to the bedroom. I smile and stand, catching on that she needs to talk privately. "We're going to bed," I say. "Everyone out. We'll see you in the morning." I meet Ryan's, then Taylor's eyes just so they know it's not that.

Breetana smiles at me as I take her hand and lead her to the bedroom. She turns to me as soon as she closes the door behind us. "I don't like Greg."

"I gathered. Every time he opened his mouth you dug your nails into my arm."

She blushes. I fucking love that. "I'm sorry, babe." She looks down at the ground.

"It's fine. I'm pretty tough."

Her laugh is musical, and I grin. "I don't want Greg to be responsible for Nikki."

"Okay. What my girl wants, she gets. You want me to call Ryan in here?" She nods. Tears sting her eyes. I walk to her and take her face in my hands. "Baby, hey. We'll talk to him, okay?" I lean down to kiss her, and then hug her for a minute while she takes a deep breath. "I'll go get Ryan."

I let her go and walk out into the suite. Rico and Pete are in a hushed conversation when I come out. I raise an eyebrow when they immediately shut up.

"Something you want to discuss?" I ask them.

"We were just thinking…," Pete begins. His voice is quiet, and he glances to the other suite as he motions me closer.

I walk over to join them. "What?"

"Something just doesn't seem right. With Greg. He seems…" Rico shrugs.

"Off. He seems off," Pete finishes.

"We wanted to bring it up to Ryan, but Greg has been here a long time."

I look up at the ceiling and blow out a breath. "Go back to the bedroom with Bree. She said the same thing. I'm just grabbing Ryan and Taylor right now."

"Yes, sir," Pete says. They both get up, and I enter the middle suite. Ryan is sitting on a chair on his phone. He sees me and holds up a finger. I nod and head to Taylor and Nicole's suite.

"Where's Taylor?" I ask Miguel.

"He took Nicole to bed." I nod and head back to the bedroom.

"I wouldn't go back there if I were you. Nicole has been horny as fuck. She's probably all over him."

"What the fuck, Greg?" Miguel says, disgusted.

I have to physically restrain myself from punching him in the face. "I'll take my chances. But I'll warn you. One more word about Nicole, and I won't hesitate shooting you in your fucking mouth. Got it?" I growl. Greg smirks, and I continue back to the bedroom. I knock on the door.

"What?" Taylor growls.

"We have to talk. Bring Nikki with."

Taylor opens the door. "Dude. She's exhausted. She's eight months pregnant. What's going on?"

"Not here. I wouldn't be here if it wasn't important, but it is." I keep my voice low.

"I'll leave her with the guards then."

My heart stops beating, and I glance down the hall before looking back at him. "Taylor. Please."

He takes a second to read my expression, then sighs. "Fine. Give us a minute."

"We'll be in our bedroom. Her security stays here."

He raises an eyebrow, and then nods before closing the door. I know even if he has no idea what's going on, he trusts me and will do what I say with no hesitation. Just like I would for him.

I walk back to Ryan's suite and catch his eye. He's ending his call, and I nod towards my suite. He gives me a nod of acknowledgement, and I keep walking.

Breetana is sitting on the edge of the bed when I walk in the room. Rico is sitting on an ottoman, and Pete is perched on the arm of a chair. I leave the door open.

"Is he coming?" Breetana asks softly.

"Yeah, baby." I sit next to her, and she takes my hand. A few minutes later, Ryan saunters into the room, followed by Taylor and Nicole. Rico and Pete both get up.

"You can sit here, Nikki," Rico says. She smiles as Taylor settles in the chair and pulls her onto his lap. Fucking adorable. Seeing them together makes me even more certain that I want everything with Breetana.

"What's up?" Ryan asks.

"Will you close the door?" Breetana asks. Ryan closes it, and Breetana stands up. She motions everyone to gather around Nicole and Taylor and keeps her voice low while she speaks. "I don't want to insult you, Ryan, but Greg."

"I know. I'll deal with it."

"No. I mean, yes. He was disrespectful to you, but that's not why I called you in here," Breetana says.

I look at Taylor. "When I went in to get you, Taylor, Greg warned me not to go back there. He said Nikki was horny and insinuated you were probably fucking."

"What? How would he know anyway?" Nicole asks dumbfounded.

Breetana shrugs. "That isn't all." She looks at Ryan. "I don't think he should be on Kiki's detail. I don't like how lightly he's taking this."

"He's... he's a good guy. He's been with me a long time," Ryan says. He looks a little torn.

"Sir, we don't mean to overstep, but he's been acting really off these past few days," Pete interjects.

"Not himself. At all," Rico agrees.

Ryan glances at Breetana, and then me before he looks at Nicole and Taylor. "What do you think?"

"I mean, does he listen to us when we're...? Because… that's just gross." Nicole chews on her lip and glances at Taylor.

"If my girl is uncomfortable, then switch it."

Ryan nods. "I'll talk to him."

"I'm sorry," Breetana says quietly.

Ryan shakes his head. "Don't. I'm the one who told you to not ignore your instincts. I meant that. I'll talk to him and assign someone else to work with Miguel."

"Thank you," Breetana says relieved.

"Of course." Ryan smiles and everyone leaves. Taylor holds Nicole down and waits.

He looks up at Breetana when Ryan shuts the door. "How long have you had that feeling about him?"

"Um... honestly? Since I met him. He just rubs me the wrong way." Breetana shrugs and glances at me before she looks back at Taylor.

"That's what I thought. I had the same feeling." He nudges Nicole up, then follows. Nicole hugs Breetana, and the two leave the room. Breetana collapses on the bed.

"Baby, you have no idea how proud of you I am. For standing up for Nicole and facing down your fears with Ben today." I watch her as a slow smile spreads over her beautiful lips.

"Come lay with me," she says softly.

I smile. "How about you and I get ready for bed, and I'll hold you close to me all night long if that's what you want."

"I'll take that deal," she says tiredly.

I pull her up, and we both get ready for bed. She pulls one of my t-shirts out of the drawer and strips off everything but her panties. She puts my t-shirt over her head and crawls into bed.

"God, Bree. You really have no idea how beautiful you are."

She smiles and pats the bed next to her. I crawl in and shut the lights out. She burrows herself into my arms. "I love you, Chase."

"I love you, too, Bree."

It takes only a minute before she's asleep. I can't help but laugh quietly as I kiss her head. My girl runs herself into the ground until she finally collapses. That's definitely something I'm going to have to get her to quit. Even if it means holding her tightly in my arms all night long.

I can't say I'd ever complain about that. Having her in my arms is my Heaven, and it doesn't take long before I myself am comfortably asleep.

Chapter Twenty One

✗ Chase ✗

Waking up the next morning to the sun streaming through the windows and Breetana softly kissing my face everywhere is how I want to wake up for the rest of my life. I grab her hips and pull her down on top of me. She giggles and kisses my neck before pressing herself against my chest.

I wrap my arms tightly around her. “I could get used to this,” I say huskily. “Waking up to you. Every single damn day.”

“I hope so. You did say you wanted to marry me.”

“And you did say yes.” I grin like a damn fool. Fuck, it’s been less than a week since we made our relationship official, but I don’t care. I know what I want. I’ve wanted it for three damn years.

“I did, didn't I?” Her smile could light up the entire city of Duluth. Probably Chicago, too.

“Fucking right you did.”

“My ring needs to be huge. Fit for a zillionaire's wife,” she says in mock seriousness.

I laugh and kiss her on the side of the head. “Well, I'm not exactly a zillionaire”

"Hmm... Too bad. I was looking forward to you flying me to the moon."

"Baby, say the word. and I'll buy you the moon."

She laughs and looks at me. Her eyes. I could drown in their depths and be a happy man. "Okay. Buy me the moon."

"Done."

She smiles and kisses me. She always closes her eyes when she kisses me. Like she's completely giving herself to me, and to the kiss. I can't get enough of her.

"Seriously, though. Your ring. I know you don't care about how much it costs, and I know you don't like big and gaudy shit. You don't even wear jewelry except the bracelet on your wrist that you never take off."

"Kiki has a matching one."

I smile softly. "I saw." I wait for her to tell me the story. I know she will. She never misses my hints.

"Our parents gave them to us. The day they were killed." I feel her shudder, and I hold her closely.

"I'm sorry, baby."

"Don't be. It's one of the best memories I have. They said they saw them and knew immediately that they were ours. So they bought them. They gave them to us for no other reason than because they loved us."

"It sounds like they were really great parents."

"The best. They loved us so much. We were a happy family."

"I wish things could've been different."

"Honestly, I can't say that I do."

"You can't mean that. Bree, you've been through a ton of awful shit."

"But if I hadn't, I wouldn't be where I am. I wouldn't be with you. If Shaun hadn't done what he did, I may have married him. If my parents hadn't been killed, I never would've moved to Chicago. Everything happens for a reason. Sometimes, it sucks, but it makes us who we are."

"Fuck. Breetana, you're a fucking warrior. I could possibly be any more proud of you."

She kisses me. "So…, you know all my darkest secrets. What about you? Taylor told me you guys grew up together, and you were both players all the way through college."

I laugh. “Yeah. We grew up together. His mom and my mom were both nurses. His dad was a cop. We lived next to each other. His parents didn't really get along. They fought a lot. Taylor was at my house more than his. My mom thought of him as a son. I thought of him as a brother. Still do. We were and still are inseparable.”

“What about your dad?”

“Uh…,” I pause and clear my throat. “Well, my dad was killed, actually. He was killed in Iraq. He was in the Air Force. The F-16 he was flying had some mechanical issues. He couldn't get out. The eject function malfunctioned, and he was stuck inside. I hadn't even been born yet. I never knew him.”

“That's so sad.”

“My mom never remarried. She's always said it's because he is the love of her life.”

“That's so romantic. Sad and tragic, but romantic.”

“She has always been both mine and Taylor's rock. She's supported us both through everything. She even helped put Taylor through school. When I started my business, she's the one who co-signed the loan. She gave me her savings and her retirement, even though I told her not to. She had that much faith in me. I took off pretty quickly. It was pretty scary, honestly, but she supported me through it all. By the end of my third year, I had her paid completely back and the loan paid off.”

“She sounds amazing.”

“She is. After I made sure my company was stable, I started splurging on things. I bought her a house. A car. Made sure she was set. She has a nice retirement fund for when she actually retires. And I made sure Taylor was set. Cops don't make much, but he always insisted he was fine. I didn't care. To me, he’s my brother. I bought him a house, too. Bought him a car. I bought myself a private jet. I own the entire building the company is in. But the money never really meant anything.”

“You enjoy taking care of those around you.”

“Those I care about, anyway.”

“I knew underneath all that cocky exterior there was a really nice, sensitive guy,” she teases.

I blink and try not to smile. “Don't let that shit out. I have a reputation to protect.”

"Really? And you think getting married isn't going to ruin that?" She smiles impossibly wider.

"You're right. We can't get married. It'll ruin everything," I tease back.

"Too late, Shaw. You're all mine." She wiggles against me.

I groan. "Keep doing that, and I won't let you out of this bed."

"Oh, honey. Do you honestly think that isn't my intention?" Her teasing tone is a huge turn on.

I grab her hips and grind her down onto me. "Do you feel what you do to me?"

"Good thing I'll be your wife soon. So we can wake up like this every day." She giggles. I slap her ass, and her eyes go wide. "Oh!"

"Shower. Now," I growl. She giggles again. I fucking love when she giggles. She climbs off me and takes off to the bathroom. I chase her and catch her, throwing her over my shoulder. She laughs as I slap her ass again. "You're so fucking hot, Bree."

"So are you, Mr. Shaw."

"Christ. You're gonna kill me." I set her down in the bathroom and turn the water on.

She quickly strips my t-shirt off her and her panties. I strip my boxer briefs and pull her into the shower. I lift her up and hold her against the shower wall as the water soaks us. She wraps her arms around my neck and her legs around my waist. I kiss her as I lift her hips slightly, and then drop her onto my hard and waiting cock.

"Oh! Fuck, Chase."

I stay still while she gets used to me. She tightens and clenches around me, moaning softly. "Ready?" I ask after a moment.

"God, yes."

"My name, Bree. I love when you say my name."

"Yes, Chase." She whispers it, and then nips my lip. I growl as I slowly begin thrusting, rolling my hips. "Oh, wow." She buries her head in my neck.

"You like that?"

"I'm in love with everything you do."

I give myself to her deeply and hard while still keeping my thrusts slow. "You're so tight, baby. So fucking good."

"Oh, Chase." She grips my shoulders tighter and kisses my neck, up my chin, and to my mouth. The angle allows me to hit the spot deeply inside her that drives her crazy with want. "Chase, you feel so good."

I hold her firmly as I thrust and lean down to kiss her breasts. "I love the size of these. Perfect."

"Mmm…," she moans, digging her nails into my shoulders. I take one of her nipples in my mouth and suck. "Oh! Oh... Chase. Fuck!"

"I love my name coming out of that sexy mouth of yours." I gently bite her nipple, and she throws her head back. I feel her start to tighten around me. "Not yet, Bree. Give me a second."

"Chase, oh my God. Oh my God. Oh!"

My thrusts become more erratic, and she smashes her lips against mine. Her pussy pulses around me. Despite the fact that we're in the shower, I feel her getting wetter for me. With each clench, she squeezes my cock until I can't fathom the idea of not filling her.

"Now. Come for me now."

She lets go and pulses around my dick. "Chase! Yes! Fuck, yes!" Her hips jerk against mine as she pulses and spasms around me.

I thrust as deeply as I can inside her and explode. "Fuck, Bree!" I nip her neck and slam into her again and again as I come. I slow my thrusts more and more, helping us ride through our release. After we come down from it, several moments later, I slowly pull out of her and let her down.

She kisses my chest. "I love you."

"I'd marry you right now if you'd let me. I love you that much." I kiss her hair, and then let her go so we can clean up.

She takes a washcloth and starts lathering her soap into it. "What if we just did it then?"

I raise an eyebrow. "Did what?" I lather up a washcloth myself and look down at her.

She smiles. "What if when we got back to Chicago, we just got married? A small, intimate ceremony. Just your mom and Taylor and Nikki. And Reese and Ryan?"

I know I'm grinning like a complete fool, but I find it difficult to care. "What about your friends? The ones you have girl's night with?"

She bites her lip and looks down. "They haven't even bothered to check in with me. I guess I haven't with them either, but I missed girl's night, and they didn't even call or text to see where I was or if I was coming. The only person who has checked in with me is Reese."

"He's a good guy. He used to work with Taylor, actually. He was a good cop, but he hated it. Taylor recommended him to me. Said I needed to hire security, or he was going to do it himself. So, I hired him. He worked with Taylor to hire a team. Been with me now for seven years."

"He seems really loyal."

"So far." We finish cleaning up and get out of the shower. We head to the bedroom as we dry off to get dressed.

"I'm serious, though. I think we've wasted too much time with being so in love with each other and not saying anything. I love you. I know you love me. I want to spend my life with you."

"I'm surprised you don't think it's too fast."

She shrugs and bites her lip. "It is fast. But I don't care. I just want you. Maybe it's jumping in headfirst, but I feel like when the stars align, you don't mess with it. We've both wanted each other for so long. It seems foolish to me to *not* do this fast."

I smile as we get dressed. When she's dressed, she starts to head to the bathroom to brush out her hair, but I grab her arm. "I love you."

"I love you, too." She smiles up at me.

"For your ring, I'm thinking a white gold band because you hate yellow gold. A princess cut diamond. Probably a half or three-quarters karat because your hands are so small. You don't like things engulfing you."

She gives me a teasing smile. "Not true. I like when you engulf me."

"Totally different. How am I doing so far with the ring? I want you to like it."

She adorably purses her lips while she thinks. "My favorite color is pink."

I laugh. "Duly noted, though I already knew that." A pink diamond. And her matching band will have smaller diamonds. Both pink and regular to match her engagement ring.

"What about my ring size?"

I take her hand and kiss it, studying her fingers. "Average is a seven, isn't it? You're smaller than that. What is it?" I ask.

"A five."

I grin. “You're fucking small everywhere, aren't you? Well, except those tits.” I smirk as I look down at them. “Which I thoroughly enjoy burying my face in.”

She laughs and kisses me. “And not expensive. I don't care about money. I just want you. It could be made of tinfoil for all I care.”

“Breetana, I'd do anything you asked, but skimping on your ring isn't going to be one of them.”

“Chase, I mean it. I don't want you to think I'm after your money.”

“You think I don't already know that? Go finish getting ready, and no more arguments on the ring.”

She shakes her head and smiles as I leave the room. I have a phone call to make. I want that ring ready when we get back to Chicago.

She's absolutely right. We've wasted too much time fighting how we feel about each other. No more. She's everything I've ever wanted. Now that I have her, she's everything to me. Wasting any more time isn't an option. It’s obvious we both know what we want.

Chapter Twenty Two

⚔ Taylor ⚔

Nicole stirs and groans. I kiss her shoulder and hug her close to me, my arm protectively over her stomach as I lean against the headboard of the bed. Nicole is sitting up against my chest.

"I'm sorry I kept you awake all night," she whispers.

"It's okay."

"It's not. You didn't ask for any of this." She gestures over her body.

I sigh. "Nicole. Stop it," I rumble warningly.

"It's true," she says teary-eyed.

"I'm here for the long haul. Sleepless nights included," I reassure her.

"Why are you so nice to me? I don't know what I did to deserve you."

"How many times are you going to make me say it?" I squeeze her tighter and kiss her head.

Her self-esteem is so low it's astonishing to me. I can't understand how in the hell she doesn't see how perfect she is. How beautiful. When I get my hands on her ex for everything he's done, how low he's made her feel, I swear he's done for. I'll end him.

"I just don't understand how you can love someone like me." Her hands fly to her mouth, and she looks up at me, eyes wide as a doe's. I smile. I do love her. God help me, but I've fallen hard and fucking fast. This girl shattered all of my barriers as soon as she looked at me. I gently grab her hands and pull them away from her mouth. "I... I... didn't mean to say that. To assume."

"Nikki. I fell in love with you the second I saw you. Pretty sure everyone knows that. I haven't tried to hide how I feel about you. I haven't tried to hide wanting to spend my life with you. That I want to take care of you. Of both of you."

"I just don't understand why. That's all." She tries to break free of my arms. It doesn't work.

I just hold her tighter. "Do you really need a reason?"

"I have to go to the bathroom. I feel like he's sitting on my bladder."

I kiss her head again. "Baby. I don't care how many times you make me say it. I don't care how long it takes you to believe me. But I'm in this. With you. Whatever you need, I'll give it to you. I'll spend every waking moment erasing whatever the hell damage your ex caused you if that's what it takes." I let her go after kissing her again. She slowly climbs out of the bed and makes her way to the bathroom.

He really did a fucking number on her. He had to have spent years tearing her down in order to make her feel like she isn't good enough for me. For anyone. To make her feel like everything she says is stupid.

I scrub my hands over my face as she turns the shower on. I smile and crawl out of bed, making my own way to the bathroom. I strip my boxers off and sneak into the shower behind her. There's one way I know to reassure her. It seems to work like a charm, and I have no problems doing it as often as she likes. I slip my arms around her.

She squeaks. "Taylor! Oh my God, you scared the shit out of me!"

"You're so beautiful, Nikki." I rumble against her neck. "I know he really fucked with your head, but I'm *not* going anywhere. I do love you. I don't think you're stupid. At all. I think you're beautiful. I think you're worth more than you give yourself credit for. And I cannot wait to meet the little one you carry, sweetheart."

"Taylor... I don't know what to say." She turns in my arms and lays her head on my chest. Her tears intermix with the hot water, and I hug her tightly. "I'm scared."

"I know."

"No. I mean. Yes, I'm scared with everything going on, but I... I'm also scared of you. Of how I feel about you. I'm scared you'll run when things get hard, and that I'll be alone again. I'm scared he'll come after the baby legally and take him away from me. I'm just... I'm scared. Of everything."

"I know, baby. I understand. You have a lot going on, and you've been through a lot. You've been hurt by the two guys in your life who should've been your biggest champions. You have no reason to trust someone you've just met." I take a deep breath.

I don't want to say what I'm about to, but whatever she wants, whatever she needs, I'll do it. I know she needs to hear this, even though it isn't something I want to say. I know it will hurt us both, but I know her well enough to understand this is something she needs.

I push her back slightly and take both of her hands in mine. I bring them up to my lips and brush a kiss across her knuckles as I close my eyes. I let my breath out, but keep my lips pressed to her skin.

I open my eyes slowly. "If this is too fast for you, then I'll back off. I don't want you to feel like I'm pushing you, or that I'm playing games with you. I don't want you to think this is just sex for me, Nicole. I really can't picture my life without you in it. Both of you. And whatever you need me to do to prove it to you, I'll do it."

I release her hands, lean down to kiss her, and leave the shower. I hear her sniffle, and my heart breaks as I grab a towel to dry off. I fight hard not to go back in there and sweep her in my arms, but this is something she needs to work through. She needs to be sure about her feelings. As sure as I am about mine.

After I'm dressed, I head out to the suite to give her space. Ryan is giving instructions to one of his guys, so I head to the balcony. I need to be alone.

"What's up?" Ryan asks seconds later from behind me.

"Five fucking seconds. A new record." I shake my head.

"I'll pretend I know what that means."

"You and Chase. You can read me like no other. Took you five seconds to come out here to check on me."

"You're my brother, Taylor. What the fuck do you expect?"

I sigh and plop down on one of the chairs. Ryan sits next to me. "I shouldn't have come on as strong as I did with Nikki. It feels like she's fucking terrified of me sometimes."

"I doubt that."

"She doesn't believe I could ever love her. That I want a future with her. That I have no problems with the fact that she's carrying a kid that isn't mine."

"She's been through a lot."

"I know. I feel like I've been pushing her. Instead of taking things slow with her like I should be, I'm being typical fucking Taylor and jumping in head first. Thinking with my dick, and not my head."

"If that's what you think is happening, you really aren't as smart as I thought."

"Fuck you, Ryan." I shake my head but smile. He knows what he's doing. He knows how to get me out of my head and back into the right frame of mind.

He grins, then laughs. "For the first time ever I'd have to say you're thinking with your heart. You love that girl, and I know she loves you. Don't take a fucking genius to see it." He pats me on the shoulder as he stands.

I lean back in the chair and close my eyes. "How the hell do you do that? You've never even been in love. Now you're giving love advice?"

He pauses. I can hear him heave in a heavy sigh. "I wouldn't say I've never been in love. Just… more in love with someone off-limits."

"Who the fuck could be off-limits to the great Ryan Crane?" I keep my eyes closed but smile.

He's silent for a moment before he sighs. "Work it out." I hear him leave the balcony, and I sigh heavily. I hate that he's right. I have to show her that I'm not going anywhere. That I want to be with her. Telling her isn't enough.

Several minutes later, I hear the door open quietly. "Taylor?" Nicole's soft voice makes me smile, but I don't open my eyes.

"Yeah, baby?"

"I... I'm sorry. About earlier."

I feel her sit next to me. I still don't open my eyes.. "Baby." I point to my lap, and she chuckles.

She stands, and then sits in my lap. "Much better," she murmurs.

"I agree." I kiss her neck. She puts her arms around my shoulders and settles her head against my chest. I put one arm securely around her waist and drop the other to her upper thigh, my hand just brushing her core under her skirt.

She sighs in contentment. "Say it again."

I smile and rub small circles on her thigh with my thumb. "I love you."

"I love you. I love how you know that's what I wanted you to say. How you just know what I need. All the time. Without me even saying it."

"Always, Nicole."

"I love how protective you are. How in tune with me you are. How you know if I'm scared. Or if I'm beating myself up over something. I love how just the smell of your cologne centers me. How being in your arms makes everything okay again."

I smile, but say nothing. I know she just needs to talk. I kiss her forehead and run my hand up to rest on her stomach. One of my new favorite things in the world is feeling him kick or move. I love Nicole's reaction when he reacts to me.

"That. I love when you do that. How you show how much you care for me and for him by doing what you're doing. I love how you sat up with me all night just because I couldn't get comfortable. How you rubbed my back and my stomach just to try and ease the discomfort, and how you didn't complain. Not even once. Even though I know you had to be uncomfortable."

"Honey. My priority in life now is you and the life you carry inside you. Is that fast? Fuck yes. Not like me in the slightest. I never envisioned my life turning out like this, Nicole. A ready-made family wasn't on my radar. I was happy the way I was." I open my eyes and gently lift her face so that she's looking at me. "I don't want to scare you. I don't want you to be afraid that I'm going to take off. I'm not going anywhere. I know that's hard to believe. Considering my past, I don't know that I'd believe me either. But things change. Baby, you've changed all of that for me. The second I laid eyes on you. And if you need proof, I'll be happy to give that to you. If you need me to show you that I'm in this with you, I'll do it."

"You have. Everything you've done. The fact that even after I acted so stupid -"

I shake my head and cut her off. "Stop. Stop. Nicole. You know better. Start over."

She takes a deep breath. "I was acting stupid."

"No, baby. Fuck, Nicole. Expressing how you feel, especially to your fucking boyfriend isn't stupid. Now. Try again," I say dominantly. She looks at me, her bottom lip quivering. I kiss her softly. When I pull back, she's smiling softly. "Try. Again."

She bites her lip, and I feel myself getting hard underneath her. Her biting her lip is one of the sexiest things she does. "Even after I pushed you away, you're still here. You're still wanting to be with me. You still want me. And you still say you love me."

"I'm not just saying it. I know it's fast, Nicole. I really am trying not to push you. But I know how I feel. You're it. You're the one."

"Will you promise me something?"

"Anything."

"Will you promise me that when Billy comes after me for custody, and I know he will, that you'll fight with me?" she asks softly.

I smile and kiss her shoulder. "Two things. First. Billy will not come anywhere near you or the baby. Ever. And second. I know you don't know Ryan well, but I doubt you'll have to worry about Billy much longer."

She exhales a long breath. "Can I ask you something?" She fiddles with the hem of my shirt as she looks at her hands.

"Baby. You know you can ask me anything."

"I don't want you to be upset. I'm not trying to accuse you of anything either… but are you part of his crew? The m-mafia?"

I laugh, and she furiously blushes. "Are you asking if I'm a dirty cop?" I ask, humored. She doesn't say anything, and I laugh again as I hug her. "I'm not a dirty cop, Nicole. I am part of Ryan's crew, but not to the extent you think. I promise. Ryan has fed me a few tips to take down some bad people. I get the credit for the takedown. He gets to peacefully take over the area. But he isn't involved with drugs or any of that shit. He's actually cleaned up the areas he's taken over, and he's provided a lot of jobs to Chicago's residents. He runs a legal mafia. Not to say he doesn't cross lines, but with everything else he does… Well, he helps us stop the bad guys."

"He's really scary, though."

"He's protective. There's a difference. So am I. I'd do anything I needed to do to protect my family. Which is Ryan, Chase, our mom, and now Breetana. You, and this baby. You guys are my family. And I'd do whatever I need to do to keep you safe. The difference is Ryan is far more upfront about it. And since I'm part of his family, he'll do whatever he has to do to make sure I don't have to cross the lines he does."

"Has he... had to kill people?"

I let out a breath and kiss her neck as I hold her a bit tighter. "Is knowing the answer to that something that is really important to you?"

"Yes. I just want to understand."

"Yes. But never unless someone he loves is being threatened, or if the people he's after are threatening innocent lives. He isn't a cold-blooded murderer. He'll do anything to keep those he loves safe. Innocent people in this world from being taken out by the bad guys."

"I always thought the mafia shook down people for money and killed people if they didn't cooperate. I guess I watch too many movies."

"You aren't far off, sweetheart. A lot of what I deal with as a cop is taking out people like that. Ryan is... different. Ryan doesn't do what he does to hurt people. You want me to show you an example?"

"Um… okay?"

I reach in my pocket and take out my phone. I show her a map of Chicago. "All of the areas in red are areas where we had some serious high crime. Murders. Drugs. You name it, it happened."

I push a couple more buttons and show her another map. "This is the same areas today."

"There's a lot less red."

"Areas Ryan has moved in and helped clean up."

"So, he really is a good guy?" Nicole questions.

"Yes. I'm not involved in that part of things. He keeps me out of the really dirty parts. I know how he does what he does, but Chicago P.D. and a lot of other departments and federal agencies turn their heads. He doesn't let us be involved with it to protect us and our jobs. So, you don't have to worry. I'm not a dirty cop. He doesn't bribe me. I'm not involved in any kind of nefarious activity."

"I don't mean to sound needy or... um…" She cuts herself off and looks down as she bites her lip. I kiss the top of her head, and then gently lift her face so she's looking at me again.

"I am not going anywhere. I won't let Billy take the baby. I won't let him touch you or the baby. I will fight *with* you. I'll fight *for* you. I'll be your fiercest protector because that's what you fucking deserve, Nicole. You deserve someone who isn't going to abandon you. Someone who will worship you, and make you feel as beautiful and as special as you are. Someone who will build you up. Not tear you down. I'll love you until my last breath. I promise."

She leans in and kisses me deeply and slowly. Our tongues dance with each other's. After a couple of minutes, Nicole reaches down and rests her hand on my length. I hiss against her mouth and moan.

"I love that I have this effect on you. It makes me feel like you really think I'm beautiful."

"You are beautiful, Nikki. Any guy who doesn't have this kind of reaction to you is crazy. Although, if they do, they face me. And I can't promise it would end well for them." I give her a teasing smirk, but I'm fucking serious. She laughs and squeezes me. I growl and unbutton and unzip my jeans. I release myself for her, and her eyes light up. She smiles dangerously and starts stroking. I close my eyes. "Fuck that feels good."

"I love how big you are."

I look around, and then run my hand up her leg once more. "I love that you're wearing a dress."

"Dresses are all I'm comfortable in right now. With it being so hot and me being so far along and huge."

I laugh as my fingers brush along her panties. "You're so fucking beautiful, Nicole." I move her panties aside and dip a finger inside.

"Mmm... Taylor." She continues stroking me, and I push my finger deeper inside before taking it all the way out and repeating the motion.

Her strokes are long. From my base all the way to my tip. It drives me crazy, but I lavish her with the same attention. I give her deep and long strokes until I feel her start to tighten. I give her another finger and bring her lips to mine. I kiss her. Our tongues twine again as she strokes me faster, and I set my thumb against her clit.

"Mmm... Right there…," she moans as she arches into my fingers while I thrust.

“I know how you like it, gorgeous.”

I'm getting close and feel she is, too. Her walls tighten around my fingers, and she starts shivering. She’s just starting to clench and pulse uncontrollably. Her breathing quickens. I rub her clit, giving her a little more pressure, and it's all it takes.

She whimpers quietly, and the sound shoots straight down my spine through my cock. “Oh... Fuck, Taylor. You're so, so good at that.”

I crook my fingers. She jerks into me. “Come, baby,” I murmur against her lips.

She lets her head fall back as her eyes close. Her hips jerk into me as she arches. Her pussy spasms around my fingers and tightens. Her hand on my dick tightens, but she doesn’t stop stroking as she comes hard, soaking my fingers.

I thrust her through as she moans and pants while she rides out her release. When she relaxes, and that beautiful, satisfied smile hits her lips, I slowly start to pull. I adjust her panties and lick my fingers as she gets off me. She lowers herself to her knees in front of me as she continues stroking. I watch her curiously and pull her hair back from her face when she takes me in her mouth.

“Oh… fuck, baby. Just like that.”

I want to let my head fall back, but I love watching her too much. She strokes me as she swirls her tongue around my tip. She gives me a few hard licks just below my tip before she deepthroats me.

“Mmm…,” she moans around my cock. Her voice reverberates through me, sending vibrations through my dick.

“Holy shit…” My dick hits the back of her mouth again and again while she strokes me. “I'm gonna come, Nikki. You gotta -” She deepthroats me again, and I lose it. My cock pulses in her mouth, and I shoot my load down her throat. She swallows, and I try to catch my breath. “My God, baby.”

“I love the way you taste.” She licks every last drop.

I can't help but shake my head with a huge shit-eating grin as I look at my watch. “Finished just in time. We gotta go.” I lean forward and kiss her. I stand and pull her up, then pack myself away.

“I love you, but I don't know how much longer I'll be able to get down on my knees when I want you in my mouth. It kind of hurts.”

"You don't need to. There's lots of other ways you can have me if that's what you want."

She cocks an eyebrow and looks up at me confused. "Like how?"

"I can stand. You can sit. You don't have to be on your knees, baby." I smile. Her eyes widen, and I laugh. "What, beautiful?" I run my fingers through her hair as I look down at her. I love her height compared to mine.

She smiles. "I don't really want to talk about my ex, but I've only ever been in one position with him. And when I gave him blowjobs, it was like that. And he never gave me anything in return. I had to finish myself off."

My mouth drops. "How in the fuck did you survive so long?" I stare down at her in a state of disbelief. She smiles and shrugs. "So he never fingered you." I watch as she shakes her head. "Used his tongue? Never made you come?" I shake my head when she shakes hers again. "I can't believe it. I'm going to make you come undone, Nikki," I vow.

"I can't wait."

I kiss her. I don't have any idea why she stuck with that douche for so long, but I have every intention of worshiping her like she deserves. "We should go. I want this house packed up so I can get you out of this place and home where you belong."

"Home… with you?" she asks a little hesitantly.

I nod. "Where you belong, Nicole. You don't belong here. You belong in Chicago. With me, your sister, and Chase."

"I really, really like that idea," she says softly. I lean down to kiss her once more. "I really love you. I'm so baffled at how much in such a short amount of time. It's only been a week."

I smile because she's not wrong. But I'm completely okay with it. "I really love you, too, baby." I kiss her again and take her hand, leading her back inside the suite.

Everyone is gathered in Chase's suite, getting ready to leave. Ryan sees our hands intertwined and winks. I smile at my luck. She's perfect, and I'm never ever letting her go.

Chapter Twenty Three

⚔ Breetana ⚔

The roaring in my ears completely drowns out everyone's voices.

The basement.

Nicole wants me to go to the basement.

I can't. I can't do it.

Chase's arms encircle my waist, and he kisses my neck. "Talk to me," he whispers.

And just like that, I'm safe. The world is right-side-up once more.

"I love you." It's a whisper. I can't give him more than that, but I hug his arms, willing him to hug me closer.

He does. Thank fucking God he does. "I love you, too. Now talk to me."

"I can't go down there. I can't."

"Okay. I'll go myself. You can tell me why later."

"Chase…, one more minute," I plead. "I can't stand up without you right now."

"Christ, baby." He kisses my neck again and keeps his grip tight. "What the hell happened to you?"

"I think I can answer that. If you're okay with it, Breetana." I forgot Sergeant Appleton was even here. All I can do is nod. "Her uncle would force her into the basement when he…"

I let out a strangled sob and turn in Chase's arms. I bury my face in his chest, and he runs his fingers through my hair.

"Oh my God. Tana, I didn't know. Really!" Nicole squeaks.

I shake my head into Chase's chest and take a deep breath, but my voice comes out in no more than a whisper. "It's okay. I didn't tell anyone." I look up at Chase as I bite my lip.

"We don't have to do this. Fuck whatever is downstairs," he says nodding towards the basement.

I vigorously shake my head. "No. Kiki needs the boxes down there. There's only a few."

"Then I'll do it myself, baby. Go finish the nursery. I'll meet you up there as soon as I'm done."

"Nikki and I will be finishing up her room, so you won't be alone," Taylor says softly. I nod as I take another deep breath.

Chase kisses me on the forehead. "I won't be long, and then I'll help you out."

"I'll go with her. Kill two birds with one stone and get the fuck out of here quicker. Ben and I are done with our meeting anyway," Ryan volunteers.

"If you need any other help, I'm off today. Nothing else to do," Ben says.

"Go help Chase. Let's get this done quicker," Ryan commands.

"Sure." Ben stands, and Chase leans down to kiss me before he follows Ben down to the basement.

Nicole and Taylor walk up the stairs, and Ryan and I follow. I head to the nursery with Ryan close behind. The further I get away from the basement, the better I feel. The more the ache in my chest eases; the memories fade into the dark depths where they belong.

"Wow. What a mess," Ryan says wide-eyed as he takes in the chaos.

"Yeah. She wants everything in here. I'm not entirely certain if I should take the crib apart the rest of the way. Taylor started it yesterday when they were in here," I say softly.

“I'll finish the crib. You finish the packing.” Ryan rolls up his sleeves, I can’t help but smile at his muscular arms. He truly is an imposing figure. I drop to my knees and start gathering clothing. “Looks like it got ransacked,” he muses.

“Kiki has never been a very organized packer. It's funny because everything else in her life is organized to a fault. She has lists for everything. But when she's packing? It typically looks like a hurricane hit. I used to call her Hurricane Kiki.”

Ryan laughs. “The name fits!”

“Boss?” My heart quickens as we both turn to see Greg standing in the doorway. I can feel Ryan immediately tense, and it causes me to become even more nervous than I already had.

“What the fuck, Greg? I told you you're on patrol. Get the fuck outside. Now.”

“Sir, I'm sorry, but we have a situation. We think you need to check it out.”

Ryan glares. “What? What's the situation?” His voice is dangerous. Greg glances at me and clears his throat. Ryan growls.

“I'll be okay,” I say nervously.

“Not a chance in hell. I'll be right outside.” Ryan looks at me briefly, and something in his eyes sets me on edge. I don't know what it is, but something. I watch him follow Greg out of the room. True to his word, though, he's right outside the door. I shake off the feeling and stand. There's some clothing left in the closet. I take it all out and close the door.

Just then, I catch a glimpse of something shiny. I cock my head as I look towards it. “What?” I look out the window and catch a glimpse of the sun reflecting off something.

A... mirror?

There's slight movement, and I stumble backwards.

It can’t be.

Can’t.

I'm too terrified to scream, so I run.

I round the corner of the room straight into Ryan. He catches me.

“He's… out… there.” The words are staggered. Barely above a whisper, though they sound so loud to my ears.

“Who?” Greg asks.

“I saw him. Ryan, I saw him.” My voice shakes. I can’t hear anything over the pounding in my ears. Ryan pulls me into him. I start sobbing uncontrollably.

“Go! Fucking search the perimeter!” Ryan yells. Greg scurries away.

Taylor and Nikki run out of her room. “What the hell?” Taylor asks, confused.

“Downstairs. Close all the fucking shades,” Ryan commands. Taylor leads Nicole downstairs with no hesitation. Ryan takes my face in his hands. “Look at me, sweetheart.” His eyes meet mine. I do, but I'm fighting to breathe. “We need to get downstairs. Think you can hold on long enough for me to get you down there?” He takes out his gun and takes my hand. All I can do is nod. “I'd carry you, but we're going by windows. I need you to stay with me, Breetana.”

“I will,” I whisper, swiping at my tears. I have to be strong.

“Take deep breaths for me, sweetheart.” His voice holds some kind of calming dominance. I do as he says. I focus on his breathing when he pulls me to his side. We walk down the stairs together. “I'm gonna close these shades, sweetheart. I need you to stay behind me until I get you to the side of the window. Okay?”

I nod staying as close to him as I can. “Okay.”

“That means I need to let you go for a minute. You need to be strong for me.”

“I will. I promise.” Strong. Have to be strong.

He pushes me behind him, and then pulls me close to his back. He walks to the side of the window, keeping his body in front of mine. Blocking me. “Duck down. Don't move until I tell you to.”

I crouch on the floor, and Ryan moves quickly to shut all of the windows in the area. When he's done, he reaches a hand to me to help me up. He keeps his gun drawn and leads me to the front room. He enters first, sweeping the room with his gun and keeping me behind him. “Okay, sweetheart. We're good.”

I run directly to Chase. He pulls me tightly to his chest. “What the fuck just happened?” he asks Ryan.

“Where's Greg?” Ryan asks one of his guards.

“Outside. He just walked out,” Pete answers.

“What did he say when he came in?” Ryan asks.

"That he needed to talk to you," Rico responds.

"Fuck," Ryan growls.

"At the risk of sounding repetitive...," Taylor begins. "What the fuck just happened?"

Ryan looks at him. "Greg came in and told me that they had reason to believe someone was outside. I asked him why. He said there were footprints about fifteen feet from the edge of Nicole's property outside of her room. They could be looking in. I was just about to tell you, Taylor, when Breetana came flying out of the nursery saying that she saw him."

"Who, baby?" Chase asks as he rubs his hands soothingly up and down my back

"Shaun." I sniffle. "And he had a gun with a scope. It was a long-range rifle. Like my dad used to have," I say finally calming down. "I saw him. Clear as day. He wasn't even trying to hide."

"Fuck! Fuck! Fuck!" Taylor drops in a chair. "How the fuck did he get by your guys?"

"I don't know. But you can fucking bet I'm going to find out." Ryan's voice is dangerously low and challenging. I don't doubt he'll find out. I don't want to know how, but I can't deny that I trust him.

"If you guys have stuff left upstairs then I want guards at the windows. Two," Ben orders.

"Couldn't have said it better," Ryan agrees.

"We need to get the rest of this house packed up and get them out of here," Ben says.

Ryan smiles. "I knew there was a reason I liked you. Ben and Rico. With Chase and Breetana. Pete and Miguel. With Taylor and Nicole. I'll start bringing shit down for the movers. We aren't coming back here, so this needs to get done tonight."

Nicole looks around panicked. "Someone has to be here tomorrow to organize the movers."

"Baby, we have thirty-four guys here. We'll send a couple up here tomorrow for the movers," Taylor says. "You're in danger here. We never should have been here in the first place. All of this stuff can be replaced. We should have just grabbed the important shit and left."

"But -" Nicole starts.

"A few guys will be here anyway helping Ben with our takeover and clean-up," Ryan interrupts. "We'll make sure it all gets taken care of, Nikki."

Nikki looks sadly around the house and bites her lip as we all head off to hurry the packing. I just want to go home. They'll follow, but at least we'll have home field advantage. We need to get out of here.

I know Nicole is struggling to let go. Everything she's ever loved is here. This house. She worked so hard for it. All of her things. She bought it all. I can understand why she wanted to save as much as she could. Why it means so much to her. But Taylor is right. We should have stayed. It's too dangerous.

Silver Bay holds nothing for either of us anymore.

Chapter Twenty Four

ᚸ Breetana ᚸ

Chase pulls me to my feet, and I bury my face in his chest. I'm exhausted. It's three in the morning, but everything Nicole needs is packed. The important stuff we need to take with us for her is in the SUVs. Everything else is set up for the movers.

"Ready to get the fuck out of here?"

"I never want to come back here again. Ever," I breathe into him.

"No one can blame you there, kid," Ben says.

I glance at him. "Thank you. I don't think I've said that yet."

"No thanks necessary. I'm just happy to be able to help now. Your case has haunted me, Breetana."

"I'm sorry." I bite my lip as I look down at the ground.

"Don't be. Don't ever be sorry. You turned into a hell of a woman and somehow got me the help I need to turn this town around. I'll forever be grateful for that. I'm proud as hell of you."

Chase sticks his hand out to shake. Ben takes it. "Thank you. Good luck. If you're ever in Chicago, look us up."

"I'm sure I'll need a vacation soon. I might take you up on that."

"We'll be happy to have you," I say tiredly.

"Tana? You guys ready to head out?" Ryan appears in the doorway on edge. Chase takes my hand and leads me out of the room. We all head down the stairs, and a sense of dread falls over me. Chase, of course, senses it and squeezes my hand. I turn to Ben and hug him.

"What's this for?" He draws me in and hugs me tightly.

"Be safe, okay? Please keep in touch. I hate it here, but I need to know that you're okay. That things are okay. I just… I need to know that."

"I'll keep in touch. Give me your phone. I'll program my number." He pushes me back slightly. I release him and hand him my phone. He shoots himself a text so he has mine and hands it back.

"I don't want to rush you, Breetana, but I want you guys out of here. I got the SUV as close to the door as I can get it, and guys will be surrounding you," Ryan says.

"Okay. You're right. Let's go." I steel myself as we get ready to leave.

"Same rules as always. I want you guys close to us at all times," Taylor directs us.

"We're ready," Nicole says.

Ryan takes a deep breath. I've never seen him so on edge. In the short time I've known him, he's always been the picture of calm and collected. "Breetana first. She seems to be the target."

"T-target?" My eyes dart to his.

"Yes, sweetheart. He was watching you," Ryan says as calmly as he can as he watches me. I swallow and cling to Chase's back.

He takes out his gun. "Straight to the car, baby. There's a lot of guys out there that will act as a barrier."

I lock eyes with Nicole and mouth that I love her. She mouths it back to me. Taylor holds her close and gives me a soft smile.

"Trust Ryan and Chase, sweetie. You'll be okay," he says. "I got Nicole. Don't worry about her. Just get to the SUV."

I breathe in Chase's cologne as Ryan cautiously opens the door. After a second, he motions for us to go. When we get to the SUV, Chase makes sure I'm in the back before he jumps in the front.

I gasp for air. "What are you doing? Chase, I need you!"

"I need to help Taylor keep an eye out while he's driving, baby. Nicole will be back there with you. It's safer for both of you." He's so calm. I don't know how. I force myself to gulp in air. Chase reaches around to caress my leg. “I'm right here, Bree. Okay? I'm not going anywhere.”

I reach down and squeeze his hand as Taylor and Ryan usher Nicole into the backseat with me. Taylor jumps in the front.

“Behind me,” Ryan commands Taylor. “Ben and someone from County will be escorting us to Duluth. We're going fast.”

“I'll keep up,” Taylor assures him.

Ryan closes the door and gets into his SUV with a couple other guys. Everyone else piles into their vehicles, and Ryan pulls out. Ben hits his lights and sirens as Taylor pulls out behind Ryan. Everyone follows. I see another squad pull up behind our convoy while another speeds up to us, staying at our side.

Nicole chews on her bottom lip, and I see her tears. I take her hand and pull her into me. I stroke her hair as we both sniffle.

“Baby, it'll be okay. I'll get you out of here. I'm sorry if I'm scaring you right now,” Taylor says. Nicole doesn't say anything. She's gripping my arm as she cries.

I hold her even more tightly. “It's okay, Taylor. Just please get us out of here. She'll be okay.” I see his eyes are filled with worry and concern as his meet mine through the rearview mirror. Just then, his phone rings.

He hands it to Chase. “It’s Ryan.” Chase answers and puts it on speaker. “What's up?”

“Saint Louis County will be taking over at their county line and escorting us completely the rest of the way to the hotel. These two squads are going to drop off, and so is Ben. It’s not their district. State Patrol is joining in. We’re about to see a whole bunch of squads.”

“Got it,” Taylor says.

“Ben said Saint Louis County has six squads. State Patrol will have four. He isn't taking chances. Just want you to have a heads up when the switch happens. Should be coming up quick.”

“Thanks.” Taylor speeds up to keep up with Ryan as Chase hangs up the phone. I catch a glimpse of the speedometer.

“Holy shit,” I breathe. He’s doing a hundred twenty-five and seems in total control.

As soon as we’re a little ways from Silver Bay, the squads shut their sirens off, but leave their lights on.

I caress Nicole's cheek. "We're okay, Kiki," I whisper.

"I'm so sorry, Bree. I'm sorry about the basement. I'm sorry I made us all stay, so I could organize all of my stuff for the movers. I put us all in danger. I was so, so stupid."

"Nicole," Taylor cuts in authoritatively. "What did we talk about?"

"I'm sorry. I really am. It's just the way I feel," she chokes out over her tears.

"You aren't stupid. You know better. Stop it. Fix the language," Taylor commands. Nicole sniffles as she hugs me, but doesn't say anything. Taylor reaches around and squeezes Nicole's leg.

"You aren't stupid, Nikki. You aren't. Please don't think you are," I beg. It hurts me that she thinks about herself as stupid. Tears sting my eyes again, and not because I'm terrified.

"We shouldn't have stayed. I shouldn't have insisted," she says, shaking her head.

"Nikki, no one here blames you," Chase tells her.

"We all know how important this is to you. That was your first home that you bought on your own." I kiss her head. "We all know that you wanted to feel like you were in control of something for once in your life. Ryan let us stay as long as he felt it was safe. He told us all that if he felt the danger was too close, he was moving us out immediately."

"None of us are upset with you, honey." Taylor squeezes her leg once more, then puts both hands back on the wheel.

"I just wanted to make sure that everything gets to Chicago. I wanted to make sure everything was neatly labeled and packed, even though I'm such a messy packer. I really am sorry for making us stay longer than we should have."

"It's hard to uproot like this. To feel like you have no control over your life," I soothingly whisper to her.

"I wanted to make sure nothing important is forgotten," she guiltily whispers.

"If anything is forgotten, we'll replace it. It's okay."

"I just worked… so hard for everything I have."

"I know, Kiki. I know how hard this is. But you aren't alone. Okay? You have me. You have Chase now and Ryan. And most importantly, you have Taylor now. We're all here for you."

"It's… so hard to give it all up. To just let everything I worked so hard for go. And start over."

"But you won't be alone, Kiki. We won't let you be." I hug her close as a flurry of squad cars join us. We continue to speed down the highway.

Chase takes his phone out and dials a number. "How soon can you be ready to get us the fuck out of here?" He pauses. "Good. Do it."

"Baby, how far along are you exactly?" Taylor asks.

"I'm just going into my thirty sixth week. Why?"

"Fuck." Taylor glances at Chase. "Can she safely fly?"

Chase shrugs. "I don't know."

I nibble my lip. "Maybe I could pay a doctor enough to fly with her. I've been able to save -"

Chase cuts me off. "I know how much you get paid. I sign your checks. There's no way you'll have enough saved to bribe someone. I wouldn't let you anyway. I'll pay." Chase takes his phone out again. "Ryan, we need to stop at the hospital. Find us someone who can fly to Chicago with Nikki." He pauses, and then hangs up. "He said he'll take care of it. We're going to the hotel. No exceptions or detours."

"That's Ryan for you." Taylor chuckles.

"Thank fucking God you decided to call him," Chase says.

"I know we said we were driving back to Chicago, but I'm so glad we aren't," I say to Nikki.

"Me too. I just want to get out of here. There's nothing here for me anymore. All my hard work was for nothing."

"No. It wasn't. You can start over when this is all over. Just a few more hours, Kiki." I run my fingers through her hair, and she does the same to me. We hold each other tightly while Taylor navigates us through the darkness.

I can't wait to be on that plane. Silver Bay has caused nothing but heartbreak for me and Nicole.

Finally.

Finally, I can get her out of here and home where she belongs.

Chapter Twenty Five

⚔ Nicole ⚔

Chase's plane is so luxurious. I've never been on a plane before, but I seriously doubt they typically look like this. I'm in awe. I sit next to Taylor and take it all in. “It's so... pretty,” I say. I know my eyes have to be pretty wide. Chase laughs.

Taylor smirks at him. “There are benefits to having family who is a billionaire. I never have to worry about waiting in lines at the airport.”

“Just drive right up to the hanger, board, and leave,” Chase says.

“I really could get used to this,” Breetana teases.

“Me too. I'm already dreaming of all the traveling I want to do. Greece, Italy, France, England, Australia.” I smile as Taylor and Chase both laugh.

“Jesus. You want to travel the world, don't you?” Taylor says, smiling down at me.

“Hey. If that's what she wants, I'll gladly make it happen.” Chase laughs.

“As long as I get to come!” Breetana says.

“Tana and I always talked about traveling.” I smile as Taylor puts his arm around me.

"Where do you want to see first?" he asks.

"We always wanted to do some kind of historical thing."

"Like Hiroshima, Auschwitz, and Pearl Harbor," Breetana chips in.

"We both have an obsession with World War Two."

"Really?" Taylor asks, surprised.

"Taylor is a history buff," Chase informs us.

"I almost majored in it." Taylor grins.

"Really?" I look up at him. "I thought you always wanted to be a cop."

"Well, not always. I was kind of a dick in college."

"He really was," Chase agrees. "Rebellious as hell. He spent the first two years fucking around more than studying."

"Still graduated with honors." Taylor shrugs and grins cockily.

"Because of me, you asshole," Chase laughs. Taylor laughs and squeezes my shoulder.

"I'm glad you aren't a dick anymore," I say looking up at him. I really can't believe how far I've fallen in love with him.

"Well…" He winks at me, and I playfully slap him in the chest. He catches my hand and kisses my palm. I look at him lovingly. I mostly can't believe he wants me. That he loves me. He leans in to kiss me, and I meet his lips. The kiss is soft, sweet, and ends far too soon.

"Nikki?" I pull away slowly from Taylor and look at Ryan. He's boarding the plane with someone behind him. "This is Doctor Chantau. He's one of the best doctors at St. Luke's Hospital here in Duluth. He specializes in pregnancy, delivering, and all that stuff."

"Doctor. It's nice to meet you." I hold out my hand to shake.

His hand is warm and gentle. "Likewise. And do we have the father with you today?" He glances between Taylor and Chase.

"Oh. Um…" I hesitate and glance at Taylor. I'm not really sure what to say.

He smiles and winks at me. "Yeah, doc. That would be me." I smile so big, my face actually hurts. Taylor leans over and kisses me.

Doctor Chantau nods. "Good to meet you, as well. Congratulations to the two of you. Nicole, I'd like to get a blood pressure and your vitals before we take off, if you don't mind."

"Sure." I smile softly at him.

"Whatever you need to do to get us in the air," Taylor says.

"I'll be quick." The doctor takes my blood pressure and other necessary vitals. He listens to the baby and smiles widely. "Looking good. You're right at the point where we say flying is risky, but I'd say we can get in the air. I don't foresee any problems. We'll have you wear an oxygen mask until the cabin pressure is stabilized. Extra precaution. We won't be that high because it's not a long flight. I pulled up your records. I'm happy you've been affiliated with our hospital. It made it easier for all of us. I don't have to ask you a bunch of questions."

"I'll let the pilot know we can leave." Chase gets up and walks to the front of the plane.

"I'll jump on my own plane. See you on the ground." Ryan winks and follows Chase to the front of the plane. He exits out the small door as Chase walks to the pilots in the front of the plane.

"Let me know if you feel any discomfort," Doctor Chantau says to me.

"Okay."

Everyone settles in as the flight attendant takes our breakfast and drink orders. Taylor takes my hand and entwines our fingers. "I know you don't do that well in the morning with eating. Do you want fruit and dry toast again?"

I look up at the flight attendant and smile. "I'll have what he said, but can you put peanut butter on the toast?"

"Of course, miss."

"Do you have any milk to go with her water? It helps with her acid reflux," Taylor asks.

"Absolutely. I'll get everything out when we get in the air." The flight attendant leaves, and I lean against Taylor's shoulder.

"Wow. You know her pretty well already," Breetana says softly.

Taylor shrugs. "I pay attention."

"Sometimes," Chase says, rolling his eyes.

I laugh. "You two really do bicker and pick on each other like brothers do."

"Chase is a pretty good guy when he isn't busting my balls," Taylor jokes.

"You usually deserve it, asshole," Chase retorts.

We all laugh as the plane begins its take-off. I grip Taylor's hand tightly. He looks down at me and squeezes my hand. "You okay?"

"I've never been on a plane before. I'm just nervous."

He lifts my hand to his mouth and kisses it. "I got you."

I lay my head on his shoulder, and he slips his arm around me.

Finally. I'm finally breaking free.

Goodbye Silver Bay.

XXX

"Babe? Hey. We're just arriving at our gate."

"Already?" I feel like I'm coming out of a haze.

"How are you feeling, Ms. Carter?" Doctor Chantau asks.

"Um… actually, not well. I…" My stomach tightens, and I close my eyes. "My stomach hurts, and… I feel like I'm going to throw up."

Taylor runs his fingers through my hair, and Breetana takes my hand. My stomach clenches again, and I nearly scream. I don't like how quickly it came on. As soon as I opened my eyes. I whimper, though I'm not sure if it's pain or fear.

"Baby, you look pale. What's happening?" Taylor asks. I grip his hand as hard as I can, and he winces as he looks at the doctor with concern. "Doc?"

"What's going on? She looked so peaceful when she was sleeping," Breetana says. I can tell she's nearly as panicked as I'm starting to feel.

"She looks like she's about to pass out," Chase says.

I swallow. "Something... isn't right." I look at Taylor, and my vision blurs as another cramp hits. I can't hold back the scream.

"There, there sweetheart. Guys, let's get her someplace she can lay down," Doctor Chantau orders.

I feel Taylor lift me in his arms and carry me somewhere. The pain is getting worse, and I scream again as I start crying and gripping his shirt with a death-like hold. "Taylor!"

"I'm right here, beautiful." He sets me down somewhere and takes my hand in his. The pain is blinding.

“Let me just hook her up. I need to know what's happening.” The doctor’s voice is calm.

“Fuck, Doc, am I glad Ryan chose you,” Taylor breathes.

“Hold her hand. Help keep her calm. Talk her through the pain,” Doctor Chantau tells him.

I grit my teeth. “Taylor…, it hurts.” I sob harder, and Taylor turns my head towards him. He softly kisses me, and then holds me close to him. I feel like my stomach is being ripped apart.

“I love you, baby. You're so strong,” he whispers in my ear.

“I love you,” I cry. The pain is so severe, I can't even scream. How did this happen so fast? It’s only been a few minutes since Taylor woke me. Not really even that long. I don’t even know. I feel myself fading, but I can't stop it. I can't fight it. “I'm so sorry.”

“Nicole!” Breetana screams. I can’t see her. “Chase! Let me go! Nicole! Oh my God!”

“Baby, let the doctor work!” Chase grunts.

“Nicole? Baby, open your eyes for me. Come on, Nikki,” Taylor whispers.

I try, but I can't.

Darkness surrounds me.

Everything goes completely black.

Chapter Twenty Six

✗ Breetana ✗

I didn't think I could possibly cry anymore, but here we are. Nicole lays motionless in my arms. At least she's breathing.

After she passed out on the plane, Doctor Chantau checked everything, including the baby. Thank God he thought to bring necessary equipment. Like an ultrasound machine. The man was prepared for every possible outcome. I guess he really is the best.

After what seemed like endless hours to me, and with Chase having to physically restrain me from running to her, the doctor gave her an all clear. The pain was stress-induced labor pains. Turns out she's exhausted and her passing out was just as stress-induced as her exhaustion. The baby and Nicole are both just fine.

She'd been in and out of consciousness for the past few hours. Doctor Chantau had decided to stay until she woke up and felt like she would be okay without him. He has been in contact with other doctors in the area, too, trying to find someone he felt was good enough to leave her care to. He constantly checks her, and we're all grateful.

Taylor comes out of the bathroom, and a few moments later, I feel a hand on my arm. "Need a break?"

I shake my head with a sniffle. “I can’t leave her.”

Taylor sits down next to Nikki on her other side and takes her hand. After checking her out, Doctor Chantau wanted to make sure she’s under his constant watch. So, we brought her to Chase's house and set her up in one of his guest bedrooms. We all feel it’s safer to stay together. We know we’re going to be followed here. Doctor Chantau has Nicole hooked up to monitors.

We’ve all been by her side ever since. Chase and Ryan are both sitting in oversized chairs, and Taylor and I refuse to leave Nikki's side.

“I didn't say you had to leave her. I just thought that maybe you'd like to go to the bathroom. Or clean up. Or eat something,” Taylor says softly.

“That would be leaving her. I'm not doing that again. Ever again.”

“She wouldn't be alone, Breetana,” Taylor says just as softly.

I shake my head. “I left her twice, Taylor. And she got hurt. I won't do that to her again.”

“You... actually think the reason she got hurt is because you weren't with her? Fuck me, Tana.” He puts his head in his hands.

“She wouldn't have been raped by that sick son of a bitch like I had been for years if I hadn't gone to that stupid party.”

“Baby. Come on. You know better than that.” Chase sits on the bed behind me.

“It's true, Chase. And then I left her again when I moved here. And then I failed her by letting her stay there packing everything. I should have made her leave Minnesota right away. We could've hired people to deal with her stuff.”

“Breetana. Enough. Enough beating yourself up,” Taylor says. I shut my mouth immediately at his commanding tone.

“There were three other people there who could've made that same decision. It doesn't all fall on you,” Chase says.

“The only reason none of us did anything is because we all knew how important it was to her to get everything organized, and make sure she had her important documents and everything,” Ryan says. “She needed that control. None of us were going to rob her of that. She hasn’t had control over her life for a long time.”

“And Ryan and his guys brought the sense of safety we all needed,” Chase continues.

"Breetana. Please listen to me when I say this because I love you like I would a sister. You can't keep blaming yourself for everything that happened. You didn't cause it. If you keep blaming yourself, you're going to destroy yourself. I've watched good people destroy themselves over shit like this too many times. Don't let yourself be one of them," Taylor says.

Tears sting my eyes. "It's so simple for you to say that. You didn't live it."

"You think I had a perfect fucking life?" His voice is still calm, but serious. "I didn't. I saw shit I wouldn't wish on my worst enemy. But I fought like hell to get through it. I had support. Just like you do. You have another thing coming if you think anyone in this room is going to let you keep doing this to yourself." Taylor's eyes flash with a little anger and hurt, but a lot of love. It throws me off.

"Baby, come on. Take a break with me. We won't be gone long. Let's go grab drinks and something to eat for everyone, okay?" Chase takes my arm gently in his large hand.

I shake my head and pull away. "I want to be here when she wakes up. Why can't you guys understand that?"

Ryan sighs. "We do, Tana. More than you seem to think. But how do you expect to be able to be here for her when you yourself are falling apart? Taylor will call you up here immediately. Or I will. Okay?"

Chase gently lays his hand on my arm again. "Please, Bree. You'll feel better. I promise."

I sigh and kiss Nicole on the forehead before allowing Chase to help me up. I don't want to do this. I don't want to leave my sister. But I'm smart enough to know that everyone here has a point.

Chase takes my hand and leads me down the stairs to the kitchen. "I'm sorry, Chase."

"For what?"

"Being like this."

"Protective?"

"How do you do that? How do you just know what I'm feeling? Even when I don't?"

"Because I've spent the last three years learning everything about you. Even though I didn't think for a second you would ever put up with my shit. I never thought we'd be here, baby."

"Chase..., you're so, so sweet."

“A side of me few have seen.” He takes my hands in his. “I love you. I hate that you're blaming yourself for everything right now. I thought you and I talked through this and you were feeling more... okay about everything.”

I sigh and lean against the counter. “We did. It's so hard to change the way I've thought for so many years.”

“I know, baby. But if you don't start, Taylor is one hundred percent right. You're going to destroy yourself.”

I look down at the ground. Chase steps in front of me and lifts me onto the counter. He parts my legs and steps between them. His hands run up my thighs and come to a rest on my hips. He kisses me.

I close my eyes and melt into him. After a moment, I pull back. “I'm trying.”

“I know. And I'm proud as hell of you for how far you've come after everything.”

“I really do think Taylor is perfect for Nikki,” I say softly.

“So do I.”

Chase kisses me again and again until our tongues are fighting for dominance of the kiss. Eventually, he wins, and he softly bites my lower lip as he pulls away. He gives me a gentle kiss before lifting me off the counter.

We make everyone sandwiches and bring them and sodas to Nicole's room. Taylor is lying in bed holding her close. He's giving her soft kisses, and his hand is slowly rubbing her stomach as he whispers in her ear. I smile as tears sting my eyes.

As soon as he sees me, he gives her a soft kiss to her lips and sits up. He tries to covertly wipe his eyes but gives up and takes the sleeve of his shirt to wipe them.

“Taylor…?” I almost whisper. He looks up at me. “Can we... talk? Out in the hall?”

“Yeah. Yeah, of course.” He stands and walks out the door. I glance at Chase. He gives me an encouraging smile as he hands the doctor and Ryan sandwiches and a soda. “What's up, Breetana?”

“I just... wanted to say I'm sorry.” I take a deep breath.

“It's fine. Really.”

"No it isn't. I'm upset with what happened. I'm beating myself up over it and making it about me and my feelings when it's not. It's about Nikki."

"What? Breetana, you have nothing to apologize about."

"Please just let me finish."

"Okay." He folds his arms across his chest and leans against the wall.

"I know it's ridiculous, but I really do blame myself for this. I feel like if I were there, none of this would have happened." I sigh and close my eyes. "But the truth is, had I stayed, I wouldn't have survived. I know I wouldn't have." I look down at the floor.

"Are you done?"

"Yes."

Taylor takes my hand and pulls me against his chest. "You and Nicole are definitely sisters. You worry about the craziest things." His arms encircle me, and I let out a breath. "This isn't your fault. You left believing she'd be okay. She was with a good family in a good home. You know that she flourished under them. She bought her own house. Owned her own business. Who can say that at her age in this day and age? You did the right thing. It can't always be about her. You have to look out for yourself, too. You did that. End of story. Okay?"

I nod into his chest. "Okay."

"So, what do you say we forget this entire thing and focus on what's important right now?"

"Deal."

"Good girl." He kisses me on top of the head, and then guides me back to the room. We both settle and all eat in silence. When we're finished, Taylor sits on the bed next to Nicole. He lifts her hand and kisses it. I sit on Chase's lap and curl myself into his arms.

"You coming back over here?" Taylor asks.

"I'll be here when she wakes up. I think you should lay with her. It's your turn," I say softly. He grins and wastes no time lying next to her and pulling her close.

Chase kisses my head. "That was incredibly sweet of you. And a sure sign that you just might be letting go of that guilt." He holds me close and tightly.

My eyes get heavy, but before I fall asleep, Nicole groans. My eyes fly open, and I run to the bed. I sit next to her and take her hand.

Taylor kisses her cheek, still hugging her tightly. “That's it, baby. Come back to us.”

Doctor Chantau appears at my side, and I start to move out of his way. He puts a hand on my shoulder. “It's okay. Stay.”

Nicole's eyelids flutter open. Her eyes meet mine, then Taylor's before her other hand flies to her stomach. “The baby! Is he okay? What happened to him?” Her eyes are pleading with Taylor.

“Ms. Carter? Do you remember what happened?” Doctor Chantau asks.

“I... I woke up and had cramps. And it hurt really bad, and now I feel nothing. Oh God. Did I lose him?”

Taylor wipes away a tear from her eye. “Shh. Baby is okay. Momma's okay. Everything is okay.” He softly kisses her, and my heart melts.

Chase runs his fingers through my hair and rests his hand on my shoulder. I stand and step into his waiting arms. The doctor takes my place on the bed.

“I've run a bunch of tests and kept you under my watch. You’re very healthy, Nicole. So is your baby. I’m concerned with your blood pressure. It's a little high. I'd like to see that come down a bit. Mr. Crane filled me in on the situation, so what I would like to do is keep you on bed rest until the delivery. I don't feel comfortable sending you to a hospital. Especially one I’m not familiar with.”

“What about when she’s ready to deliver?” Chase asks.

“Then I will accompany her to the hospital. She’s under my care, and it will stay that way.”

I hug Chase. I’m so thankful for him. I don't know what I would do without his strength. His calm demeanor. Without him to ask questions for me when I’m freaking out.

“I'm so happy to hear you say that.” My voice cracks.

“I want guards. I don't want to be there without guards.” The fear that fills Nicole’s face breaks me. I tighten my grip on Chase, and he kisses the top of my head. This should be the happiest time of her life. She should be loving every second of this. Ryan appears on the other side of the bed behind Taylor. Nicole looks up at him. “Will you please still keep people there with us? I feel safe with Taylor, but even more safe with you and your guards around us."

"Sweetheart. You don't even have to ask. Taylor will be in delivery with you, and he'll be armed. I'll have guys outside the delivery room. When you get up to your room after the delivery, I'll have guards with you. And we'll have guards on the baby if they don't allow him in the room with you."

"Which I will insist on," Doctor Chantau assures her.

"Chase is making sure you have a private suite," I tell her.

"It's easier for us to make sure everything is secured if you aren't in the main hospital," Taylor says as he runs his fingers through her hair.

"I'll make sure you're in a VIP room," Chase says.

"So you're staying, Doctor Chantau?" Nicole asks quietly.

He smiles. "Yes."

"But what about your patients? And pay? I don't think my insurance covers any of this!" We all watch as Nicole's heart rate spikes on the monitor.

Chase hugs me as I fight to run to her. "Shh. It's okay. Doc's got it under control," he whispers.

"Don't worry about any of that, my dear. Between Mr. Crane and Mr. Shaw, I am well taken care of, and so is your care."

Taylor rubs Nicole's stomach lightly, and she almost instantly calms down. "Thank God for you, Taylor," I say. "You have such a calming effect on her."

"Always. I always will." He kisses her cheek and continues rubbing her stomach. I wipe a tear away and hug Chase.

"Thank you." It's a whisper for only him.

"For what, baby girl?"

"Taking care of her. And the doctor. For bringing me to get her. For everything."

"I love you. I'd do anything for you and her."

"I know. But thank you anyway."

He holds me while the doctor examines Nicole. I don't care about anything else going on around us. All I care about is Nicole and the baby being okay; the people in this room.

Everything else... Joe, Shaun, Billy, the cartel. None of them matter to me right now. Just my family.

Funny. After our parents died, all I had was Nicole. She was my family. In a matter of a week, I found family again.

I found home.

As soon as Doctor Chantau finishes examining Nicole, I slip out of Chase's embrace and sit next to her on the bed again. Taylor is still wrapped around her.

I smile at Nicole and lean forward to kiss her head. "How are you feeling?"

"Relieved. Glad to be out of Minnesota. I just want to put everything behind us." She shifts, trying to sit up and Taylor nearly falls out of the bed.

I almost laugh, but hold back. "Chase? Can we put them in another room with a bigger bed?" I ask instead.

Chase nods. "Yeah. This was the most convenient at the time. Even though it's upstairs, it's the closest to the door we came in."

"Maybe putting us next to the Doc would be a good idea," Taylor says.

"Ground floor would be convenient for you, Nikki. You'd be close to the kitchen and living room. And there's a private bathroom. This room doesn't have one," Chase says.

"Since she's on bed rest, I would prefer she limit her movement and not have to deal with stairs," Doctor Chantau says.

"It's settled. We move Nicole downstairs to the center room next to Doc," I say.

Ryan stands and stretches. "I'll make it work with the guards."

I look at him quizzically. "Why wouldn't it work with guards?"

Ryan glances at Nicole, and Taylor gives him an almost imperceptible shake of his head, but I see it. I narrow my eyes.

"Nothing. It's good. I'm just saying I'll let the guards know," Ryan says. Nicole beams up at him. I make a mental note to ask him what that means later.

"Let's get everything moved and set up downstairs with the equipment. I want to have it available if it's needed," Doctor Chantau says.

I sit with Nicole while everyone starts moving everything downstairs. She smiles up at me. "I'm happy I'm not in Minnesota anymore. That I'm here. With you and Taylor. Even Chase and Ryan."

"I'm happy you're here, too. I'm so sorry for everything that happened to you."

"Don't, Tana. Please? If none of that happened, I wouldn't be here. Who knows what would've happened? Everything happens for a reason. You're the one who taught me that."

I touch her cheek as I softly smile. "I did, didn't I?"

"You're the best older sister anyone could ever have. I'm so lucky you're mine."

"I'm the lucky one, Kiki. You've kept me from falling apart so many times over the years. You're the one who is the best sister anyone could have." I lean down and hug her. We stay like that for several minutes until we hear Taylor clear his throat.

"Sorry to interrupt, but are you ready to move?"

"Yeah. I'm ready." Nicole scoots to the edge of the bed, and Taylor helps her sit up. She slowly begins to stand, but winces. "Ow…"

"Want me to carry you?"

"You can't carry me. I'm too heavy." She shakes her head.

I laugh. "You're crazy. You've always been small. You still are."

She furrows her eyebrows. "Have you seen my stomach?"

Taylor laughs. "Baby, how do you think you got up here? You certainly didn't walk." He bends and lifts her with ease. She stares at him in shock.

"Told you," I smirk. Taylor takes Nicole downstairs. I follow.

Chase is talking to the doctor, and I stop next to him. "Thank you. For staying. And being so understanding about the craziness we call life."

"Think nothing of it."

"I hope you aren't being kept away from anyone," I say. I'd really hate if anyone was missing him.

"No. No family. No wife. The job has always been most important to me."

I smile a little, and then take a deep breath. "Can I ask something?"

"Of course."

"When Nikki was getting up from bed, she was in pain. Is that... is that normal?"

"There's really nothing to worry about. The baby is sitting a little lower than we like to see, but there is no danger to her or the baby. The fact that he is sitting lower is the reason I want her on bed rest."

“Is there a chance of her delivering early?” Chase asks.

“There is, but it wouldn’t be that early. She’s full term. We like to see babies delivered around thirty-nine to forty-one weeks. That’s average. But some deliver now, and the babies are perfectly healthy. That's one of the reasons I want her on bed rest. I know with the situation, stress is inevitable, but I want to try and keep it as low as we can and keep that baby inside for a couple more weeks at least.”

“Maybe they'll be nice and not attack until after the baby is born,” I joke.

Chase smiles. “Thanks, Doc. We really appreciate you doing this and staying here with her. Despite the danger.”

“Frankly, son. Having a doctor around during a time like this may be a really good thing.” He smiles, then disappears into Nicole's and Taylor's room.

I yawn. “Not sleeping is catching up to me.”

“Want to go take a nap?”

“Yes. I really do. Let me just tell Kiki.” I pop in and tell Nicole we're going to bed for a few hours, and then Chase and I go to his room. I strip all of my clothes off and crawl under the covers.

Chase looks at me incredulously. “Seriously? You're sleeping like that?”

“Yes. I'm too tired to put anything on and I’m done with all things clothes for the day.” I look up at him as he gets into bed next to me. I smile. “You're so incredibly perfect. A beautiful man.”

Chase laughs as he pulls the covers up over us. His hard length is pressed against me. He chuckles. “I promise to behave. Since you're tired.” Feeling him against me instantly wakes me up, and I reach down, taking him in my hand. I start with slow lazy strokes. He moans. “Baby…”

I kiss his chest. He reaches down and finds his way between my thighs. “Mmm…,” I murmur. He runs one long finger from my clit to my entrance as I give him long strokes. I love how I can make him so hard.

“God, baby. You're soaked already.”

“See what you do to me?” I tease. He growls and flips me over, climbing on top of me and plunging into me in one sure thrust. “Fuck, Chase!”

He stays still and buries his head in my hair as he wraps his arms around me. I wrap my legs around his waist and my arms around his shoulders. "I needed this."

"Me too." He starts slowly moving, his hard cock filling me in ways I never imagined.

I match his rhythm and begin moving my hips against his. After a few moments, my body is practically begging for him. "Chase… Harder…," I moan against his lips.

"Gladly." He reaches down and lifts my hips as he gives me harder thrusts.

"Yes! Oh yes!"

His delicious thrusts are both deep and the perfect pressure. When he pulls all the way out and slams himself deeply inside me again and again, his cock hits every spot that drives me crazy. I don't know how he does it, but I swear he's somehow dragging his dick over my clit with each thrust.

"Bree. My Bree. You're so fucking wet and tight, baby girl. You feel so good. So damn good." His thrusts become faster and harder.

My nails dig into his shoulders as my hips meet his. Our skin slaps together. His dick pounding my pussy makes the filthiest of noises that make me blush. He feels so good. So big. He fills me just right. He is as much made for me as I am for him.

"Chase! Oh my God, don't stop!"

He reaches down and starts rubbing my clit. "Fuck. Fuck, baby girl. I'm about to come. Come for me, baby. I need your pussy tightening around me," he growls into my neck.

"Chase… Oh, Chase!" I tighten around him at his command. He flicks my clit as he rubs, giving me the perfect pressure. Seconds later, my release hits, and my whole body shakes. "Chase! Oh! Oh God, Chase..." My entire body quakes against his.

He thickens inside me then explodes. "Oh, holy fuck, Bree!" He buries his face in my neck and hugs me even tighter as he spills all he is into me, continuing to thrust as we ride out our orgasms.

After a few minutes, Chase has slowed until the thrusting stops. We've somehow managed to catch our breath, but neither of us want to move. Maybe I'm strange, but his weight on top of me, even though I know he's holding a lot of it off of me, makes me feel so content.

He kisses my neck as he slowly pulls his dick out of me. I moan at the feeling of his cock and whimper at the loss.

Chase pulls me close to him as he settles. “I love you.”

“I love you. I'm glad we're home.”

I smile and burrow into his arms. I love being wrapped up with him. I feel so safe. Loved. Protected. I'm asleep moments later thinking of only one word, and how safe and happy it makes me feel.

Chase.

My home.

Chapter Twenty Seven

⚔ Chase ⚔

(Four Days Later)

I've spent the better part of my day in my home office dealing with emails and fires that need my attention. Even on vacation, the CEO is never really on vacation.

Fuck. Who am I kidding? This isn't a fucking vacation anyway. Some of this shit could wait until I'm back in the office, but I need time away from everything. Ryan's guys invaded my house. Breetana and Taylor are fussing over Nicole. Even the doctor is getting annoyed, and I heard Nicole yell at both of them at least once.

It's chaos. And the only way to keep myself sane is to distract myself. Typically, a nice distraction would be Breetana, but her attention is definitely not on me.

I glare at my phone as it rings, but I pick it up anyway. "Shaw?"

"Mr. Shaw? I'm calling to let you know your ring is ready."

"Pierre." My mood immediately improves. "I'm glad to hear this. The set? Or just the engagement ring?"

"The set, sir." His slight French accent is barely noticeable these days. He's been in the U.S. for many years. I've been working with him since I was a teenager.

"And my band?"

"Ready to go, sir."

"Good. You'll be coming to drop it off?"

"Yes, sir. Whenever you're ready."

"Now is fine. I'm home. Call when you're close. Things are crazy, and security is tight, so I'll have to meet you by the gate."

"Yes, sir."

I hang up. At least one thing is going right. Breetana and I will soon be married. And with any luck, this bullshit will be over soon.

"Babe?"

I smile as I close my laptop. "Yes?"

Breetana closes the door and walks to my desk. She hops up on it in front of me. "Do you intend on being in here all day? I miss your lap."

I laugh and tug her into my lap. "My lap is available to you anytime, baby."

"I didn't want to bother you. I know you're busy. Though, why I'm not doing any of this…"

"Nope. I'll take care of it. But I do need a distraction. All of this can wait."

"I need a distraction, too. I love my sister, but I think she's going stir crazy. She hates being in bed all day. She just called the doctor a terrorist and poor Taylor the spawn of Hades."

I raise an eyebrow and rub my thumb lazily over her thigh. "Hades? Not Satan?"

"Nope. Hades. Satan is too simple for Nikki." She smiles. I chuckle and kiss her shoulder. She turns her head to me and kisses me on top of the head. "Still need a distraction?"

I smile and run my hand down her core. I rub over her jean cut-offs. "Do you know how sexy you look in these?"

"Hmm…" Her smile grows lustful. "No. Why don't you tell me?"

I kiss her neck and cup her pussy in my hand. She moans and puts a hand over mine, pushing it harder against her. "I love the way you look in these. Your perky little ass." I rub her harder, and she gasps. "You're sexy as fuck legs." I reposition her so her back is to me. And that sexy little ass is against my hardening cock. "Enjoy the ride," I whisper in her ear.

"What?" She tilts her head. I unbutton her shorts with one hand as I slide my other one inside and under her panties. I slip a finger inside her tight pussy as I unzip the shorts. "Oh!" She grinds against my hand and my cock.

"Wet for me already?" I say into her hair.

"Oh fuck! Chase…," she moans. I slide my middle finger inside her and out of her while I rub my palm against her clit. "Oh my God, Chase…"

I slide a second finger inside her unable to resist because she feels so fucking good, and she rubs her ass against me. My dick sprints to attention and hardens. "God, Bree. That feels good."

"You feel good. So, so good!" I push a second finger inside her and thrust deeply while I start rubbing her clit with my thumb. "Mmm... You know just where to touch me."

"I know what you like. I know the way you like it." I keep giving her deep thrusts while rubbing her clit, and she pushes her ass harder into me. "Shit… that feels so fucking good."

"Oh my God. I'm so close…" I kiss the back of her head, and then give her a little more pressure on her clit. She leans forward and puts her hands on my desk. "Chase! Mmm…"

I feel her clench around me. "That's it. Come for me. Let me feel it, baby."

"Mmm… Chase…"

Her release hits her, and I pull her ass back to my cock. "Not done with you yet." I pull my fingers out of her and nudge her off my lap. When she's standing, I pull her shorts and panties down to her knees and part her legs slightly.

"Mmm... I like where this is going."

I stand and unbutton my jeans. I drop them low on my waist and pull out my throbbing dick. "Bend."

"Oh…" She bites her lip and bends, and I gently push her down so her breasts are flat on my desk. I tease her with the tip of my cock, rubbing it between her slit until she's writhing against me.

"I love when you're so wet for me."

"Chase. Please. I can't take any more."

I grip her hips, then plunge inside her, unable to deny my girl anything. She screams in pleasure, but muffles it against her arm. I continue plunging inside her, hard and fast as she grips my desk. "Damn you feel good. So fucking tight."

"Oh… Mmm!"

She pushes herself back into me, and I go deeper inside her than I've ever been. "Fuck. Oh God, baby. I've been waiting all day for you."

She loses complete control and meets each and every one of my thrusts. I love when she does that. When her pussy, already so wet, gets wetter. When she clenches and pulses erratically around me, squeezing my cock with each thrust. The feel of her ass slamming into me sends me straight to the edge. I reach around and start rubbing her clit.

"Oh my God. Oh…" She grabs my hand and pushes it harder against her. She keeps her hand on mine as she meets my thrusts, not missing a single beat.

"Fuck, baby. You're so hot. So fucking hot. Come for me, Bree."

Her thighs start to shake, and she grinds her ass into me while I fuck her. Her walls tighten around me, and I know we're both done. I feel her release and let go, slamming into her again and again as we both come. I'm making a mess of us both, but I don't care.

"Chase!" she cries out.

"Fuck…" I fill her pussy and moan with her as I collapse on top of her.

We stay in that position for a while as we catch our breath. I pull out slowly and pack myself away. She lays sprawled on my desk, and I bend to kiss her lower back while I pull her panties and shorts back up.

She sighs and turns towards me. "Wow." She wraps her arms around my neck.

I lean down to kiss her. "Thanks for the distraction, Future Mrs. Shaw."

"Anytime, Future Husband."

I kiss her again and hold her for a few minutes before pulling away. "So, when do you want to marry me?"

"Now."

I laugh. "I'm not completely opposed. I know the wedding will be small, but no way are we doing some Justice of the Peace thing." I kiss her head. She smiles and lowers her eyes. "Tell me."

"Well, I always kind of liked the idea of a destination wedding."

"And where would you like the destination to be? Hawaii? We could do it on the beach."

"I love the beach."

"I know. That's why I suggested it."

"You know me well."

"I try." I kiss her.

"The waters in Hawaii are pristine. And I've never been there, but it's been a dream. Pearl Harbor is there."

"Pearl Harbor is a good place to marry. Anything you want, Bree. I'll give you the world if you ask me for it."

She smiles adoringly up at me. I would give her anything she wants. I hate that the one thing she absolutely wants, for this to be over, is the one thing I can't give her.

An hour after Breetana's beautiful distraction in my office, I'm standing at my gate between two guards waiting for Pierre. I know she wants to marry me, but I'm still wringing my hands together. Giving her this ring and her saying yes is all I want right now. The wait is killing me. I'm more nervous now than when I was building my company.

Finally, after what seems like another hour to me but is probably only a few minutes, I see Pierre pulling up to my gate. I breathe a sigh of relief. I start walking to his car, but one of the guards stops me. I growl.

"I apologize, Mr. Shaw, but we have to check him out. Mr. Crane's orders."

I shoot him a glare. "He's my fucking jeweler. What the fuck is he gonna do? Throw a diamond at me?"

The guard bites back his laugh. "We have our orders, sir."

"Fuck. Hurry up. I don't want Bree to see." The guards search a wide-eyed and shocked as hell Pierre and his car. I stand with my arms folded across my chest. They both step back and let him approach me when they're done. "No cleaning cloths he can smother me with?" I call to the guard.

The guard fights hard but cracks a smile. "No, sir. He's all clear."

I shake my head with a grin and hold out a hand for Pierre to shake. Pierre smiles nervously. "Goodness. You weren't kidding, were you?"

"Been a crazy ass week."

"I can definitely see that." He glances uneasily around at the numerous men patrolling my property.

I can't help but shoot him a grin. "We're all good, Pierre. No need to worry. How about them rings? I'm dying to see how my design came out."

"Of course!" Pierre pulls out two velvet boxes.

He opens one, and the smile that breaks out over my face could light up the world, I'm sure. The wedding band is made up of pink and white diamonds. The engagement ring is a single three-quarter karat diamond on a platinum band. It's exactly what I wanted.

"Wow. Fucking gorgeous. She'll love it. Turned out even better than I thought!"

"I'm glad you like them!" He hands me the box, and I close it and put it in my pocket.

"This one mine?" I nod towards the other box he's holding.

"Yes, sir. I know you were apprehensive about how this one would look, and if it would be too feminine for you, but I think it turned out well."

He's right. I'm apprehensive as fuck about this ring. Having it match Breetana's may not be possible if it looks like a woman's ring. I love my girl, though. I want to at least try. "You have the backup in case?"

"I do. But I really think you'll like this one." He opens the box.

I smile widely. "Wow. That… you're right. It turned out great." The band is platinum to match Breetana's. In the middle is a small pink ion strip that goes around the entire ring.

"We're going with this one then?"

"Yeah. Absolutely."

He hands me the box, and I put it in my other pocket. "You outdid yourself, Pierre. Quick work. Just as spectacular as the necklace I got mom for Christmas."

"That was one of my best pieces. I enjoyed making it."

I smile and hold out my hand to shake his once more. He takes it. "You have my information for payment?"

He nods. “Yes, sir. I'll process it as soon as I get back.”

We part ways. I head back into my house. Having the rings in my pocket is a great relief. The problem now is that I don't know how to ask. Or when. Or if I just give it to her. She already said she wanted to get married. Technically we’re already engaged.

I sigh as I walk in the house. Taylor is just coming out of the kitchen. “Got a sec?” I ask. There’s not getting past the hopefulness dripping from my voice. I need my brother.

“Sure. Let me just get this milk to Nikki.”

“How's she doing?”

“I don't know if she wants to rip out my hair or her own. But she’s pissed about being put on bed rest. Tana just asked if she wanted to read a book together or do a puzzle, and Nikki shot daggers. She is absolutely not doing well with this.”

“It's for her own good.”

“She doesn't see it that way. She feels like she's being held hostage. She was crying last night and wouldn't let me hold her to comfort her at all. Broke me apart.”

“She's got to be feeling pretty stressed about everything. Being pregnant and having to deal with those hormones on top of it? I'd hate that.”

“Yeah.” He lets out a breath and sighs. “I'll be right back. Probably best to get this to her before she grows a second head.” He attempts a laugh, but I can see the bags under his eyes. He's probably slept about as much as I have. Which is hardly at all. I walk into the kitchen and sit at the table. A few minutes later, Taylor sits next to me. “So? What's on your mind?”

“I got the rings.”

“Yeah? Let's see 'em. How did yours turn out?”

“Better than I thought. It actually looks pretty fucking fantastic.” I show him both sets, and he whistles.

“You definitely did good.”

“Think Bree will like them?”

“Dude. That girl would be fine with aluminum on her finger if it meant marrying you. She'll love these.”

I chuckle. “Good. The question now is how do I give her her ring? I already asked her. She already said yes. We've even decided on a destination wedding. Taking her to a nice dinner or doing some fancy proposal seems kind of ridiculous at this point."

"Honestly, Chase, Breetana doesn't seem like the type to want a big, elaborate proposal. She's a very down to Earth woman. She could care less about money, or what you could buy her, or how elaborate you could make a proposal or a wedding."

"She's never cared about money. You know when I bought her the Camaro so she didn't have to drive around in that death trap she called a car?"

"Yeah."

"She refused to accept it. When I finally convinced her to take it, she decided the only reason she would do it is if she considered it a business vehicle. And when she said she quit? She had every intention of giving it back."

"Doesn't surprise me. At all. She told me that."

I sigh and look down at her ring. "I don't want to just hand it to her. She deserves more than that. This means more than that."

"Well don't just thrust it into her hand. But, and this will sound cliché, just do what feels right."

I smile. "Pretty damn cliché."

"But damn good advice." He stands and stretches as he yawns. "I think I'm going to lay down. Attempt a nap."

"You look dead on your feet. A nap is probably a good idea."

"Yeah... I'm... just glad this isn't forever. I love Nikki. I really do. But I swear to God. I can't keep up with her. One second, she's all over me. The next she wants to kill me." Taylor pats me on the back. "Don't wait too long with that ring."

"I won't."

Taylor leaves the kitchen, and I stand. I put the ring back in my pocket.

Tonight. That's when I'll give it to her. Gives me time to think of a way to surprise her and show her how much she means to me.

Chapter Twenty Eight

⚔ Breetana ⚔

I rinse my plate off from dinner and put it into the dishwasher as my phone rings. It's been a long day, and I'm really not in the mood to talk to anyone, so I ignore it.

Nicole has been so stressed and upset, and I just don't know how to help her. I feel so bad for Taylor because he's been the one with her the most and taking the brunt of her wrath.

I walk back out into the living room and turn on the TV. I find a movie that looks good and curl up. Chase and Ryan are walking around the outside of the house, and the guards Ryan has inside, including Greg, are all in different parts of the house. I'm grateful to be alone for a few minutes.

"Hey. Mind if I join you?" Taylor's deep voice rumbles.

I jump a bit, and then sigh. So much for being alone. "Sure," I say softly. He drops heavily on the couch next to me and lets out a heavy breath. I smile. "Needed a break?"

"I just got her to sleep, actually. She hates this bed rest thing."

"I'm sorry she's taking it out on you."

"I know what I signed up for. I'm not mad at her. She's going through a lot. Being pregnant above and beyond all this other shit has got to be really hard on her."

"She's so lucky to have you. We all are. You're so sweet with her. And you take her shit in stride. You don't let it get to you."

"I wouldn't say that. Her not allowing me to comfort her. That gets to me."

"It won't be long. This will be over soon."

"Yeah. I know." Taylor glances down at my phone when it goes off again. "Are you going to answer that?"

"I hadn't intended to." I sigh again and take out my phone, glancing at the caller ID. "Oh! It's Ben." I answer it. "Hey, Ben!"

"Hey there. I tried calling a couple times, but you didn't answer."

"Yeah… I was sort of ignoring my phone."

"I get that. Hey. I was trying to get a hold of Ryan. Is he with you?"

"He's doing a perimeter check with Chase. His phone is here on the table charging."

"I see. Well, I hate to tell you this, but they're on the way. Billy, Shaun, and Joe jumped a plane to Chicago. They should be there within a couple hours. I texted Ryan the flight information."

My face falls. Damn. I really wish they had waited. "I'll tell Ryan."

"Good. Have him call me, would you? I have some information he requested."

"Sure." We say goodbye and hang up.

Taylor is looking at me concerned. "You okay?"

"They're on a plane. Ben texted the information to Ryan."

Taylor turns Ryan's phone on, then stands with it in his hand. "I'll get him."

"Thanks."

Taylor doesn't get far. Chase and Ryan walk into the room. "I just turned your phone on. Ben called Tana. They're on the way. He texted the flight information to you."

"I'll send some guys. We'll follow them," Ryan says.

I ignore them as they all start talking about a plan. I don't want to hear anymore about more guys coming for security. More motion sensors. Alarms. The cartel. I can't take any more.

I lay my head on the arm of the couch and sigh as I close my eyes. All I want is to start my life with Chase. But instead of being able to do that, I have to deal with my crazy past. The one I thought I'd left behind.

"Babe?" Chase asks as he sits next to me.

"Hmm…?"

"You're crying. You okay?" He brushes a tear away with the pad of his thumb.

"I'm just upset about so much stuff."

"Want to go upstairs and talk about it?"

"I don't want to keep harping. Same shit as usual." I shrug.

"Bree. Come on. Let's go upstairs. I don't care how many times I hear it. You need to talk about it. Get it out."

I smile and take his hand. He pulls me up and leads me upstairs. I really, really love this man. "I love your bedroom."

"Our bedroom, baby."

"Right. Ours. I still can't believe it."

"Believe what?"

I start getting undressed and ready for bed. Chase follows my lead. "That you're really finally all mine." I smile softly at him. "Do you have a t-shirt I can wear?"

"Why? You like smelling like me? And yes, babe. I am all yours."

I bite my lip. "I do love your scent all around me. Makes me feel safe."

"In that case…" He waves to his dresser with a grin. "Top drawer. Take your pick."

I laugh and find a t-shirt to put on. I've been wearing things I usually wear to bed. Panties and tank tops mostly. But I prefer Chase's t-shirts. After I get it on, I crawl into bed. Chase is fiddling with something, but quickly hides it in the drawer of his nightstand.

I raise an eyebrow. "You okay?"

"Perfect." He crawls into bed, under the covers. "Come here. Talk to me."

"You are an amazing man." I crawl on top of him.

"Mmm…," he groans. What the hell are you trying to do to me? Do you know how hard it is to listen to you when it would be so easy to slip inside you and make you shatter?"

"Maybe it's a test. See if you can listen to me and understand when all you can think about is fucking me."

"Fuck, Bree. You turn me on even more when you talk like that."

I can feel his hard cock against my thigh, and I kiss his chest. His arms wrap around me while I lay my head on his solid chest. I know he's teasing. He'd happily lay here like this with me and let me talk all night long if it's what I needed.

"I just wish Nicole didn't have to go through this. Especially being pregnant. And poor Taylor. He's so sweet for taking care of her, even though she pushes him away."

"He's tough. And he loves her. He'll get through it. As for her. Well, she's pregnant. This is hard, but it has to be harder for her right now."

"You're right. Of course." I smile against his muscles. His methodical caressing of my back and hair relaxes me. "I just can't wait to start my life with you."

"Speaking of…" He reaches into his night stand and takes out a box. I instinctively know what it is.

"Chase…"

"You know how much I love you. I'd do anything you asked."

Tears sting my eyes. "Yes."

"And I know we already talked about it. We're already engaged. But…" He pauses and opens the box.

My heart flutters. "Chase…" The light in the room reflects off the diamonds and makes them all sparkle and shine. "It's so pretty. It's the most gorgeous ring I've ever seen. And pink! You remembered my favorite color."

He smiles. "Of course I did." He takes the ring out and places it on my finger.

"It fits."

"It's sized already."

"I love it."

"It's like it was made for you," He teases as he smiles.

I giggle happily. "Knowing you, it probably was."

He laughs. "You got me. I had it designed."

"I love it, Chase. I love you."

I kiss him. I can't help thinking how perfect it is. How it was made just for me. But most importantly, no matter how crazy life is right now, I have Chase. And he has me. We're in this. Together.

For the rest of our lives.

Chapter Twenty Nine

✗ Nicole ✗

I may actually go completely insane. If I have to spend one more single solitary night in this bed, I will freak the hell out. I can't do this.

I groan and sit up as Taylor comes into the room. I frown and bite my lip, looking away from him. I'm so ashamed of how mean I have been to everyone, but especially to him. He's been my rock through all of this, and all I've done to thank him is be a bitch.

"You okay, babe?" He sits next to me but keeps his distance. I can't help but feel even worse. I wouldn't be surprised if he decided he didn't want to be with me at all after the way I've treated him

The thought makes me nearly start sobbing. I choke one back, but the tears come anyway, and I put my head in my hands. "Please don't leave me, Taylor."

"What? Baby, what are you talking about?" He immediately closes the distance between us and pulls me close to him. "I'm not going anywhere. Why would you think I'd leave you?"

"I know I've been so mean to you and difficult."

"Nicole. Come on. You're pregnant. You're stressed the fuck out with everything going on." He gently rubs my back and kisses me on top of the head. "I'm not going anywhere. I already told you I'm sticking with you. You're mine, Nicole. I love you."

"You... still want me even after I was such a bitch to you? You still want to be all mine?"

"I don't want anyone else. I don't want to be anyone else's. I know when I have something good. Something real, and something worth it. I'm not letting this go. I'm not letting you go." He continues holding me while I cling to his shirt.

"I really don't deserve you."

"You are definitely wrong about that. You deserve the entire fucking world." He kisses my neck as his phone goes off. I kiss his shoulder as he pulls back. He looks at the caller ID and then shoots me an apologetic look. "I have to take this. It's one of the guys on the taskforce I lead."

"It's okay. I understand." I smile, and he leans in to give me a quick kiss on my lips before he answers.

"Hey, Zeke." He leans down to kiss me again before he leaves the room. I take a deep, incredibly relieved breath. He still loves me. Thank God he still loves me.

I slowly stand and take a few shaky steps. I'm relieved there is no pain. The pain has been dissipating over the past few days, and I finally got Doctor Chantau to agree to let me go for short walks.

I smile as I open the door and step out into the hall. The sun room in the back of the house has quickly become my favorite room. Chase has a pool in the back, and his house overlooks the lake. I haven't seen Taylor's house yet, but I really, really hope that he has a sun room like this.

I round the corner to the sun room but stop quickly when I see Greg. He's pacing nervously and talking on the phone. His eyes keep darting around, and I quickly duck back behind the wall before he sees me.

"I told you, my boss is fucking good. He has eyes all over this place." He pauses. "That's not what I signed up for. You guys need to find your own way in," he hisses. I cover my mouth with my hands. "Fine. Give me a bit. I'll call you back."

I hurry down the hall in search of Ryan, hoping Greg doesn't see me. I don't know what I just heard, but I don't think it's good. Not what he signed up for? Their own way in? His boss is good? What the fuck is happening?

I see Ryan leaning on the kitchen counter. He's looking intensely at his phone, and his expression is haunted. I don't know if I should approach him or not. I sniffle and take a deep breath, daring to look over my shoulder. Greg is nowhere to be seen.

"You okay?" Ryan asks. I jump and look up at him. He has an eyebrow raised and is looking at me, confused.

"I…" I look back over my shoulder. "I don't want to bother you. You seem like you need to deal with something."

"It's…" He trails off and sighs, looking down at his phone again. "It's a girl I've become fucking infatuated with. But she's off-limits, and I'm trying hard to fight my damn feelings off. Despite my feelings, though, I vowed to protect this girl and keep her safe. She's having a hard time right now, and I'm not there."

I look down, guilty. "I'm sorry."

"Hey, Nikki. No. You have nothing to apologize for. She's not in danger. She just needs someone to talk to. She's fine with me texting and being on the phone with her. I just…" He closes his eyes a moment before opening them and looking up at the ceiling. "I want to be there with her." He looks back down at me. "You know? Be more of a comfort than just a voice or words on a phone."

I smile softly. "I get it. It's hard being away from someone you care so deeply about."

"Yeah…" He looks down at his phone one last time before looking back up at me as he takes a deep breath. "Anyway. What's up?"

"Can we talk somewhere alone?"

"Uh… sure." He glances around. "Looks like we're alone."

"I mean not out here. Somewhere private."

"Nikki, what's going on?"

I bite my lip and plead with him. "Please, Ryan? Not out here." I'm whispering and glancing around nervously. Ryan nods and takes my arm. We walk into Chase's office, and he closes the door. I walk to the far end of his office as far away from the door as I can.

Ryan watches me, but follows. "Nikki?"

I take a deep breath. "I... don't really know if what I heard means anything. But I think it does, and it scares me."

"Okay. Nicole, talk to me."

I pause a moment before deciding to plunge ahead. "I heard Greg… He was on the phone with someone. At first, he said something about his boss. I assume he meant you. He said his boss is really good and has the whole area covered. And then he said that isn't what he signed up for. I don't know what. And he ended the call saying to give him a bit, and he'd call back."

Ryan looks at me. I look down at the ground and wring my hands together. I wouldn't blame him for not believing me. It's not like I have a good track record of people believing me. Even though what I say is true.

"Nikki. Look at me."

I do, but can't quite meet his eyes. He steps forward and raises my chin the rest of the way, forcing me to fully look at him. "I'm... I'm sorry."

"You don't need to be. I know what you're thinking right now."

"You... do?" I swallow.

He nods. "What I don't get is why you automatically think people will think the worst of you. Why you think I wouldn't believe you." He lets go of my chin and smiles. "I want you to trust me, Nikki. If you feel like something's up, I want to know about it. And you need to feel like you can trust me enough to come to me."

I don't hesitate. I hug him. A huge weight is lifted off my shoulders instantly. He wraps his arms around me. "I'm so happy you believe me. I'm not used to people believing me."

"I know what you went through. But you have to understand something right now. Me, Taylor, Breetana, and Chase. We aren't like the assholes you were around in Silver Bay. Okay?"

I nod into his chest. "Okay."

"I mean this when I say it. You may have been alone up there, but not anymore. Taylor really is like a brother to me. I hope that you'll trust me enough to start thinking of me like family to you, too."

"My family is a little messed up. Except Tana."

"What you had wasn't a family. This, what you have in me and the others, this is what family is, Nikki. We trust. We love. We laugh. We fight and make up." He squeezes me a little bit before pulling away. "I told Breetana to trust her instincts. I'm telling you the same thing. Okay? I'll check into this thing with Greg. I'm already keeping a close eye on him anyway because of everything in Silver Bay.

"Thank you."

He leans down to kiss me on the cheek. “Anytime. Now. Forget about all of this. Why don't you drag Taylor out to the pool?”

“Oh. Um… what about the dangers of… you know.”

“I have more guys out there than I care to tell you, sweetheart. Taylor has constant patrol around here. You're safe.”

“O-okay.” I give him a hesitant smile as we leave the office. I search for Taylor and find him grabbing a beer from the refrigerator in the kitchen. I slip my arms around his waist from behind resting my forearm on the gun on his hip and my head on his back. I never thought I'd say it, but I’m getting used to his gun. It's become a source of comfort to me.

“There you are. I was wondering where you went.” He places his arms over mine and hugs me close.

“I love you.”

“I love you.” He takes my hands, raises them to his lips, and grazes his lips across my knuckles before he turns to face me, the beer he was reaching for long forgotten.

I smile up at him. “I don't want to ruin the moment, but... I was walking to the sun room when I saw Greg,” I whisper.

He visibly stiffens. “Oh?”

“I heard him talking to someone on the phone. It sounded like he was planning on how to help them get past all of the guards. I told Ryan.”

He hugs me tightly. “Good girl. What did he say?” he whispers in my ear. I know his eyes are scanning for anyone listening.

“That he'll take care of it.”

Taylor relaxes in my arms. “Good. He will. He doesn't take betrayal lightly.”

“He believed me. No questions. I'm not used to that. No one but Tana has just believed me before. Well. And now you and Chase.”

“Of course he believes you, baby. He's not like the fucktards you had to deal with. None of us are. It's going to be different now.”

“I know. I just need to get used to it.”

Taylor pulls away and leans down to kiss me. “The three of us are loyal to a fault, Nikki. Chase and Ryan are a lot alike. It's why they hit it off so fast. Between the three of us, you and Breetana are going to learn what it's like to be treated the way a woman should be treated. You're going to learn what it feels like to have a family, baby. A real one.”

"Our parents were like that. Loyal. Protective. Loving. Sometimes, I wish they were still around. But, like Tana says, everything happens for a reason. I wouldn't have met you otherwise."

"Well, I don't like the circumstances, but I can't say I'm unhappy about having met you."

His heart-warming smile makes me melt. I wrap my arms around his neck and stand on my tippy toes to kiss him. I still can't reach him and he stands tall, teasing me. "Taylor!"

"What?" He grins.

"Let me kiss you."

"What's stopping you?" he teases.

"Your height! You tower over me!" I squeak with a giggle. I love when he teases me. He laughs and leans down just enough so I can reach his lips, but I still have to be on my tippy toes. "Mmm... So much better."

"You know, I don't mean to sound like a petulant child, but you haven't let me touch you in four days. Since we got here."

I wince slightly. "I've been really mean, huh?"

"You've been stressed, babe. Huge difference. You've also been in pain. You know I'm kidding around." He grins. "But if you want to make it up to me…" He bites his lip and looks down at my pussy.

I laugh. "Intriguing offer from an incredibly skilled man…"

He smirks cockily. "With incredibly skilled fingers, and a talented tongue." His eyes meet mine once more.

"Take me to bed, officer," I say in my best sultry voice.

"That's Lieutenant to you." He grins playfully at me and points to the badge attached to his belt. "See? Chicago P.D. gave me a shiny badge and everything."

I laugh and squeal as he picks me up and carries me to bed. I know he understands the reason I didn't let him touch me was because of the pain and fear of the pain. I can't help but be excited at the prospects he promised, but I really love that he is so respectful and waited for me to be okay again before he even tried.

He's so perfect, and for a little while, he makes me completely forget about the dangers that lurk outside these walls.

Chapter Thirty

⚔ Breetana ⚔

I wake up in the middle of the night feeling like my mouth has a cactus growing inside it. It's so dry that I feel like I may throw up.

I gently remove Chase's arm from around my waist and wait for a second before I silently slide out of the bed. I know he hasn't been sleeping well, and I don't want to wake him up. He continues softly snoring. I head to the master bathroom and down some water.

"So much better," I whisper to myself.

"You okay, babe?" Chase asks groggily from the door.

I jump slightly. "I needed some water. I didn't mean to wake you."

"It's okay. Come back to bed." He holds out his hand. I take it, and he leads me back to the bed. We both crawl in, and he wraps his arms around me. "I had a pretty bad dream. Woke up, and you weren't here."

"Aww... I'm sorry, my love." I hug him close and run my fingers through his hair. "What was the dream?"

"I don't want to talk about it. It's never happening, so it's not worth repeating."

"If you're sure."

"I am."

"If you need to talk, though."

"I know, baby." His grip on me tightens. "Will you do something for me, though?"

"Anything, baby."

"If you have to get up in the middle of the night, wake me up?"

"This dream really scared you, didn't it?"

"Please, Breetana." Chase rarely ever uses my full name. He usually calls me Bree, so I know he's serious.

"I promise."

Chase pushes me onto my back and lays his head on my stomach. He wraps his arm around my hips. "I'll apologize ahead of time for this. I'm not going to leave you alone. Not until this is over. I'm sorry that I'll come off as a possessive fucker."

"Babe. Don't. I understand. I'm just as stressed as you."

"I can't wait until this is over."

"Where is this coming from?"

Chase sighs as I run my fingers through his hair. "What Nikki said today. About what she heard. It just... confirmed our suspicion."

"It's kind of scary. But I know I have you. And Taylor and Ryan. Sure, I'm scared, but I know you'll protect me."

"I love you. I love you so damn much, Breetana. If anything happened -"

"No. No, Chase." I sit up and force him to look at me. "You and I have been through too much for it to end like this. It took us three years to get to this point."

"Bree -"

"Chase. Listen to me. We're going to be fine. We're going to get through this. Our love is going to get us through this."

He smiles at me. "Bree. My Bree. Always so confident."

"Not always. There have been times when you've had to keep me going. And now it's my turn."

"I love you."

"I love you, too."

He kisses me and pulls me down on top of him. His arms wrap around me, and I wrap mine around him. "I can't wait to see you in your mom's dress standing on that beach as you look up at me and say 'I do'."

"I can't wait to become Mrs. Chase Shaw."

"Who's going to be there?"

I smile, sensing he needs the distraction. "Taylor and Nikki. Ryan. Reese. Your mother. And I hope you aren't upset, but I invited Ben and his wife."

"Not upset at all. We could do a nice dinner afterwards. All of us. To celebrate, if you want."

"Do you want to pick a location out together? I mean, I know Pearl Harbor, but where?"

"Maybe later. Right now, I just want you close to me."

"I'm not going anywhere, Chase."

"Damn right you aren't." He tightens his grip on me.

I kiss his chin. "Chase." It's a quiet command. I feel like he needs to talk.

He smiles, but I know it's forced. "Ryan said not to ignore instincts. Well, my instincts are telling me that this is going to get really bad very soon."

"But we'll get through it. We can get through anything."

"Remember when Taylor said he was training me how to protect myself because I refuse to hire security?"

I chuckle softly. "Yes."

"I never hired security because I'd never been threatened. No one I loved had ever been threatened. I felt like I was unreachable. Untouchable." He runs his hands absently up and down my back. "I should've listened to Taylor."

I look up at him and furrow my eyebrows. "Are you... blaming yourself for this?"

"I feel like I can't protect you, Bree."

"How can you possibly feel like that? Chase. You spend seven days a week in the gym. You go every Sunday to the range with Taylor to shoot. You know how to fight. You train. I feel safer with you than I've ever felt with anyone."

"I would do anything for you."

"I know."

"No matter what it is."

I reach up to touch his cheek. "I know, my heart."

I understand what he's getting at. I know he's trying to say he'll give up his life if it means saving mine. It won't come to that. I won't let it. Losing Chase isn't an option. Not when we finally got together.

He's like the missing piece to every part of me that was broken. Everything about him just fits with me. Chase makes me better. He fulfills me.

I won't let *anyone* take him from me.

Chapter Thirty One

⚔ Chase ⚔

I've spent the day hovering unnecessarily close to Breetana, and I've noticed Taylor is just as on edge. He hasn't left Nicole's side.

Surprisingly, neither of our girls are upset in the slightest. Both of them have taken it in stride and haven't questioned us.

To my surprise, even Ryan seems on edge. I haven't seen him less than vigilant since I met him, but he seems to jump at every noise. He investigates everything on his own.

"Babe?" Breetana asks softly.

"Yeah?"

Breetana is just coming out of the bathroom in our bedroom after taking a shower. "I asked if you were okay. You didn't answer."

"Oh. Sorry. I'm fine." I'm sitting on the edge of the bed. Breetana kneels in front of me and pushes my legs apart so she can sit between them. She wraps her arms around my waist, and I smile as I wrap my arms around her and kiss her on the head.

"I know you better than that."

Fuck. She really does. I should know better than to try and keep anything from her. I've never been able to. She can fish information out of me better than even Taylor can.

"I'm just on edge, sweet girl. The longer this goes on, the worse it gets. I love you. I don't want this to be happening. You don't deserve this, Bree. You or Nikki. You both deserve so much better."

"I know. But it is happening. We have to get through it."

"Just promise me you'll fight, Bree. No matter what. That you'll fight."

"I promise. As long as you promise, too."

"I promise."

She sighs. "What was the dream?"

"Don't worry about it." I won't tell her. She doesn't need to be worried. I won't tell her she died in the dream. I won't tell her that I wasn't there.

That's the reason I haven't left her side today. Because in my incredibly vivid dream, she was killed right in front of me. They got to her because I wasn't there.

Breetana shifts and runs her hand along the front of my jeans. I groan and smile down at her. This is Breetana getting me out of my head in a way only she can. "Looking for something?"

"I am. Usually your jeans house something I crave."

"Is that so?" I chuckle and lean back a little.

She smiles up at me as she slowly runs her hand over my hardening length. "Found it!" she says victoriously.

"I don't think it was hiding very well," I tease.

"I don't think it's possible for you to hide it. You're far too big."

I laugh. "You're not wrong," I say with an arrogant wink.

She shakes her head and bites her lip to hide her smile. "So modest."

"One of my best qualities." I grin.

She laughs as she unbuttons my jeans. Carefully holding my cock down, she unzips them. I lift my hips. She pulls them and my boxer briefs down. I kick out of them. She shoves them aside and takes my cock in both hands. She begins stroking as she looks up at me through her lashes. So fucking beautiful. Just the feel of her hands against my skin sends all of the blood in my body straight to my cock, making me forget about everything but her. But it's those eyes of hers that always do me in. Big. Doe like. Sexy as hell.

"Why, Mr. Shaw. I believe you might be happy to see me." She gives me a devilish smirk.

"You have no idea." I hold her hair back as she smiles and takes me in her mouth. "God, baby." Her mouth is warm and wet. She takes as much of me as she can until I hit the back of her throat. She knows exactly how I like it.

"Mmm... You taste so good." She flicks her tongue across my tip as she looks up at me again.

"Keep talking like that, and you'll get all of me in your mouth."

"Mmm… my favorite snack."

"Fuck, Bree. Watch your… oh… Holy shit," I gasp. She deepthroats me, moaning and sending vibrations through my entire length. I lean back on my elbows and throw my head back.

"Watch my what?" She strokes from my base to my tip, and then takes me in her mouth again until I, once again, touch the back of her throat.

"Fuck... Oh fuck, baby…" I groan, nearly forgetting my name, but then I grin. "Your mouth. It's gonna get you in so much trouble, baby."

She hums against my cock, and I jerk at the sensation. "Challenge accepted." Her strokes become more insistent and slightly harder as her tongue swirls around my tip. She lightly grazes just underneath it with her teeth, and I nearly come undone.

But not yet. She feels way too fucking good.

My stomach clenches as my back tenses. "Fuck, baby. Where the hell did you learn that?"

"I didn't. I'm just figuring out what you like." She lightly scrapes her teeth along the vein running up my cock, and then runs her tongue down it.

"Goddamn…," I breathe as I tangle my fingers in her hair. My cock throbs under her touch, and before I can say anything, she takes me in her mouth again. Without warning, I shoot my load down her throat, and she swallows, sucking me dry. "Fuck. Fuck, Bree." I lay all the way back and take a couple deep breaths.

Breetana stands up and removes her towel. She climbs into the bed, sits on her knees, and waits for me. I laugh as I sit up and throw my t-shirt off. I crawl into the bed, stalking her.

"You're so sexy when you're crawling across the bed to me." She tries to be pouty, but it just makes her look adorable.

I laugh and grab her around the waist, pulling her on top of me. She sits up, giggling. and rubs herself against me. I'm almost instantly hard again. She guides me to her, and then drops, plunging me deep inside her warm, wet walls.

She closes her eyes and bites her lip. "Wow…"

I smile as I look up at her. "You like that?"

"God, you feel so good. So hard. So big." She opens her eyes and looks shyly at me. I smirk at her and put my arms behind my head. She raises an eyebrow. "What are you doing?"

I shrug. "Ride me."

Her eyes widen even more adorably. "Oh God…" She gently puts her hands on my abs and starts moving against me. I bite my lip, watching her. Her pussy is so wet. "I don't... know…" She moves awkwardly, nibbling her lip.

I grin and grab her hips. I lift her up and let her drop, plunging myself deep inside her once again. "Just like that." I keep my hands on her hips to help guide her. She has no idea how much I want this.

She smiles shyly and mimics what I just did. "Mmm... yes…" She continues lifting herself up and dropping herself as I grip her ass and rock her over my cock. "Oh, Chase!" She gets wetter and wetter until she's dripping down my cock.

I love it.

I love all of her. The faster she rides me, the more her tits bounce. My dick gets impossibly harder and thickens inside her. I love watching my girl lose control and give into nothing more than what feels good. She twists her hips. Her hands roam her body until they're tangled in her hair.

And still, she doesn't stop.

"Fuck, baby girl." I squeeze her ass and thrust into her pussy. She pulses and clenches around me with each and every thrust she meets.

"Oh… Chase, I -" She doesn't even complete the sentence before she shatters.

“Shit, baby.” I watch as she soaks my cock. Her pussy spasms around my throbbing dick. Her hips jerk against mine erratically. I hold her in place while my load explodes from me into her. “Fuck, Bree!”

I shoot jet after jet of hot come inside her pussy, filling her until it’s dripping out of her and down my cock. I slam into her again and again as we both lose control. Breetana collapses on me, moaning and whimpering as we both pant.

I kiss her deeply. I haven't pulled out of her yet, and after a few moments, my sweet kiss has turned hot. Our tongues twine with each other, and our hands are all over each other's bodies. I start getting hard once more.

“Mmm... Chase…”

I grip her hips and flip her so that I'm on top. She wraps her legs around my waist and takes my face in her hands. She licks her lips, and it’s all it takes for my mouth to crash into hers as I start pounding her pussy again.

XXX

Hours later after both making love to Breetana and fucking her several times, I wake to a light knocking at the door. Breetana is wrapped around me, exhausted and passed out from our early exertions. I kiss her lightly on the forehead before untangling myself from her body and slowly getting out of the bed. She doesn't stir. I grab my jeans and slip them on, buttoning them as I walk to the door. I quietly open it to see Ryan standing on the other side.

“Grab your gun.” He whispers it, but I hear the urgency, so I rush to grab the gun on the nightstand and hurry back to him. “You got a lock on this door?”

“Yeah.” I don't question him. I've come to trust him as much as Taylor. I lock the door and follow Ryan to Taylor and Nikki's room. He softly knocks.

Taylor answers, sleepily. “What?”

“Lock her in here. Get your gun.”

Taylor doesn't question him. We both follow him to the kitchen. “What the fuck?” Taylor asks when we get there.

“One of my guys just called me. Said Greg was outside but couldn't see what he was doing.”

“You think he's making a move?” I ask.

“Yep,” Ryan confirms. “We’ve been watching him. I want him taken down at the same time everyone else is.”

At that moment, Rico walks silently into the kitchen. “I have Pete by the front door. Miguel is in the back.”

“Good.” Ryan turns to me and Chase. “Rico is my second in command. Hasn't been with me long, but he's trustworthy. I promoted him after we found out about Greg's betrayal.” Ryan rubs his eyes. Taylor and I both nod. “Rico, go with Taylor. Do what he says. To you, he's another me.”

“Sure thing, boss.”

“I want you two with Nikki,” Ryan continues. “I think Greg’s making his move, and I have pretty reliable intel that he's working with Joe, Billy, and Shaun.” Ryan looks at me. My heart sinks. I share a look with Taylor. He puts a hand on my shoulder and leads Rico out of the kitchen. I look at Ryan. Reading me, he says, “She'll be okay. I'll be with you every step of the way.”

I take a deep breath and nod. “Let's do this.” We head out of the kitchen and towards the stairs. I catch a glimpse of something towards Taylor's and Nicole's room but figure it's Taylor and Rico. Not paying attention, I run directly into Ryan's back. “What the hell, bro?” I say in nothing more than a whisper.

“Shh!” Ryan points at the ground, and I see Pete facedown. Ryan crouches, and I immediately raise my weapon to cover him. “He's alive.”

Just then, we hear gunshots.

My heart kicks into overdrive and jumps into my throat. “Shit! Taylor!” I start running towards where I saw the movement, but Ryan grabs me.

“We're okay! Get Breetana!” Taylor yells.

Ryan runs up the stairs, and I'm close on his heels. Halfway up, we hear a door being kicked open. Breetana screams.

“Bree!” I practically shove Ryan out of my way as I run by him. “Bree!”

She screams again. “Chase! Help!”

I don't think it's possible for my heart to beat faster, but it does. "Hold on, baby! Almost there!" Images of my dream come back to me. Of my beautiful girl bleeding out in my arms. By the time I reach the room, Ryan right at my side, I can hardly breathe through the panic. "No! Let her fucking go!"

My gun is aimed at the head of whoever is holding my princess. The gun to her head is the only thing stopping me from taking him out.

Behind me, Ryan shoots, and a guy drops to my feet. I look down for less than a second, slightly startled.

Suddenly, pain shoots through my stomach.

"Chase! No! Chase!" Breetana screams.

"Chase! Fuck!" Ryan yells.

Another shot rings out.

I watch Breetana sink to the ground as everything goes black.

Chapter Thirty Two

⚔ Breetana ⚔

"Chase!" I scream. "Chase!" I fall to the ground. Shaun falls on top of me. He's so much bigger than me. Heavier. It's like trying to move a ton of bricks. "Chase!" I sound like a wild animal, but I can't help it. I just watched Shaun shoot Chase and Chase fall to the ground. "Chase!" I can't get Shaun off. I'm flailing and pushing as hard as I can. Tears are streaming down my face. "Help! Help me! Chase!"

Chase is being surrounded by people, and I can't see him anymore. I'm screaming and yelling. I'm kicking and flailing as I cry. This has to be a nightmare. It can't be happening. It can't be.

With all of my strength, I shove Shaun off me.

"Chase!" My voice doesn't even sound like my own anymore. It's high pitched. Everything that comes out of my mouth is a scream. "Chase!" I scramble to my hands and knees after getting Shaun off me. I stand and run towards Chase, but I crash into Ryan. "Chase!" I fight against Ryan's stone body. "Let me go! Chase! Chase!" He's too big. Too strong.

But I don't give up. I won't. I scream and fight him as hard as I can trying to get to Chase.

"Breetana! Let the doctor work!" Ryan commands as he holds me tightly to his hard body.

I struggle against him. I fight to get free. "Let go! Let me go!"

"Breetana, let him work!"

I can hear myself screaming as Ryan keeps his arms tightly around me, pinning my arms to my side. He doesn't give me an inch to struggle. "Let me go!"

"Not a chance in hell. You have to let the doctor work," he whispers in my ear. Soothingly. He sways with me gently. "Shh…, Tana. Shh…, sweetheart."

"We have to get him to a hospital. Immediately," Doctor Chantau says as he looks up.

"The bullet went through," Taylor says.

"What? Chase! Chase!" I try to get away again. I can't breathe. My chest is collapsing. Am I even crying anymore? I can't feel anything but my heart being squeezed in my chest.

"Breetana! Stop it!" Ryan says dominantly enough to cut through some of the panic. But it's not enough. "It means the bullet isn't in him," Ryan says.

"What did it go through, then?" I shriek. "Ryan! Let me go!" I try to push off him. "Chase!"

"Breetana, listen to me!" He lets me go, but keeps a hold of my arms. I try to break free to get to Chase, but Ryan is too strong. "Focus! We need to get him to a hospital. How do we get to his helicopter?" He forces me to look at him. "Tell me how. How do we get the helicopter? We're too far out of town for him to be driven. Come on, honey. He needs you." Ryan's brown eyes are filled with strength. I take a deep breath as he makes me look into them. "Come on, honey. Focus."

"It's on the r-roof." I hiccup over the sobs.

"I know." Ryan says calmly. "Tell me how to get up there."

I need calm. He's calm. Calm. I gulp in air. "He… I don't…" I shake my head. Focus. Focus. I can do that. Chase needs me to.

"Focus, honey. I can fly it. Can you get me up there? How do we get up there, Breetana?"

I focus on Ryan. "You'll get him there?" I whisper.

He nods. "I'll get him there, sweetheart. Just get me to the controls. Get me to the helicopter."

I sniffle and nod. Hospital. Chase needs the hospital. "Th-there's a room. At the end of the hall. I th-think the stairs to the r-roof are there." I start shivering uncontrollably. Or maybe I already was.

"She's going into shock, Ry," Taylor rumbles. I keep focusing on Ryan. I have to.

"I'll take care of her, Taylor." He doesn't take his eyes off mine. "Let's get him up there, okay? Can you help me get him to the helicopter?"

I nod. "Y-yes."

"Good girl. There's the warrior I know." Ryan takes my hand and leads me out of the room, keeping Chase from my view. The shivers are violent now. But I keep my mind on the task. The helicopter. "Focus on getting me up there, Breetana. Okay? We have to get him to the hospital. You need to help me."

"We… yeah. We. Together." I stumble, and Ryan pulls me to his side.

"Get me to the helicopter, Breetana. Come on. I need you. So does he."

I shake the haziness away and take more deep breaths as Ryan opens the door. "I've never been up h-here."

"It's okay. We'll do it together." We both climb the stairs and get to the door.

It's locked.

"Oh God! No!" I cry out.

"Hold it together sweetheart. It's okay. It's just a deadbolt." Ryan unlocks the deadbolt I'm too panicked to see and pulls me out onto the roof. "You're doing great. Just focus. You need to help me get him there. That's your task."

"I'm focusing on you," I tell him. "If I don't, I'll pass out."

"Then focus on me if that's what you need. Just hold it together for me." He leads me to the helicopter and helps me in.

"You can really fly this thing?" I ask, unsure but hopeful.

"Benefit of coming from a really rich family. Jason, Nick, and I all had lessons." He finishes strapping me in as Taylor and the doctor load Chase into the helicopter.

"I'll take Nikki and Rico. We'll meet you there," Taylor says to Ryan.

"How's Pete?" Ryan asks.

"Fine. Your other guys are calling a clean-up crew."

"Stay away from that part of it, Taylor. I'm serious. Let me handle it. I don't want any blow-back on you." Ryan jumps behind the controls. Taylor says nothing. "I mean it, Taylor!"

"Just save my brother!" Taylor yells as he heads back into the house.

Ryan closes the door and starts up the helicopter. "How's he doing, doc?"

"He's stable, but we need to hurry."

Moments later, Ryan has the helicopter lifting off the ground, and my stomach lurches. I grab Ryan's arm and squeeze my eyes closed.

"Stay with me, Breetana. You're safe. I promise."

"The hospital. We need to call them." My eyes are still closed, and I'm still squeezing his arm.

"Taylor is doing that, sweetheart. It's taken care of. They'll be waiting," Doctor Chantau informs us.

"Where am I landing, Doc?" Ryan asks.

"Taylor is texting me that information when he gets it. I'll let you know. How far out?"

"Seven minutes," Ryan says. I open my eyes and take several deep breaths as I let go of Ryan's arm. He takes my hand. "Trust me, sweetheart. I won't let him -"

"Don't. Please don't say it." I shake my head. He squeezes my hand. I squeeze his back and don't let go. We fly in silence for a few minutes, Ryan never letting go of my hand. Finally, I look over at him. "How did you know Chase has a helicopter?"

"He told me. When we were walking his property."

"Oh. I didn't know," I whisper. "That he had one. I've never seen it."

He squeezes my hand. "You can't see it unless you're near the edge of the property. It's not visible unless you're at the back of the house. But he told me." He smiles. I smile softly back.

"Got the text," Doctor Chantau says, relieved. "They have a spot in the parking lot they closed off for some work starting tomorrow. They'll have a couple doctors out there with lights to help you land. They said the chopper will be safe to leave there."

"Thanks, Doc," Ryan says. "Coming up to the hospital now." Sure enough, I can see someone with a red light of some sort as Ryan nears the lot. "We're kind of close to the parking ramp. This is going to be a little rough, sweetheart. I need both hands. You can take my arm if you need to."

Ryan nears the hospital and starts descending. The helicopter seems to jump in the air, and I can't stop the small scream that escapes. "Oh, God!" I grab Ryan's arm and squeeze my eyes closed again.

"Almost there, honey," he says.

The helicopter seems to be fighting wind of its own making, and I bite the inside of my cheek to stop myself from screaming again. Ryan seems to be in complete control. I take as much comfort from that as I can. Finally, I feel it touch the ground. Ryan moves quickly to shut everything down.

Doctor Chantau opens the door to meet the other doctors. "Bullet went through. Seems to have missed all organs. We need to get him to an OR. Make sure everything vital was missed and there are no fragments."

I gasp at the idea parts of the bullet could be inside him. Ryan helps me out of the helicopter, and we hurry after the doctors.

"Doctor Chantau, are you staying with him?" I ask nervously.

"I won't leave his side, Breetana."

"Thank you. Thank God for you." I watch them take Chase away and collapse against Ryan.

"It's okay. Let's get him checked in, okay?"

I nod. I can't do anything else. Anything I can do to keep my mind off what's happening to him right now. Anything I can do to help in whatever way I can. I know I need to call his CFO, who is acting CEO right now. Chase won't be back for a while. He'll be healing.

Healing from my horrendous past.

Just as we are finishing the paperwork, Doctor Chantau comes out.

"Is he okay?" I ask. I'm exhausted. I'm not even sure the words came out of my mouth or if they're in my head and I just thought I said them.

"He'll be just fine, sweetie. I have him being moved upstairs to a room for observation now," Doctor Chantau says.

"Private?" Ryan asks.

“Of course.” Doctor Chantau begins leading us to Chase when commotion near the emergency room entrance makes us stop.

“She went into labor!” Taylor is carrying Nicole in his arms. She screams.

“Oh my God!” My knees buckle. Ryan catches me. Nicole screams again as doctors rush to her.

Doctor Chantau forces his way through the crowd. “Back up. Back up! I'm this woman's personal doctor!” Ryan pulls me back to him as Nicole, Taylor, and Doctor Chantau are rushed off. “Room 9865! It's on the VIP floor. You're both on his list!”

Ryan takes my hand and leads me to the elevators. As soon as we’re inside and the doors close, I burst into tears. Ryan hugs me. “Hey. Hey, he's okay, honey. They both are.”

“Thank you. Thank you for being here. For getting him here. For treating us like family. We'd all be dead if not for you.”

“You're a fighter, Breetana.”

I shake my head. “I'd be dead if not for you. Shaun shot him. In cold blood.”

“And I shot Shaun. But I wouldn't have been able to do that if you hadn't punched him.”

I look up at him. “What? I didn't -”

“Oh, you did. As soon as he shot Chase, you punched him as hard as I think *I've* ever punched anyone. He stumbled and dropped his gun. I shot. He fell on top of you, but I needed to keep Chase alive until the doctor could get to him, so I left you there. You fought him off before I could get to you. It was probably less than a minute, but you fought like a fucking bear, sweetheart.”

“I was just thinking of getting to Chase.”

The elevator doors open and Ryan leads me out, keeping his arm firmly around my waist. Security sits behind a desk.

“Can I help you?” the security officer asks.

“We were sent up here for Chase Shaw,” Ryan says.

“And you are?”

“This is Breetana Carter. His fiancé,” Ryan says.

He checks his list and nods. “I have you here. And you, sir?”

“Uh... Ryan. Crane. His…” He hesitates. He needs a relationship in order to get in. I can see that from the list. The guard looks at him expectantly.

I clear my throat, slightly touched at Ryan’s hesitation. “Chase's security and brother.”

He looks down at his list once more. “Ah. Yes. I have you, as well. Let me get you badges.” The security guard gets us our badges and lets us in. “Mr. Shaw is in room 9865. The nurses will show you the way.”

Ryan clears his throat. “Thank you. For that. I don’t know why I couldn’t get that out.”

“You keep saying we’re family to you.” I hug his arm.

“I do.” He smiles and falls silent, but I know he’s thinking about the impact of those words. Considering someone family is one thing. Having them consider the same thing is something else entirely. I should know.

As soon as we get inside Chase's room, I rush to his side. I take his hand in mine and bring it to my lips. “I love you. I love you, Chase. Please, please don't leave me.” I kiss his hand. He squeezes mine, and I almost squeak. “Chase?” I look at him.

A small smile lifts his lips. “You aren't… mmm… getting rid of me that easily.” Chase shifts. Ryan helps him.

“You want the bed up a little?” Ryan asks.

“Please,” Chase says with a wince.

Ryan moves the head of the bed up and helps Chase shift so he's more comfortable. I climb into the bed with him. I don't care if a doctor yells at me. I'm not leaving his side.

“I'm okay, baby. I promise. The bullet didn't hit any organs. It went right though. Mostly my side. I passed out from the shock over the blood loss. It doesn’t really hurt much. Just when I move.”

“I'm never leaving your side again. Ever. I'm so sorry.”

“Bree. Don't. I'm more worried about you. I…” He swallows and puts his arm around me. “I saw you go down covered in blood.”

“Shaun's blood,” I sniffle. “Ryan killed him.”

“Wouldn't have been able to if your girl didn't punch him.”

Chase smiles and gives me a weak squeeze. “You punched him?”

“Ryan says I did. I don't remember. All I was thinking about was getting to you.”

Chase rubs my arm a moment. “I shouldn't have left you. I had a bad feeling all day.”

“That isn't on you. Greg wasn't the only one involved. The guy who called me was a distraction. I thought we had time to set up. I didn't know Greg was already in the house.”

“So you had two people who were working for Shaun?”

“They've both been dealt with. Taylor shot Greg. Rico shot Billy and my other leak.”

“What about…” Tears sting my eyes. Chase holds me close to his side. I can't say his name.

“He's gone, honey. He tried a sneak attack. I shot him before he had a chance to do any harm,” Ryan says.

I bury my face in Chase's shoulder. “Thank God. Thank you, Ryan. For everything.”

“We wouldn't be here without you.” Chase says as he looks at Ryan.

He bends down and kisses the top of my head. “I'm going to check on Taylor and Nicole. See if I can get some information for you.”

“What happened with Taylor and Nikki?” Chase asks. I can feel him tense.

“Nikki went into labor. Taylor's okay. Doctor Chantau is in delivery with them.” I smile softly, and Chase breathes a sigh of relief.

“I'll be back.” Ryan leaves, and I lean my head back on Chase's shoulder once more.

“I fought. Just like you said. I kicked him. Joe... hit me and grabbed me. I bit him. I didn’t know where he went after. Shaun had me after him, and I fought.”

“Bree. I'm so sorry I wasn't there, honey.”

“But you were. All I could think about was you. You got me through it. Your voice telling me to fight.”

“I'm never leaving you alone again, Bree. Never. I'm installing key card access to our floor. I'm tearing down the walls of my office. No one is getting up to our floor without an escort. I don't want you out of my sight.”

“Chase... You don't have to do that. I'm going to be okay. We're… we’re going to be okay.”

“It's not optional. I'm doing it. I already called the contractors. Reese is supervising the changes.”

I kiss his chest. “I love you.”

“I love you, too, baby. And you’re right. We’re going to be okay.”

We hold each other as tightly as we dare, unwilling to let each other go. For the first time in years, I actually believe the words that I said.

I’m going to be okay.

We.

We’re *all* going to be okay.

Chapter Thirty Three

✗ Taylor ✗

"You did such a good job, baby. You're so fucking strong." Nicole is holding my hand trying to catch her breath as I am stroking her hair back from her sweat slicked face.

"I don't hear any crying. Is he okay? What's happening?" Nicole asks, looking over at the doctor.

"Doc is with him, baby." I watch Doctor Chantau working with him, a huge smile on his face.

"Taylor, what's happening?" Nicole asks frantically.

I turn to Nicole and kiss her. "Shh… he's just cleaning him up and suctioning his nose. Let him work." I kiss away a tear as our baby boy starts screaming. *Our*. Never thought I'd say those words. "See? Sounds pretty damn healthy to me, beautiful!"

She beams up at me, her smile brilliant and bright. Doctor Chantau bundles our baby up and brings him to Nicole's waiting arms. "Oh my God! Taylor, he's perfect. So perfect." She nuzzles him as happy tears flow freely from her eyes. Out of the corner of my eye, I spot Ryan at the door. I lean down and kiss both the baby and Nicole.

"Ryan's at the door, baby. I'll be right back, okay?"

"Okay." She looks up at me, pride in her beautiful blue eyes. I smile down at her and meet Ryan at the door.

"That was fast," he muses.

"Yeah. Her water broke at the house. Rico and I rushed her to the car. Her contractions were fucking close."

"You got here a lot quicker than I thought. Now I know why."

"Still fought early morning traffic. Got an escort that last few miles, though. Never been so fucking happy to be a cop. How's Chase?"

"Still resting. You get my text?"

"Yeah. Right before Nikki delivered." I can feel myself smiling like a moron, but I don't care.

Ryan smiles at me. "How's it feel to be a dad?"

I grin even wider. "Never in my life thought I'd see this day, but it's fucking amazing, bro. She was so amazing in there. She was too close to delivering, so they couldn't give her anything."

Ryan's eyes widen. "Holy shit! She did that with nothing for the pain? Is she okay?" He looks around me at a smiling and cooing Nicole.

"She's good. She's the strongest person I've ever met to get through that with nothing. I admire the hell out of that girl."

"Damn. Me, too!"

"Well? You wanna come in and meet your nephew?"

"Thought you'd never ask!" He exclaims. I lead Ryan into the room.

Nicole looks up at him. "How's Chase?"

"He's good. Tana's with him. I thought they might want to have some time alone," Ryan says. "The bullet went through his side. Mostly just a flesh wound, but the loss of blood sent him into shock.

Nicole smiles warmly, and her eyes sparkle. "Come meet your nephew."

Ryan's entire face lights up as he plucks the baby from Nicole's arms. "And who do we have here?"

Nicole chews on her bottom lip. "We... don't exactly have a name for him yet."

"Couple ideas though," I say softly.

The baby is totally content in the crook of Ryan's arm. I reach over and trace his tiny hand. He latches on to my finger, and my heart melts. I've been slowly warming up to the idea of this little life being mine, but as soon as I saw him, that was it. I'll go through whatever process I have to if it means he's just as much mine legally as he is in my heart.

"You should see your face right now, babe. You look so... awed," Nicole says smiling brightly.

"I am. I am in awe." I smile at her.

Ryan hands my bundle of joy to me and pats me on the back. He leans down to kiss Nicole on the cheek. "I'm gonna check in with a few people. Doc has you guys transferring up to a room next to Chase in the VIP area."

Nicole and I both smile at him as he leaves. I lean down to kiss Nicole and put our baby on her chest. He cuddles into her.

"I'm so proud of you, Nikki." I lean down to kiss her again.

"I really thought I would've decided on a name by now." She looks at me shyly. "We."

"Well, you know my preference, but ultimately I'm happy with what you decide." I kiss her forehead.

"Hate to do this, kids, but we need to take the baby and get vitals and everything. By the time you get set up in your room upstairs, your baby boy will be with you," Doctor Chantau says. Nicole frowns and reluctantly gives up our baby. "You'll have him back soon, sweetheart."

XXX

Later, after we are in our room and have checked in with Chase and Breetana, I put our sleeping baby into his little bed. Nicole, as exhausted as she is, looks radiant. I crawl into her bed with her and wrap her in my arms.

"Tait," Nicole says softly.

I smile. "After your father. I was hoping you'd say that."

"And for the middle name… Nathaniel."

I take a deep breath and kiss her hair. "Ryan will be happy about that. Using his middle name."

"He saved Breetana and Chase. I'll never be able to thank him enough."

"Tait Nathaniel Carter."

"No... Tait Nathaniel… Reddick."

My heart stops beating. "You're… you want to give him my last name?" I hug her a little tighter, slightly floored. Who the fuck am I kidding? Totally floored.

She laughs and touches my cheek softly with her satin soft hands. "If you'll let me. If you'll have him… Us. Unless… you… Do you not want me to?" She tilts her head at me, hesitation in her eyes. "I shouldn't have -"

"I... I'd love you to. But I don't want you to feel pressured."

She takes a deep breath. "I know it's really soon. We haven't known each other long. But you… I guess I just thought you'd be okay with it. Since we've been discussing us… It's okay if you aren't!" She looks both flustered as she waves her hands and like she's about to cry.

I smile and softly kiss her. "Honey. I'm honored you would even suggest it. I was hoping you would. I won't lie. But I wanted that to be your decision."

"So…, you're okay with it?"

"Yes, Nikki. I'm more than okay with it. I'm fucking ecstatic." I chuckle a little. She throws her arms around me and buries her head in my chest. I reach into my pocket while she's distracted. "Nicole…, uh…" I've never been more nervous in my life. "I've been really thinking about this. I don't know if it's too soon. But I know how I feel. I know I've never felt this way about anyone before. I... um…" I chuckle and close my eyes, letting out a breath. "Fuck, it's only been a couple of weeks.

She looks up at me. "I do believe my brave as hell tough guy is nervous."

I know she's teasing me, and I have to laugh as I open my eyes. "Never been more nervous in my life," I rumble. She kisses my chin. "Marry me. I know we haven't really even given this whole thing a real shot, but… damn, baby. I know what I want. I want you. Tait. A family. A real one. Marry me."

My heart pounds as I wait for her answer. She searches my eyes like she's looking for any type of deceit. Like she's waiting for me to tell her I'm kidding. I can hear my blood rushing through my veins.

Finally, she smiles softly, and I hold my breath. "Where's my ring, Lieutenant Reddick?" she teases. "I can't say yes until then. It needs to be official." She bites her lip to keep from laughing as her eyes sparkle.

"You mean…" I hold up the ring in my hand. A one karat diamond sits in the middle of a smaller blue diamond with tiny butterflies. It's on a white-gold band. "This one?" I grin as her eyes widen in surprise. "What? Didn't think I'd come prepared?"

"You haven't left my side! When did you find the time to do this?"

"I may have enlisted the help of Chase's jeweler."

Her mouth drops as I slip the ring on her finger. "It has butterflies."

"I remembered their significance to you. The reason you have that sexy as hell butterfly tattoo on your side." It's because to her, butterflies represent freedom and beauty. She got the tattoo after her break-up. As a way to help her get over the hurt and move on.

"It's so pretty."

"I hope you like it."

"I love it, Taylor." She can't stop looking at it. Her smile is as radiant as the sun. Her eyes sparkle like the ocean.

"You're breathtaking, baby." I lean down to kiss her. I pour all of the passion and love I can muster into the kiss. When I pull away, we're both breathless.

"The blue. You had the ring designed. What does the blue mean?"

"I guess to me it represents protection. Family. And you being mine… Well, it represents you being mine to protect. To love. You're my family. You. The baby. Our son."

"I love it. It's perfect. For us."

"We don't have to get married right away like Tana and Chase. I know they're doing it because they've wasted so much time. They don't want to waste more. We don't have to do that, but I do want you to know that I'm ready when you are. I'd marry you right now if that's what you wanted."

"Tana has always wanted a small destination wedding. Only a few people there. Just those closest to her. I've always wanted a big wedding. Surrounded by loved ones, family, and friends. But we don't have to do that."

"Anything you want, Nicole. I'll give you a fairytale wedding, or I'll marry you in Vegas in front of Elvis. You name it. It's yours."

She laughs. "You really want to marry me?"

"More than anything. And you're fucking killing me. You gonna give me an answer or make me wait?"

"Oh my God!" She covers her mouth, and I grin. "I really never answered?" Her eyes widen. I shake my head. She throws her arm around me and kisses me. "Yes! A zillion yesses!"

I kiss her again and pull her close to me. I'm thankful she isn't hooked up to any machines so I can hold her without the fear of setting one of them off.

My Nicole.

My Tait.

Nicole and Tait Reddick.

My family.

My perfect family that I will never leave. That I'll never scream at or abuse. That I'll never threaten. That I'll always, always protect.

I'm going to be a far different father than my sperm donor was.

Chapter Thirty Four

⚔ Breetana ⚔

(Two Weeks Later)

The day has finally arrived. The first day of the rest of our lives.

It's only been two weeks since Joe, Shaun, Billy, Greg, and whoever else was working with Greg were taken care of by Ryan and his crew. Two weeks since Chase was shot.

It still hurts to say that. To know he was shot because of me. Because of his love for me. I'm thankful every single day that he survived. Even more thankful that he still wants to be with me. That he still loves me. Wants to marry me.

"Are you ready to marry your sexy billionaire?" Nicole teases as she giggles.

I laugh. Nicole is helping me get ready. Her two week old baby is currently at her's and Taylor's home under Doctor Chantau's watchful eye and masterful care. Her and Taylor joined us in Hawaii along with Ryan, Chase's mother, and Reese.

"I've never been more ready for anything. I'm so ready to marry him."

"You look beautiful, Tana."

I look down at my simple long white dress. It's light and perfect for a wedding in Hawaii. It's a halter-top with a plunging neckline. I love how it flows when the breeze catches it.

"Thank you. You do, too, Kiki. I love that dress on you. I'm so glad you found it." The dress is a knee-length, sweetheart neckline, strapless dress. It's rose pink, and Nicole looks amazing in it.

She hugs me and we both hurry out of the room we are in. Nicole gives me one last hug before hurrying off to find Taylor.

Reese appears at my side. "You have no idea how happy I am that you decided to give Chase a chance. He's a good guy. You actually listened to me for once."

"First time for everything!" I tease.

Reese takes my hand and spins me in a circle. "Beautiful."

I blush. "You have to say that. You're my best friend."

He laughs and gently hugs me. "I think that gives me leeway to be honest and tell you if you look like shit. Which, in your case, is only on Saturday mornings when you're hungover." He grins. I laugh and playfully swat his arm. He teasingly fends me off. "Alright, alright! You ready to get married?"

"So, so ready."

"Are you sure you're okay with me giving you away?"

"Reese. You're my best friend. You've always been here for me. For the last three years anyway. You know everything about my past, and you didn't judge me or turn me away. And even when it got totally crazy, you were still here for me. Checking in. Making sure I was okay. You stepped in to supervise Chase's remodel. You came to the hospital to visit every day. I want you to be the one to walk me down the aisle. To my future."

He smiles down at me and kisses me on the forehead. "Then let's get you married." He holds out his arm, and I take it.

He guides me out of the building, and I gasp at the sight. The few chairs are covered in a deep pink covering. There's light and dark pink rose petals all down the aisle. The small altar overlooks the ships that are docked in the harbor; the ocean is just beyond.

"Chase." I choke up. "He really outdid himself."

"He may have had a little help."

I look up at him, surprised. "You did this?"

He smiles softly at me. "A lot of it."

I hug his arm. "Thank you."

He leads me around the corner and down the aisle. My eyes catch Chase's, and I'm lost. Lost in his eyes with nothing but the sound of the water softly lapping against the breakwall behind him.

Chase.

My Chase.

My Chase… waiting for me in his loose black slacks and white shirt. His deep pink tie matches the theme.

Chase shakes Reese's hand as we reach him. He takes my hand in his and pulls me to him.

The ceremony itself speeds by in a blur. I'm drowning in Chase's eyes, unable to look away from their depths. Chase never breaks contact with me for a second. Not even when we exchange rings. The only time my eyes close is when the officiant tells him he can kiss his bride.

Bride.

Finally.

He's finally mine.

All mine.

And I'm all his.

I can't wait to begin the rest of our lives together.

The End

Next In The Crane Family Series

The dark and sexy Crane Family Series continues with ***Protecting Her***.

I didn't always want to be a cop. That would mean stepping into my father's shoes, and I hate him.

Little did I know, choosing the profession would be the best thing that ever happened to me because it led me to the love of my life.

Nicole.

I fell hard and fast for my girl and the baby she carried. They both quickly became not only everything I wanted, but also everything I didn't know I needed.

When Nicole's life is threatened by an unknown gang in my city, I vow to her that she'll be safe. I throw all of my resources at the unknown threat, but come up empty-handed. My wife's growing fear pulls at my heartstrings.

In order to keep her from harm, I find myself crossing lines I'd always been shielded from. But I'll do whatever it takes to protect my family.

Even if it means being pulled into a dark underworld I can never come back from.

~ This book is a steamy Cop/Mafia Romance that has dark and violent themes, physical violence, body-shaming, bullying and taunting, is an age-gap, and has strong language that may not be suitable for all readers. ~

Order ***Protecting Her*** Today!

The Crane Family Series

Available Now

The Reluctant Mafia King
Sweet Lies
Billion Dollar Love Story
Be Mine
Protecting Her
Dangerously Forbidden Love
His Heart
Love In The Dark

Box Sets Available

The Crane Family Series

Other Books By Melony Ann
The Beautiful Dream Series

Available Now

Loving You
My Love, My Heart
Softening Lyric
Undercover Temptations
Captain Charming
Breaking Boundaries
Crashing Into You
Tactical Inferno
Ravishing Our Queen
Cherished By The Texan
Unveiling Our Passions

Box Sets Available

The Beautiful Dream Series: Box Set: Part 1
The Beautiful Dream Series: Box Set: Part 2

The Deimos Trilogy

Available Now

Connor's Legacy
Aryan's Alpha
Kade's Redemption

Box Sets Available

The Deimos Trilogy

The Forbidden Temptation Series

Available Now

The Detective's Forbidden Temptation
The Running Back's Forbidden Temptation

The Lucinio Family Series

Available Now

Rising From The Ashes
The Player's Rebel
Encrypting My Heart

Multi Author Series
Piper Falls: Firehouse 49

Available Now

Ignite My Fire by Melony Ann
Regain My Fire by Kindra White
Playing With My Fire by D.L. Howe
Fight My Fire by Darley Collins
Against My Fire by Anneke Boshoff
Relight My Fire by Louise Murchie
Harness My Fire by Ayana Lisbet
Quench My Fire by Havana Wilder

Let's Be Friends

Follow me on

Bookbub

Facebook

Goodreads

Instagram

Tik Tok

Visit my website
www.melonyannauthor.com

Subscribe to my newsletter and get a FREE never-seen-before NOVELLA just for subscribers!
https://www.melonyannauthor.com/exclusive-content

Join my Facebook Reader Group!
Jason's and Melony's Sizzling Book Nook

The official Crane Family Series Playlist on YouTube
https://youtube.com/playlist?list=PLGEiD5wbQmDc78K7gNeODh-janqmIFiie

Dedication

The world is tumultuous, but we know we're yours.

Acknowledgements

Brad - You're my everything. I love you beyond reason, and probably more than that.

Laura - There really aren't words to express my love and adoration for you. You honestly are my sunshine.

Jay - Thanks for all of your love and wisdom. Even when I don't listen. Which is more often than not… I love you with all of me.

Ayana - Thank you so much for always being here for me.

Anneke - Thank you for always giving me a hug when I need it. Even from so far away. Love you!

Jason - When my head is spinning, you somehow know how to bring me back to myself. Thank you for never running away.

To the Bookstagram Community.

To my family.

To all of those who believe in me and support me.

To all of those who don't.

Cover by: Carter Cover Designs

Edited by: Alyssa Skaggs

About Melony Ann

Melony Ann began writing short stories and poetry as a child. She continued honing her craft over the years until she took the plunge and began publishing her work, despite having severe anxiety.

Melony writes contemporary romance stories that are full of suspense and a lot of steam.

When she isn't writing, she is loving her family and working to make her life something she deserves.

Melony believes that if her writing can inspire just one person, then all of her hard work is worth it.

Her hope is that her writing allows each and every one of her readers to escape for a little while. To dive into a different world one book at a time.

www.ingramcontent.com/pod-product-compliance
Lightning Source LLC
LaVergne TN
LVHW020707110826
845149LV00012B/2140

9781961966284